LATE IN THE DAY

Mr. Raymond's new novel, told in scenes of high comedy, is the story of a few years in the life of Mr. Stephen Blaize. We first meet him, at the age of 64, walking along the Menin Road, to revisit the scenes where, forty-odd years before, playing his part in the great battle for Passchendaele, he stood upon the one really great peak of his life.

Next he enjoys the treat he has always promised himself: a visit to Paris. And there in Paris an astonishing thing happens which shows him that his character is an unsatisfactory mess which he must really do something about. And so Mr. Blaize begins his stumbling efforts to achieve within himself an integrity which he can respect. Back in the unending streets of London, he is drawn towards the Quakers—till he comes up against their doctrine of Pacifism, and this doesn't mix at all with his feelings about Passchendaele. To all attempts at goodness there is a notable obstacle in his old father, nearly ninety, a general burden, but a delightful figure of fun in the story. Mr. Blaize's final solution to the problem of his old father has little to do with goodness, nothing to do with Pacifism, but quite a lot to do with the convenience of all.

At a Quaker meeting Mr Blaize encounters a most unwilling Quaker, one Wally Bletcher, whom he discovers to have been a gunner in the Passchendaele battles. Wally becomes his good friend, and together they return, still searching for a solution to Mr. Blaize's difficulties, to the old Ypres Salient where once they had known the most momentous experiences of their lives.

BOOKS BY ERNEST RAYMOND

NOVELS

A London Gallery *comprising*

We, the Accused	*Was There Love Once?*
The Marsh	*The Corporal of the Guard*
Gentle Greaves	*A Song of the Tide*
The Witness of Canon Welcome	*The Chalice and the Sword*
A Chorus Ending	*To the Wood No More*
The Kilburn Tale	*The Lord of Wensley*
Child of Norman's End	*The Old June Weather*
For Them That Trespass	*The City and the Dream*

Other Novels

One of Our Brethren	*The Old Tree Blossomed*
Mr. Olim	*Don John's Mountain Home*
The Chatelaine	*The Five Sons of Le Faber*
The Visit of Brother Ives	*The Last to Rest*
The Quiet Shore	*Newtimber Lane*
The Nameless Places	*The Miracle of Brean*
Tell England	*Rossenal*
A Family That Was	*Damascus Gate*
The Jesting Army	*Wanderlight*
Mary Leith	*Daphne Bruno I*
Morris in the Dance	*Daphne Bruno II*

BIOGRAPHIES, ETC.

Paris, City of Enchantment	*In the Steps of St. Francis*
Two Gentlemen of Rome	*In the Steps of the Brontës*
(The Story of Keats and Shelley)	

ESSAYS, ETC.

Through Literature to Life	Back to Humanity
The Shout of the King	(with Patrick Raymond)

PLAYS

The Berg	*The Multabello Road*

Late in the Day

A Novel by

ERNEST RAYMOND

CASSELL · LONDON

00688770

CASSELL & COMPANY LTD

35 Red Lion Square · London WC1

and at

MELBOURNE · SYDNEY · TORONTO

JOHANNESBURG · CAPE TOWN · AUCKLAND

———

Set in 11 on 12½ pt. Bembo type, and printed
in Great Britain by Cox and Wyman Ltd.,
London, Fakenham and Reading
F.264

For
PAMELA FRANKAU
and
PEGGY WEBSTER
With love and admiration

Contents

Contents

I

The Peak

THE small man in the dark clothes and the black velour hat, walking
along the straight highway, looked with fascinated eyes over the
green fields on either side of him. Probably he was unaware that
occasionally he swung his rolled umbrella round and round like a
walking cane, less because he was full of high spirits than because he
was charged with excitement; with this fascination. Sometimes as
the cars and lorries and autobuses sped past him along the wide road
he looked down at the squared setts of the pavé and was as fascinated
by these as by the far-stretching fields. Why should these squared
stones so draw and hold his eyes? Because in all this green landscape,
stretching from sky to sky, they were the only old and immemorial
things. The houses he had passed, the farmsteads on the swelling
fields, even the tall poplars that marched with the road like a guard
of honour, were comparatively new. But these stones, or cobbles,
had been there when he and his battalion had tramped over them
through a night of more than forty years ago; and they were old
then. How many men had dropped wounded or dead upon them
during four years of war, here in the Salient? God alone knew. For
this was the Menin Road.

What a name! The Menin Road. What haunted syllables.

I have called this fascinated visitor to the Menin Road 'small'.
In fact he was not much beneath middle height but he seemed small,
possibly because his shoulders were narrow, his legs short, his chin

recessive, and his spectacles so large that they made his mild kind eyes look large. But I do not know; I simply do not know why Mr. Stephen Blaize, late of the Civil Service, had usually been known by his colleagues as 'Little Blaize'. You could have called him a spare man, but this again was hardly true. He knew, and he alone, that his double-breasted jacket no longer met to the extent of buttoning over his stomach, and that, curtained by the back of the jacket, there was now a triangular gusset in his trousers so that they at least should close and button. Besides this apparent spareness, other things made him look younger than he was. His hair, if thin, was still brown, his face, now full, was not greatly lined and his gait—especially today—was as quick and eager as a boy's. And yet he was nearly sixty-four.

It was because he was nearly sixty-four that he was walking along this road. Only the other day he had retired from the Civil Service in which forty years of dutiful and unadventurous work had carried him to no higher rank than that of a senior executive officer in the Ministry of Internal Relations. So he had never had much money or time to spend on foreign travel, but throughout these years he had always promised himself that in the first days of his retirement he would come back to this place. He would walk along the Menin Road again. And he would find and stand at one certain spot in the heart of these fields.

'I want to stand there again once. Stand there or wander about for an hour. It will be incredible to believe I am standing there again.'

All the roadside houses were now behind him, and the hedgeless landscape filled the visible world. And not one distant yard of it but fascinated him (was it not the old Salient?) so that his heart was compact of all the deep and trembling emotions he had known he would find here. Mostly the countryside was quartered into fields of beet and mangolds and tobacco plants, their leaves large and high and crowded, for it was October. But some of it was pasture with the brown cows cropping it or lying in company together. A gentle, fertile country, and so empty that in the whole landscape only one figure was in sight, a woman bowed over the earth to gather potatoes, perhaps, or beets. So empty, and yet once it had hidden armed men in its earth by the hundred thousand, where beets and mangolds rooted now. And so silent, though they always used to say in those days, 'The Salient is never quiet.'

Mr. Stephen Blaize walked on. It was because he had now retired that his shirt collar lay open at the throat and over the collar of his jacket. As he had said to Gwendolyn, his wife, who had not come with him to the Salient (after all, she had not been there in the Third Battle of Ypres) but would meet him later in Paris, 'Stevie's free now, Gwen my dear, and off for a holiday, and he's going to wear his ne'glee'jay.' His French was vile. 'But not when you join me in Paris, Mrs. B. God forbid that I should put you to a public shame.'

Mr. Blaize had his own ideas of humour.

He passed on his left a field of arable, newly overturned by the plough, and this especially interested him. Heart-stirringly familiar was the texture of this grey earth, so clayey that when dry it cracked and when beaten with rain turned into mud and pools and tarns. At any rate, in his day, and in the fourth year of artillery fire, it had been nothing but mud and puddles and wide glistening tarns, a wet, watery tundra stretching from sky to sky.

Slowly, as he walked, the road and the country sloped upward. Oh, ever so gently up towards a sweep of higher ground. This stretch of higher ground, nowhere much more than a hundred feet high, swept in an arc some five miles long round a saucer of earth beneath it. Today it had tall woods and farmhouses on it, but then . . . then it had been the Ridge. The terrible Ridge half encircling the Salient with its guns and slaying, like Saul and David, its thousands and its tens of thousands.

The Ridge. . . .

His eyes, leaving that murderous Ridge, looked ever northward for one spot below it; reaching, searching, ransacking the country for one place in the distance. It was the place where he wanted to stand.

3

'I know I shall come to it. Instinct will lead me. There was a rough road that branched at an angle from this main highway. We turned on to it and marched through the night half a mile or more. Then we came to it. I shall find the place, even though it was midnight then.'

Yes—a thrill!—here was an unhedged side-road, turning away at an angle and wandering about the country as carelessly as this high road, with its undeviating rectitude, drove on and on, over the Ridge, to Menin.

This excited turn on to a side-road swung his eyes in the direction from which he had come, and there in the evening haze, two miles away, soared the dreaming towers of Ypres: Cloth Hall, Cathedral, St. Jacques and St. Pierre, all rising proudly into the sky, though they had been but rubble and fangs forty-odd years ago when the young Lieutenant Stephen Blaize (twenty then and slim, not sixty-four and pear-shaped) marched by them with his platoon.

On along this country road through beet fields and arable. Again the ploughed-up earth took and held his eyes. It was dry now and cracked after warm October days. But more often his eyes reached, straining, ahead for that one place he must find. It should be a low oval tumulus not fifty yards east of this very road. Bellewaarde Wood it had been called, though nothing was left of the wood except stumps and spikes and splinters, listing aslant on a hillock of mud. Ahead of him now there *was* a tall dense wood on an oblong hill, but was it possible that trees could have grown again so thick and high in forty-four years? Could Bellewaarde Wood be a wood again? Forty-four years was nearly half a century. It could be the place. It could be It. . . .

And never in all Mr. Blaize's sixty-four years an emotion like this, when, of a sudden, he saw a notice board which said 'Bellewaarde Wood' and pointed with an arrow straight at hillock and trees.

Heart pumping, hammering, he walked over rough herbage to the margin of the trees. 'I am here again. Standing here again.' He

4

walked to the corner of the wood. 'God! It must have been somewhere here that they laid me.'

§

He stood there and relived, as he had promised himself to do,
that day in the past. A day in Ypres Three, the Third Battle of
Ypres, in '17. Of his wounds he remembered little. . . An early-
morning attack, and they had been staggering and slumping through
the mud and the pools in a hopelessly broken line towards Zonnebeke, the bullets hissing and plumping around them, when two
from a machine-gun's spray got him in head and leg, the head
wound little more than a glance but the leg wound deep in his right
hock, so that he fell into the swamp and could not move. A while of
lying there, in no great pain so long as he kept still, and then five
noble stretcher bearers, sometimes knee-deep in mud, came slosh-
ing and sploshing towards him.

'What-ho, chum!' said the one who with many an oath struggled
to him first. 'Got it bad, eh?' ('Chum' was the usual mode of
address to one who needed a stretcher. Mr. Blaize was an officer,
and, had he been upright, they must have called him 'sir', but
as one of their suffering patients he was 'chum'.) 'Head wound,
eh?'

'No. Head's nothing,' said Lieutenant Blaize with a smile. 'It's
my leg really.'

'Leg? Well, that's fine. A nice leg wound means Blighty. Home
to Blighty. Jesus Christ, I envy you. Sid, here's a real lucky bloke
with a Blighty.'

'We'll all have Blighties if we don't hurry up,' said Sid. 'Or we'll
all be stiffs.'

Kneeling there, so that sometimes a leg sank thigh-deep in the
mud, they dressed the wounds imperfectly, saying, 'For God's sake,
let's get a jeldi on. We must get him away from here. And ourselves
too. That'll have to do for the moment, chum. We'll get you back
to Belly Ward Wood, where there's a dressing station. Or, better
still, where there's a bit of a road and ambulances.'

5

'Bellewaarde Wood's two ruddy miles from here,' said Sid.

'Never mind, we'll get him there. Somehow or other. Come along on to the old stretcher. Easy does it. All right, are you?'

'Quite all right.'

'Fine. That's fine. First steps to Blighty.'

And they brought him back, four of them, through the endless pudding of mud, the plunging bullets, and the spread waters, till at last they came to the duckboards. These reached only as far as the 'line' which the attack had left in the morning. It was easier on the duckboards though these narrow ways had room for only one man at the stretcher's foot and one at its head. These two tried running on the boards while the others ran behind ready to take the burden when their mates wearied. Every step took them into a zone that was safer from small-arms fire, though not from shells. And so they got him to Bellewaarde Wood.

Now, fifteen feet under the roots of Bellewaarde Wood were long mine-like galleries, tunnelled by sappers, with boarded dug-outs branching off them for men to sleep in or for an orderly room, a dressing station, a latrine, or a Battle Headquarters. Perhaps a thousand men were sometimes accommodated down there while they awaited their share in a battle. For two nights before today's battle Mr. Blaize and five other subalterns had slept down there in a dug-out with wire-netting bunks and electric light. There were two steep adits, or stairways, down into this mesh of corridors and cabins; two lest a shell closed one of them. Both with their gas-blanketed doors looked away from the enemy and towards Ypres. His bearers laid Mr. Blaize by the northern adit, and one of them said gently, 'Just half a mo', mate, and I'll nip down and see if it's the dressing station for you or an ambulance. Much better go in an ambulance to the Advanced Dressing Station at Potizje. They'll do you proud there. You quite comfy?'

'Quite.'

'Okay. You're well out of Jerry's sight here. The hill hides you. We put you here because there's a bloody battery the other side of the hill and Jerry may have the range of it.'

The lad—he was not twenty—ran down the stepped adit to the populous catacombs below, and after a few minutes returned.

'No, they don't want you, mate. Got their hands full. I wasn't at all popular down there. They've phoned for an ambulance. Look: we'll get you down these bloody stairs if you like, till it comes. Or will you be all right here?'

'I'll be all right here. Don't trouble about me.'

'Yes, I think you will, mate. It's on its way.' He was clearly relieved. Getting a stretcher down those steep stairs was a cumbersome job. 'Come on, sods. We'd better go back into the fun. So long, mate. Wish I was you. Give my love to Blighty.'

They left him, and he lay there, and the ambulance did not come. He began to be apprehensive. Not that he was in much danger here, but he was 'in the open', and every man was apprehensive when he had to be above ground anywhere in the Salient. They remembered the Ridge. They thought of shrapnel. 'Why doesn't it come? Why the hell? Please God no shell has destroyed it, men and mules and all, on the Potizje Road.'

The morning was quiet beneath the mild October sun; even the day's battle had gone silent in the distance; and he seemed alone there, till suddenly the battery on the far side of the hill opened fire. He heard an officer's voice, 'Number One Gun—*fire*.' The gun fired, and Number Two, Number Three, Number Four. Then, at one and the same time, the ambulance came tossing over the shell-torn road and a high-explosive shell dived into the battery, shooting up a high gush of blackened earth and brown smoke on the far side of the hill, and blasting the air around his stretcher. It was a German thank-you to the battery.

The driver arrested his ambulance; he did not want to come closer. The men in it jumped out and ran round the base of the hill to the battery, curiosity stronger than fear. They were out of sight for a time and then they came slowly back towards their van. Mr. Blaize called out to them. 'Here! I'm here.' Astonished to see him lying there, they came to his side.

'Christ in heaven, chum! Who were the mutts who left you here?' asked one of them, a lance-corporal.

'They expected you any minute.'

'Anyone who expects anyone any minute in this war ought to indent for a new brain. It's you we've got to pick up, is it? Get him in, chaps; and let's get away.' This man was not quite the hero the stretcher bearers had been. Or perhaps his next words explained this desire to be away. 'There's nothing we can do there,' he said to Mr. Blaize, jerking his head in the direction of the battery. 'All dead. The whole of one gun team.'

'Good ... God! ...'

'Yes, well, come on! We don't want you dead too.'

'And here am I, standing here again; not even dead yet. It must have been just here that I lay and they picked me up. I was young then, and lightweight. Old now. And rather fat. And needing these headlamps for glasses if I'm to see it all properly. That's the road along which the ambulance came—nicely metalled now. Ghosts. Surely there are ghosts about here. Many of them. The gun team, perhaps. ...'

Hammer, hammer. Tap, tap. And tap again. Coming, it seemed, from the far side of the wood where the gun team had stood. An eerie sound. Even frightening in the silent evening. What was it? Someone at work in the wood? Near him in this silence?

Hammer, hammer. Silence again.

He walked round the trees towards this intermittent sound. So still was the evening that not one leaf on these crowded trees, on ash or maple or willow, moved. Not even the fanwise leaves of the poplars, usually unresting, stirred.

Tap, tap. He was near it. It drew him round the oval wood to its southern side. And there he saw what it was: a French or Flemish mason in blue dungarees and black beret repairing the pedestal of a white memorial cross. There were one or two such monuments standing in the fields. Erected by families to dead sons, they had already a forgotten look, a little like those few monuments on the field of Waterloo—for which who cares now? But this cross was

8

different. By the path of exquisitely kept turf leading to it, by the perfect turf around its base, by the mason tending it after nearly half a century, Mr. Blaize knew it for something in the devoted charge of the War Graves Commission. Hence too that sign and arrow pointing to Bellewaarde Wood.

Mr. Blaize walked up to the rails around the cross, and the mason rose from his bent posture to learn who or what it was that had materialized out of the empty evening.

'Bon soir, monsieur,' said Mr. Blaize.

'M'sieur.' The mason, a man of fifty, his face powdered like a clown's with dust from the cross, acknowledged this greeting.

'J'étais ici il y a'—what was the French for forty-four?—'il y a quarante-quatre years ago—années, I mean. In dix-neuf, dix-sept. Nineteen seventeen. Ypres Trois.' These were words he had been longing to say to people he'd passed on the Menin Road. Now at last he could say them. 'Ici.' And with the ferrule of his umbrella he pointed to the wooded hill. 'Sous la terre. Down there. Dans les—les galeries de mine.'

'Ah, oui. In ze tunnels,' said the man, speaking his little English with pleasure. 'Oui, oui.'

'Wee, wee,' Mr Blaize agreed enthusiastically.

The man pointed to the cross. 'Look,' he said.

Mr. Blaize peered at the inscription on the monument. It said, 'Beneath this spot lie the bodies of Officers and Men of the 177th Tunnelling Company who were killed underground during the defence of Ypres.' Since they were tunnelling sappers they had been killed, presumably, while driving their galleries under the wood. If so, they were men who had died that thousands of others might rest or work in shelter beneath the slaughter-grounds of Ypres.

'You were too young to have a part in that war,' said Mr. Blaize to the mason.

'But yes, monsieur.' In '14 he was a child and a refugee from Ypres, m'sieur.

At the name of Ypres Mr. Blaize turned and looked again at those splendid grey towers soaring high above a lowland plain.

'I suppose,' he asked in stumbling French, 'there are very few people who have any interest in these memorials now. It's all so long ago.'

This was true of his countrymen, the Belgian said. They'd had another war since then with a German occupation of Ypres. It made them forget. 'But the English, no. Always the English come back. No longer in great numbers, but one or two. They return, like you.'

'Old men, I suppose, like me,' said Mr. Blaize, hoping this would be taken as a joke. He had wanted to say, 'old boys like me' but didn't know how to put this gaiety into French.

'Mais oui,' said the man. 'Les vieillards.'

This word was a disappointment to Mr. Blaize. He could never believe he looked old. And he was sure he never felt so. Whenever he used the word 'old' about himself he used it as a joke.

'They used to come in their hundreds, the English,' said the mason, chipping at a stone with which to patch a broken corner of the pedestal. 'Often bringing their wives with them. But not now. Only a few now. Some of them come and wander round in the spring or the summer—the old ones who are still alive.'

Nor was this sentence wholly pleasant in the ears of Mr. Blaize. He thrust it away from them. 'J'étais woundé ici—blessé, I mean.'

'Ah?' queried the man.

'Wee,' said Mr. Blaize, and with his index finger he pointed to his head and his knee. 'Ici and ici.'

'So?'

'Wee. Pendant la battaille pour Passchendaele.' He pointed with his rolled umbrella over the country to the green Ridge in the east. 'It was near Zonnebeke.'

'Ah, Zonnebeke?' said the man.

'Yes, we were trying to capture it.'

'Ah, so?'

'Yes, and they got me back here.' In his halting French he was struggling to tell how he had lain on his stretcher on the other side of the wood, when he noticed among the trees and the undergrowth a crater astonishingly wide—wider than shell or bomb could have made it.

'Qu'est-ce que c'est?' he asked—the one phrase he was always at ease with. 'Kesker say, m'sewer?'

The man shrugged, not knowing, but pointed to another such crater, apparently no less wide, at the wood's edge.

Hastily Mr. Blaize walked to the lip of the nearer crater, and stood looking down into it, leaning on his umbrella. It was as deep as its width had suggested; like an empty upturned cone, its sides were massed with brambles, nettles, high grasses, and saplings, self-sown. In its very bottom far below, at the apex of the cone and beneath the tangled wilderness of weeds, was a disc of black mud, reflecting the sky.

How his heart leapt in a poignant recognition of that glistening mud. It was the old mud, and that disc lay there like a black coin from long ago.

He wondered what these craters might be; he could not remember them there among the shell-holes and tarns in the old days. Perhaps they had been there; or, more likely, the British sappers or the German sappers had blown them before the great German thrust of '18, when the British armies had retreated upon Ypres again, but never, never, yielded it up. The Battle of the Lys, they had called that last advance, but it might well have been called Ypres Four. So he was looking straight down into the deep of the earth where those galleries had been, all lit by electric light, with cells, latrines, orderly rooms and a dressing station opening off them. Nothing there now but brambles, nettles, the rioting grass, and that disc of mud.

He stood on the rim looking down, unable to draw himself away. The mason went on tapping and chipping. Not in him to know what Mr. Blaize was feeling then.

§

This crater might be an inverted cone, but, beyond question, Ypres was the opposite, a conical peak, the one great peak, in the life of this man in the black velour hat and the large spectacles, leaning on his rolled umbrella. The twenty years before it, and the stretch of forty years after it, were flat or only lightly heaving ground. Not an unpleasing stretch of ground, that forty years, but after Ypres so commonplace, prosaic, undistinguished, unlit by any high, exciting, tremendous interest. No, the only peak was here, in the centre of the Salient, and sometimes, as now, in meditative mood, he would wonder how it was that for multitudes of town-bound men civilization could provide no full accomplishment of their manhood except in war.

He had lived all his life in the London borough of St. Mary Upbourne among the unending pavements. At sixteen he had become a junior clerk in a banking hall. He was not unhappy in the bank, but, as with a million others, his desk and the pavements seemed to imprison him, with only rare paroles, from adventure, excitement, travel, drama—even from heroism—and he hungered romantically for them all. This was in '13 and next year, in the warm August, it looked as if a gate had opened to all these things. But he was only seventeen and could not enlist, as he wanted to do, in the New Armies, for he was small and looked younger than he was. October of '15, however, brought his nineteenth birthday and with a lie or two he managed to enlist a few weeks before it. Just about this time Authority, shocked by the massacring of teen-age boys in France, ordained that no youth under nineteen should be sent to the front, so it was not till the autumn of '16 that Stephen Blaize, commissioned now as a Second-Lieutenant, found himself on the Somme battlefield, at Beaumont Hamel, Beaucourt-sur-Ancre and Ovillers-la-Boiselle, but the battle was dead then, or dying, and Mr. Blaize, though excited by it all—gazing with a heart almost stilled by the thrill of it, at the boundless desolation which had been the battlefield—spent that winter in little but trench warfare, never once 'going over the top' except for some night patrol or labour in No Man's Land.

But in the summer of next year, when the earth was ripe for battles again, his battalion was sent to Ypres. To Ypres, by now the classic battlefield of the war. To Ypres Three, which was the battle for Passchendaele.

Because of that hunger for drama and excitement the thrills of the Ypres Salient, already haunted when he got there, were greater than all the fears, the horrors, the unconceived discomforts, and all the sudden death around him. He had been proud when wounded, even delighted; proud when he lay on his stretcher by the door of Bellewaarde Wood. So it had been then, and now in memory the horrors were all dimmed or dismissed—or they were knit into the texture of his memory of Ypres, making it the more wonderful and dramatic. So romantic did it all seem that he found it difficult to recall the cynical despairs when they sang in their dug-outs, 'Oh my, I don't want to die, I want to go home', or

'Far, far from Ypres I long to be,
Where German snipers can't snipe at me.
Damp is my dug-out, cold are my feet,
Waiting for whizz-bangs to send me to sleep.'

He could see that this romantic conception of war was a dangerous lie, and yet ... and yet ... somehow less than a lie when you remembered the physical elations of a body trained into high health, the strange satisfaction of sharing hardship and danger with other men, and the secret pride that one was at last doing a full man's job under the sky instead of a poor mutt's at a desk. The dreaded minenwerfer; iron death screaming always through the sunlight or the rain; gas death coming down the wind; cold steel and knives only yards away; fear all round—but fear was at least a heightened intensity of living; it was akin to drama; it was not life within the grey brick of London. Death, death all round, but even death was drama.

Thus Mr. Blaize, 'Little Blaize', unable to come away from standing on the site of Bellewaarde Wood, and staring, staring through big tortoise-shell spectacles at placid, clover-sweet, fruitful fields on almost every foot of which a man had died.

§

That evening, towards nine o'clock, when it was already dark in Ypres, he stood within the great Menin Gate which spans like the arched roof of a Roman basilica the Menin Road where it enters Ypres. The traffic of lorries and cars streamed noisily through the 'nave' of the white basilica, and on the footways the pedestrians pattered by, into or out of Ypres. After all these years they could have but little thought for the fifty-six thousand names of unfound British dead inscribed on the temple's white walls. Why should they pause as they went out to look up at the old British Lion on the summit of the Gate staring out at the Salient? At the Ridge. At Passchendaele.

But two young men with silver bugles came into the Arch; they were young firemen of Ypres who could not have been born till years after Ypres Three. And two Belgian policemen, heavier but not much older, took up their positions, one at the outer entrance, one at the inner entrance, to the Gate. They stopped all traffic from passing through. Silence. A strange respectful silence after half a century. The clocks of Ypres struck, and the two young men, standing in the centre of the Arch with their faces to Ypres, raised their bugles to their lips and began the British Last Post.

As an old soldier Mr. Blaize, at the first note of the great call, whipping off his black hat, came smartly to attention and stayed so till its lovely close, chin up and chest out, hands in line with the seams of his trousers and his eyes swerving neither right nor left.

II

What Happened in Paris

NEXT day he took a remarkable route to Paris. A few days in Paris
with his wife was to be his second 'treat' for the first days of retirement. It would be a lower excitement than Ypres, but an excitement
still. Paris! He got into an autobus at Ypres which would carry him
to Roeslare, thirteen miles to the north-east—hardly in the direction
of Paris, which lay due south. *But*—the bus would ascend gently
on to the Ridge and pass through—of all places—Passchendaele.
Passchendaele, once a little slumbering red village around an important cross-roads, then rubble in the mud, had given its name to
the battle for the whole Ridge on which its rubble stood. And here
in the bright morning Mr. Blaize's autobus, having left Zonnebeke
behind, went rattling through a little town very clean and new,
delivering passengers on to its pavements, and turning at that same
cross-roads where, believe it or not, a policeman stood.

'Got to Passchendaele at last,' thought Mr. Blaize in that hurrying
bus. 'Forty-four years too late.'

All too soon it fell behind him, behind his turning and straining
eyes: Passchendaele, a new red village with new shops, new
shoppers, and a policeman on duty at the cross-roads, and an
immortal name.

He arrived in Paris late that evening and managed, much to his
pride, to find the right Métro and get into the right train for Concorde, near to which in the Rue Cambon was his little hotel. Days

ago in London he had studied this difficult operation for hours, happy, engrossed hours, and made notes on a pad and marks on a map. Never having had much money in his life, he didn't spend it easily on taxis; besides he had little confidence in his power to explain his needs to a Parisian taxi-driver. So go like an expert by Métro. And brag to Gwen tomorrow of having done so. All these thoughts were secrets to himself. Mr. Blaize was a secretive little man, and knew it, often with some shame. So much of his life was lived in the midst of a small round theatre in his skull, where he alone, unaccompanied even by his wife, watched the daily dramas of his career.

Standing in the Métro train, notes in his hand, and a press of home-going workers crowding against him, he tried to improve his French by reading the advertisements and notices on the walls. One especially interested him, and he read it more than once because he was so pleased to have translated it and so impressed by the humanity behind it. It said:

Il est pénible pour les personnes âgées de rester debout. N'oubliez pas de leur céder les places assises en cas d'affluence.

This was certainly a 'cas d'affluence' and as he was reading this a young French labourer, a magnificent young man in soiled trousers and a singlet, rose from his seat, bowed to Mr. Blaize, and offered the seat to him.

For a first experience in Paris this was a moment of shock to Mr. Blaize, and of pain. Did he look a 'personne âgée'? Trying to believe he looked only fifty-five, he said a sad 'Merci' to the polite young man and sat down. But—'âgée'! Oh, let him hope the young man was going to get out at the next station and had simply got up so as to get nearer the door. Yes, that must be it, surely. Not 'âgée'. But, oh dear, they passed the next station and several more with the young man still standing there, holding on to a bar. He had generously given up his seat to an aged person and stabbed him to the heart.

'Personne âgée!'

It was late when he arrived at the little hotel, and after a wash and after unpacking his bag—'personne âgée, oh dear'—he went out to find the cheap restaurant in the Boulevard des Italiens, of which a friend had told him. Map in hand, he got himself through the warm soft Paris night into the vast grey arena of the Place Vendôme. Here in this great cobbled octagon, empty, as it seemed, of all but the ranks of parked cars and Napoleon's column rising pompously into the sky to house that little Caesar on its crown, he felt suddenly alone and small. He was crossing towards the column when he became aware of a car coming behind him at no more than a walker's pace. Almost as if to join him. He turned towards it, and it drew abreast of him and kept at his side: a small Citroën driven by a hatless young woman with her hair, in the bouffant style, standing about her head and face like a golden beehive.

'Bon soir, m'sieur,' she greeted him through the car's open window, while keeping it in his company.

'What?' asked the surprised Mr. Blaize, too surprised to speak anything but English, even if he could have remembered, in so strange a situation, what was the French for 'what'.

'You come with me, no?' inquired the lady, recognizing his English. 'Yes?'

'Come? Where? Pardon, mademoiselle, but je—je ne comprends pas.'

'I give you a good time, yes?' said the lady, to enlighten him. 'Mais oui?'

Mr. Blaize had no answer yet, so she further inquired, 'You like it, no?'

'Like it ... I ... yes ... what?'

The small French car and the English pedestrian went on across the square, side by side.

'Yes, you come with me?'

'Ah, non, non, non,' said Mr. Blaize into the car window. He was quite bewildered by this mechanized method of street-walking, a thing of which he had never heard. And at the moment he was far

more frightened by her invitation than stimulated by it. He wanted
to hurry from the side of her car, to *run* from it; but it was not
offended morality that would drive him out of her reach; it was
fear. And fear reinforced by dislike of spending big money on
what might prove only an embarrassing business. In all his sixty-
four years fear had kept Mr. Blaire from the street-walkers' doors;
he preferred erotic reveries in the little secret theatre of his mind
to any unnerving experiences.

'Non,' he said firmly, but with a smile so as not to hurt a young
lady's feelings.

'But I give you a vary good time.' They were now passing the
pedestal of the column. 'I like you. I like you vary much. You give
me a good time too. One sees that clearly.'

Flattering, but no solvent for his fears. 'Non, madame. Je suis
sorry.' What was the French for 'sorry'? 'Je suis fâché. Je vais à
diner. A un restaurant.'

'Oh, but I dine with you, n'est-ce pas?'

This finally destroyed Mr. Blaize's nervous interest in her talk.
A man who disliked spending money on a taxi wasn't going to
spend it on a dinner for a tart. 'Non, non.'

'Mais oui?' she persisted.

'Mais non,' he said firmly. 'Non. Allez-vous-en.' But, thinking
this hurtful, he altered it to—oh, what was the French for 'good-
bye'? Not 'au revoir'. Certainly not that in these circumstances.
'A Dieu,' he said, separating the syllables into 'Ah Dew'—as if
commending her to God. 'Je ne suis pas intéressé. Je suis fâché
about that, but bon soir, madame.'

And he turned at an angle and walked through the stationary
cars along a channel too narrow for her Citroën. When he was on
the pavement he saw her car, with its burden of rejection and
resignation, speeding into the Rue de la Paix. He walked slowly
till he was sure it was engulfed in the traffic by the Opéra; then
himself went into the Rue de la Paix.

And there, of a sudden, the pleasure struck him. *She* hadn't
thought him a personne âgée. '*You* give me a good time too.'

Good girl. Weighing her in the scales with the well-mannered young man he decided that her sanguine invitation showed a sufficient credit balance in his favour. Paris within an hour had provided him, first with an alarming experience and then with a pleasing one. He walked on happily to his lonely dinner, more ready than ever to enjoy it.

§

He would have two nights in Paris before Gwendolyn joined him. This he had arranged, saying that he didn't know how long he would need for his visits around Ypres, but knowing very well, in the secret mind, that one whole day would be enough, and that he wanted at least two nights by himself in Paris so that—yes, so that he could make sure of visiting one of those notorious and naughty shows of which there was no need to make mention to Gwen.

In the morning, then, he did not go to see the pictures in the Louvre, which was near by, but to the Concert Choiseul, which was far away on the slope of Montmartre. Here, after buying himself, not without embarrassment and some private shame, a ticket for the evening's performance, he discovered that the little theatre's vestibule was another picture gallery, very small compared with the Louvre but containing pictures which proved more interesting than those in any civic art gallery and held him much longer per picture.

They were photographic 'stills' of the show he would see in the evening. They hung along the walls of the vestibule and were more shocking than anything he had imagined. He found himself studying them one after another carefully but furtively, with quick anxious glances at the plump, blonde, and presumably shameless young woman in the Bureau de Location from whom he had bought his ticket. He didn't want her to see him considering them at such length, however shameless she might be. She was knitting in her box and apparently interested only in her needles and her stitches, but how could you be sure of this when your back was to her and your face to a picture? This was a pity because he would have liked to dwell in front of one or two of them longer than seemed possible. Even so he did feel compelled to return once and again to the more flagrant of them, whatever the position of the tricoteuse's eyes.

From wall to wall across the corridor hung a banner saying, 'The Nudes of Jean Auguste Ingres, An Exhibition for Lovers of Art', and the 'stills' were 'tableaux vivants' of the Grande Odalisque, the Venus Anadyomene, La Source and, most arresting, seductive, and holding of all, the Bain Turc, with some twenty nude girls contorting or relaxing their figures in varying attitudes of desire or satiety. He came back more than once to the Bain Turc, and cast many a further glance at the exquisite girl-child who was the model for La Source, feeling quite a little love for her as well as less admirable emotions.

The pictures were not limited to the works of Ingres. One portrayed Leda and the Swan; a nude Leda supine on a rock with a magnificent swan in a position—well, this was assuredly the most pornographic picture he'd ever looked at.

'Hmm . . .' he said to himself, standing with his umbrella in front of it. 'Hot stuff. Definitely hot stuff . . . A bit thick. Definitely a bit thick. . . .'

And he found it almost as difficult to come away from this picture as from Bellewaarde Wood, but *that* emotion had been wonderful and without shame, whereas this . . . But why be shocked, as in truth he was? Why feel shame? He tried to tell himself that there was no reason, really, to be ashamed. 'It's all nonsense to say one ought to be ashamed of one's interest in . . . in these matters. It's just human nature. This interest was planted in us by God, and it's nothing to worry about, provided it doesn't lead to anything really wrong. Just accept it and enjoy it.' Which reflection set him thinking how much easier for him was commerce with pictures like these than would have been any commerce with the living woman who accosted him last night. 'No, I'm not ashamed. It's all perfectly natural. Merely the result of being human.'

And, thus fortified, he went again to look at the Bain Turc.

But he hadn't convinced himself. He knew he wouldn't give Gwen or anyone else an exact account of what he was doing now. And when at last he came away he shot an anxious and shamed glance at the lady in the box-office. But she was still knitting with her eyes on her wool, apparently accustomed to these gentlemen who were lovers of art.

§

Towards five o'clock the following evening he was sitting on the terrace of a café in the Place de la République, waiting for Gwendolyn's arrival in the airline coach. Sipping a Pernod and feeling rather a dog, since this was Paris and an aperitif and the open street, he was thinking about his character. For all his friendliness and goodwill towards others, and his fair happiness with Gwen, Mr. Blaize was at heart a solitary. A shyness fenced him in from easy communication with any but those near to him; and partly because of this no hermit could devote much more time to introspection than he. He could give many an hour to fascinated dissection of himself. And just now, though the roaring cacophony of the Place de la République was all about him, he was taking comfort in the thought that, even if the lower parts of his character had been in command last night, sending him to that squalid little show at the Concert Choiseul, a finer part must be on top now because he was feeling this great eagerness to give Gwen a thrilling time in Paris. Nothing selfish about this, surely. A good thing for once. Less selfish of course had been the fact that he had learned by heart the sentences in his French Phrase Book with which he purposed to address a taxi-driver and impress Gwen. No, selfish, that; and so also the fact that he had deliberated whether to take her by the Métro to Concorde so that he could display down there in the bowels of Paris his skill with tickets, platforms and 'correspondances'. But—and here surely he was back again in unselfishness—he had resolved, no matter what the cost, to take her by taxi past some of the sights of Paris, going by a roundabout route to their little hotel. He was looking forward to pointing out Les

Halles, St. Eustache, the Palais Royal, the Louvre and the Invalides —and to exhibiting his knowledge of Paris.

Oh, he could see perfectly well, when sitting in his strictly private theatre, what a self-showman he was. Rehearsing there some show which he'd just produced for Gwen or for the public, he would apply pleasantly derisive names to the producer, such as 'Mr. Blaize the Showman' or 'Showman Stevie'. He knew well that when he told Gwen the story of his visit to Bellewaarde Wood he would heighten and improve it where necessary, saying that he had said this or that to the mason, or had felt such and such on the Menin Road, although in fact it was only later in his bed that he had thought of things he ought to have said and emotions that he had somehow missed. And whenever he 'improved' a story like this he would, so to say, stand aside and, listening, dub himself 'Mr. Blaize the Raconteur' or 'Liar Blaize'. Did he make some happening very much finer than it had really been he would, while enjoying the moving tale, and gulping with tears over it, call its author, 'Mr. Blaize, the Poetic Liar'.

The coach! Yes, the airline coach. And Gwen sitting near the back, as she always did lest the driver crashed into something and the engine caught fire. A grand moment for Mr. Blaize when with a helping hand he welcomed her on the soil of Paris and, taking care of her in the street, displayed much expertise and learning.

Gwendolyn was a woman of fifty-seven with an exuberantly big body. Her dress always seemed to hang loose like soft curtains from the square shoulders and the large pendulous breasts. So cosily inflated did the whole big cuboid body seem that the word 'heavy' hardly applied to it. The high-coloured cheeks, full and very round, the small nose, the large, soft, ox eyes, and the over-sweet smile gave her face a girlish freshness. Had you seen her face alone without the broad and lavish figure below it you would have thought her a dozen years younger than she was.

'Come, Mrs. B. Bienvenue à Paris.' He liked when merry to address her as 'Mrs. B.' or 'Mrs. Gwendolyn' or even 'Mrs. G.' and to speak of her as 'Mrs. B.' to his friends. 'Nous trouvons un

22

taxi pour vous. Où est vos bagages? I mean, I mean, Où sont les damned things?'

'Isn't this wonderful, Stephen? Fancy! I'm nearly sixty and never been in Paris before.'

'Well, I'm going to show you a lot of it now.'

'Did you have a nice time yesterday in Paris?'

'Yes . . . quite interesting.'

'Do tell me everything. What did you do?'

'Nothing very exciting. I went to a concert. It was wonderful in Ypres—more wonderful than anything yesterday. But now, dear —maintenant nous—oh, où the hell are the taxis? Monsieur'—this to a passing pedestrain—'où sont les taxis?'

The man, without a word, turned and pointed behind him.

'Où,' repeated Mr. Blaize, feeling no wiser.

'There. That row of cars there,' said the man in easy English.

'Oh, I see,' said Mr. Blaize, smiling to please this informant. 'Merci.'

He had not expected this row of small coloured cars to be taxis. He had expected something big and square and black like a London taxi. He walked to a little orange-coloured car at the head of the row. 'Attendez-moi ici quelques minutes, chauffeur.' From the French phrase book. For Gwen's cars.

The driver, a hatless, surly-looking fellow, answered nothing but equally made no objection to Mr. Blaize putting Gwen's bags into his car. He offered no help in this business but just leaned back at ease in his seat.

'Bags aboard,' said Mr. Blaize to Gwen. And to the driver, 'A l'Hôtel Cambon. Rue Cambon. Près de la Place de la Concorde.'

'I know eet,' said the driver indignantly.

'Pardon. You *what*?' Mr. Blaize thought for a moment the man had said 'I no cat'; and wondered what that fact had to do with anything.

'I know ze place.'

'Oh, you know it? I see. I'm sorry. Yes, of course. Well, I want you to—je veux que vous allez par le Rue de Rivoli et le Place du

23

Carrousel—see?—and then par le Pont Royal et puis—puis par le Pont des Invalides'—was Gwen listening?—'parceque je veux montrer Madame Le Louvre at les Invalides et les Champs Elysées.'

His pronunciation of this last was 'Shaw's Eleezay'.

'I see,' said the driver in English. And sourly it seemed. To Mr. Blaize's discomfort.

So, to please and perhaps soften this dour man, he said with a smile, 'Merci. . . .' And 'See voo voolay. . . .' And to his wife,' Get aboard, Mrs. B.'

'Oh, this is so wonderful!' Gwen was struggling to insert her large, full body into the tiny car, and then gazing out at the Paris streets.

Gwen with her big eyes and over-sweet smile was, he liked to say, the most succulent flatterer in the kingdom. And he was thinking now that her name Gwendolyn, spelt prettily like that, matched well with her luscious and blossoming flatteries. These syrupy sweetnesses, pouring out over her friends, could almost sicken him sometimes, so that he wanted to run from them; to escape from the tea-party which was hearing them. Addressed to himself, they were more bearable. And her fund of outrushing flatteries was available for him, as well as for others, on good, sunny days. As today, when there was certainly sunshine in her heart.

'But, Stephen! How wonderful you are. How do you know all about Paris like this?'

'I read a lot, as you know. And I've read a great deal about Paris in my time.' This was certainly true of the homework he'd done last night and this morning to impress her.

'And you speak French so well.'

'Oh, no,' he demurred, as a modest man should. 'I can make myself understood; that's all. I *read* French fairly easily'—Liar Blaize, he thought—'but I have no great fluency in speaking it.'

'You seem to me to speak it wonderfully.' And with that Gwen really began to talk. Gwen always longed to talk and talk, and here she was—talking, talking—just when he wanted to point out Les

Halles Centrales (and to call them this, pronouncing beautifully).
But it was a remarkable quality of her talking that at times it included
listening at length. And this readiness to listen at length to him,
with lips parted, could often amaze him, since, as a rule, he was
rapidly bored by listening to her. She said now, even as they passed
Les Halles, 'Tell me all you've been doing. You say you went to a
concert. What sort of concert?'

'Well, it was called a concert, but it was really more of a revue.
I must say I was astonished by some of the acts. Extraordinary the
French idea of entertainment. Look, this is St. Eustache.'

'Oh, but what sort of acts?'

'Well, lots of nude women dressed only in three stars, placed
in discreet positions, ha, ha, ha.'

'Oh, you bad old man!'

'But I wasn't greatly interested in it. It all seemed rather pointless,
one naked woman being remarkably like another. Boring, on the
whole, to an old married man like me.'

This led him to tell her with plentiful laughter about the 'cruising
tart' in the Place Vendôme. 'I had a job to get away from her.
Following me everywhere with a car. Wasting her time on a
thoroughgoing old puritan like me.' (H'mmm. . . . Perhaps not Mr.
Blaize the Liar. But say Mr. Blaize the Minimizer.) 'Yesterday I gave
to the Louvre. It was for this that I came to Paris. The most wonderful collection of pictures in the world.' (That was a wonderful
collection in the Concert Choiseul too.) 'A real education.'

'You were there all day?'

'Well, yes. It's a big place.'

It saddened him that she was plainly less interested in the haunted
fields of Ypres than in this surrounding city of Paris. But that old
war—why should she be as interested in it as he, she who had
been but a child when he was in the mud of Ypres Three? He had
long discovered that people were bored by old men's memories
of the First War which, anyhow, had been largely eclipsed by the
Second and very different war. So he had resolved to say little
to friends about Bellewaarde Wood and the Menin Road and the

Menin Gate. He would bore no one with things that meant so much to him. But to Gwen—she ought to be made to listen.

So he told her the whole story, adding those enlargements to it which had only occurred to him in bed. For example: moving words that the mason had said to him, times when he had felt the ghosts around him at Bellewaarde Wood, times when he'd almost heard the guns speaking again, and his wonderful thought beneath the Menin Gate that perhaps there were fifty thousand ghosts listening to the Last Post. (Mr. Blaize the Raconteur. Not to say, Mr. Blaize the Poetic Liar.)

'I tell you the tears were in my eyes during that Last Post. I sometimes wonder if I feel these things too much. But if I'm sentimental I'm not the least ashamed of it.' (Mr. Blaize the Showman.) 'I assure you of one thing, however. I'm not telling all this to anyone but you. We old boys of World War One are now old bores. Let's forget it. That's the Invalides where Napoleon's buried.'

'You don't say!'

'I do. And now we'll go over the Pont des Invalides to the Shaw's Eleezay.'

She gazed out.

'This is it. The most beautiful highway in the world. And there is the Place de la Concorde where the guillotine was.'

'You don't say!'

'And our little hotel is quite close. Wonderful to have found a cheap hotel in the very centre of Paris.'

'Oh, I do think you have been marvellous.'

Once again, before the door of the hotel, the driver made no attempt to help them with their baggage, but just lolled in his seat till they should have completed their labours. Mr. Blaize dumped the bags on the pavement and looked in at the driver sitting in sidelong comfort.

'Combien vous dois-je?' The Phrase Book again.

'Four hundred and fifty.'

'Four hundred and fifty what?' asked Mr. Blaize, shocked.

'Francs.'

Mr. Blaize did not exclaim 'God!' He was shaken but dumb. In fell clutch of circumstance he did not wince nor cry aloud. Practically ten shillings! Nothing to do but pay—with Gwen standing there waiting and watching and admiring his competence. He handed a note to the driver, who felt in his pocket for change. 'Non, non'—to impress Gwen—'vous pouvez retenir la change.'

Instead of saying thank you the driver gave him one surprised look, then thrust in his gear and drove quickly out of sight. Leaving Mr. Blaize on the pavement.

And the awful knowledge impinged on him. Shaken by the price, he had handed the driver a five-thousand-franc note instead of a five-hundred. '5000' looked so like '500'. And the thieving scoundrel, on being told to keep the change, had taken him at his word and rushed off with five pounds or more. Mr. Blaize stood looking through his big spectacles at the corner round which his five pounds had gone.

'Was it dear, darling, the taxi?'

'Not very.' He wasn't going to disclose his mistake after all her praise of his competence. 'Under ten shillings.'

'But that's a lot.'

'Well . . . I don't regret it. I wanted you to see Paris.' (But, oh God! Oh God! How and where save four-pounds ten?) 'I'm glad we took a taxi and didn't go by Métro.' (Liar Blaize in part. Showman Blaize *in toto*.) 'Come along, dear.'

He picked up the bags and walked miserably into the hotel.

§

He had supposed that the outstanding memory of this visit to Paris would be the Louvre or the Conciergerie, or their day at Versailles, but it was something very different. It was a dream.

You must understand that in their little London home Gwen and Stephen slept in separate rooms. The overt reason for this was that he was a light sleeper and the smallest movement disturbed him, but this doctrine covered also the fact that he was half a hermit who often sought solitude in the day-time and preferred it at night.

When at the hotel's Reception he had booked a separate room for his wife, the fat proprietor and the two chic young ladies behind the counter had, he thought, gaped with surprise, but as he didn't know how to say in French, and with decency, that his wife's movements in bed disturbed him, he curtained the difficulty behind a genial smile. And the fat proprietor, keeping any astonishment to himself, allocated them two small rooms overlooking the cour.

It was in his small lonely room, and in the deep of the night, that he dreamt. Even Paris all round him was silent for his great hour. He had fallen comfortably asleep, happily fatigued by a long day at Versailles. This was their last night before returning to England, and they had treated themselves to a grand meal in an expensive restaurant where Mr. Blaize had mounted a fine show of French, after secretly memorizing sentences from his Phrase Book. He slept heavily at first and then began to dream. It was a terrible dream; a dream that seemed to enclose within itself an ultimate horror. He was exploring with a dim torch the dark grottoes of a low underground cavern whose pendent roof almost touched his head. It is likely that the dream was suggested by those old lost galleries beneath Bellewaarde Wood, but these grottoes were much deeper down and lower-roofed than they. He was wandering cautiously forward when suddenly the roof crashed around him, leaving him imprisoned within walls not two feet from his hands and under a 'ceiling' not two inches above his head. The torch was still alight, but dimming; in a few seconds it would be out. He stood alone and upright in a deep subterranean hole, far from the hearing of any man. Any moment the torch would be out, and there would be nothing but a total blackness, and the walls almost touching him. It went out.

Half knowing that this was a dream, he stormed and fought to wake from it—to break from that dark upright tomb through the dense superincumbent earth, into an open world with horizons in the distance.

He awoke, heart hammering as if to escape from *its* imprisonment, sweat moving on brow, face, and breast, and a sickness of total despair laying waste all thought. The room on which he opened his eyes, heart banging, head dripping, was as black as that tomb —or seemed so. Overlooking the cour, it was never very light, and he himself had drawn the heavy old velvet curtains across the window so as to enjoy a perfect sleep.

He leapt out of bed into a standing position since he could not lie beneath the bedclothes with horror forcing sweat from brow and breast. How get out of this reasonless despair which the dream had left? He dashed the top light on, and this helped a little. He switched on the bedside light to help more. He walked up and down, hands gripping each other behind his back. The hotel was as quiet as a crematorium at night; Gwen was probably sleeping peacefully next door.

Mouth open, breath short and panting, he felt near mad with despair. He had experienced by virtue of a dream, a total and ever-inescapable loneliness, and learned that it was something not to be borne. He had been shut in by walls a thousand feet thick, with no room for movement, and the horror of it was still possessing him. A remarkable part of this embracing horror was the thought that he would never, *never*, see Gwendolyn again.

It was this small speck of light (for this proof of love and involvement was the one pleasing thing in the blackness) that gradually led him out of the horror. Offering a hope of healing, a faint prospect of happiness again, it seemed to take him by the hand and lead him out.

It led him into a revelation. The despair of which the human heart was capable was not to be borne unless—and here was the revelation, so simple—unless one had built up a mastery of oneself, a pride in oneself; but one could have no such pride if, in the secret places of one's heart, one knew all about one's lies, and deceits and dissimulations, one's meannesses and hypocrisies; if one knew that there was really little in oneself but self-love.

Death. For some moments, while in the power of the dream, he had experienced dying, and he saw that one could only bear it *if* . . . if one had built this proud mastery of self and a consciousness that one had tried to cast away the deceits and shames and some at least of the self-love. He was sixty-four, and at sixty-four dying was not so far off. At sixty-four one must get acclimatized to dying.

How had he lived till sixty-four without this sight of the truth —the truth that (as he put it crudely, walking up and down) he was 'really a bit of a stinker'. He had had a revelation of himself and a startling sight of the only road of escape. He had seen tonight, with a final clarity, that up till this time of retirement he had been content to remain at the mercy of childish impulses and desires. These deceits and shams before wife and all the world—how had he tolerated them in himself, without any effort at self-captaincy? Never had he struggled to force himself out of infantile egotisms into the altruism proper to an adult. For sixty-four years he had been a spiritual jellyfish (he was pleased with this phrase, 'spiritual jellyfish'). Mastery? Why, he had been uncontrolled till sixty-four. A bit late in the day to be seeing the truth. Half a century late. But he was happy to be seeing it, and to be thinking that he had perhaps a dozen years left to him in which to do something about it. He was also rather pleased to think that the great majority of men, (including most in the places of authority and governing us all), were still driven by infantile desires, and that he was about to be better than they. Good to think that he was no longer like unto them, whatever he had been yesterday and for the previous sixty-four years. He felt superior also to Gwendolyn sleeping next door, who, he was sure, had never experienced Revelation. He felt, may we say, 'chosen'. A little like Saul of Tarsus who became St. Paul. Or like other enlightened ones of whom he had read. Like Buddha, 'The Enlightened', for instance. In a smaller way, of course, but the same in kind; Buddha under his Bo-tree, and Mr Blaize in his little Paris bedroom.

He got into bed as happily as he had leapt out of it in horror. He put out the bedside light and drew the warm bedclothes around him. He was looking forward to the battles with himself tomorrow. Tomorrow he was going to begin to be adult. Tomorrow, at sixty-four, he would start being grown up, with a proper mastery of himself.

'A bit late in the day, but begin being fully adult tomorrow.' The thought amounted to exultation; and with such an exultation warming him he slept.

III

Sapper Blaize

IN the coach to the airport next day he sat bumping along very
happily; more happy than he'd expected to be, now that a long-
awaited holiday was over; he had never expected to be sitting like
this in an exalted state because he was a man to whom Revelation had been accorded. He had left home infantile, and was
returning adult; he had left London a spiritual jellyfish, knowing
this and despising himself, but now ... now great things were in
train.

It was a pity Gwen would talk so much in the coach when he
wanted to be alone with this very secret happiness, and there were
moments when he felt ready to snap at her chatter like a dog, till
he remembered that he was now practising self-mastery ... that
he was no longer the old stinging jellyfish ... whereupon he left
her to do the talking, which she did all the way to the airport,
while he listened to some of it, answering 'Yes, dear,' and 'No,
darling,' but for the most part sank back into this happy sense of
dawning adulthood. Astonishing the pleasure it gave him to think
that he had a religion at last, and a code of morality. It would be
hardly too much to say that one traveller in that coach, the one
with the rolled umbrella between his knees, and the spectacled eyes
looking out at the last of Paris, was feeling full of sweetness and
light.

§

Back into the grey brick of London. Back into the dun, and dusty, streets, never ending. Back into the stucco of Victorian London and all the long roads of tall houses, ageing without and divided within into flats or maisonettes. Left the far-spread fields of Ypres, haunted but beautiful, and the high silent woods on the heaving Ridge around. Here was his own long residential street, Denlow Road, one of how many hundred others in the crowded boroughs of North London? The taxi unloaded them, not at the romantic entrance to a Paris hotel, but at their familiar doorsteps. Eight stone steps led up to their door in the tall house.

Their home was a ground-floor and basement flat, more properly called a maisonette. The large front room, once a Victorian family's dining room, was now their ample living room and reception room; the large garden room behind had been adapted into two bedrooms; down steep basement stairs there was a large kitchen-cum-meals-room facing the area; a study for Stephen looking up at the garden; and a small room for a guest.

On the morrow of their return Mr. Blaize stood at the window of the large front room looking up Denlow Road. He was waiting for the Family who were coming to take tea and hear all about the holiday. The Family, as he always liked to call it, consisted of his father, Mr. Morley Blaize, an extremely robust old man of eighty-seven, deaf and booming and burdensome; Peggy Diver, daughter of Mr. Morley Blaize's wife's sister; and Sidonie Diver, Peggy's daughter, a young woman of thirty-four who kept house for, and 'looked after', her great-uncle Mr. Morley, and who, being his great-niece, was Stephen Blaize's cousin once removed—we hope this is right. Mr. Blaize was never certain of the right term for the relationship. Nor Sidonie. She called him 'Uncle Stephen', and her great-uncle and burdensome charge 'Uncle Morley'.

Behind the watching Stephen, on a gate-legged table with a crocheted lace cloth, stood the Blaize Plate—so he called the silver teapot, jug, sugar basin, tea spoons and cake knives, all wedding presents of thirty years ago; they too were waiting for the Family.

Even as a watched pot never boils, so people watched for

from a window do not come; and soon Mr. Blaize, while staring out at Denlow Road, was deep in dreams. Denlow Road, that long vista of grey brick and stucco at which he had looked out for thirty years. October now, and the shadows of the tall houses, aslant on the carriage-way, were already long because the afternoon sun was low. At the corner of Denlow Crescent the single London plane hung out leaves of green and gold; worn old privets, darkened by a smoky London summer, peeped above the dwarf walls of basement areas; a virginia creeper patched with its autumn crimson the grey wall of No. 44; but these, plane and privet and creeper, were the only green things, the only struggling beauty, that the road could offer him ... and the rolling Salient had seemed so unbrokenly beautiful within its enclosing rim of sky.

All his life, so London-bound, he had dreamed of being a vagrant, a wanderer through green, enchanting meadows and along paths through summer-spangled woods or over mountains where his feet would be high above the timber line and the homes of men. In the depths of him he had never known a strong desire to work hard and make big money. Give him enough money to live on, and let him take to the road and the stretches of green solitude and the loneliness of woodlands and hills. Sometimes he would leave Denlow Road and go for comfort to Kew Gardens or Richmond's river or the rose parterres of Regent's Park but in all of these there was artificiality enough to offend him. Where there were asphalt paths, he would say, there was never the perfect healing he wanted.

Today, at the window, because of a picture he had just seen, he was imagining a life in some small croft on a Hebridean island, with nothing in sight except rough stony hills and the sky falling into a great sea around; nothing heard except the crying of gulls or the melancholy call of a curlew overhead.

Dreams never to be enjoyed, because Gwen liked town and society, and now, more than ever, when he was doing battle with self-love, he must consider her first.

§

Ah, this would be they: a small Ford car was coming up the road and, yes, he could distinguish Sidonie driving it with his father at her side.

'Here they are, darling: Sidonie and Sapper Blaize,' he called to Gwen in the bedroom. 'Finish powdering your nose and doing your face.'

'Oh, dear!' from the bedroom, Gwen being less than ready.

'Yes, Sapper Blaize and his chauffeur. And Peggy too, I think.'

'Sapper Blaize' was the designation which Stephen Blaize, always wanting to be the household humorist, applied to his father, but only in the hearing of Gwen and Sidonie. Its origins lay fifty years back in history.

In the great darkened year of 1914 Mr Morley Blaize was thirty-nine, and eighteen years married. A young thruster, if ever there was one, he had stormed into marriage at twenty-one. And now nearly forty, married, and the headmaster of his own prep school, he had felt certain he sat among those who would not be called upon to go and fight, and free therefore to expound the urgent duty, hotly sometimes, of all younger men to go and do so. But next year, 1915, the Government began to realize that they could never sustain their effort in the war without compulsion, and they began by asking all men, married or unmarried, to 'enrol' —somewhat to the alarm of Mr. Morley Blaize. This at first was no more than a move to frighten slackers into enlisting voluntarily. It didn't induce many to do so; and it didn't induce Mr. Morley. He still believed they wouldn't call him up, because he was a schoolmaster, and most schoolmasters were 'starred'. But as the months went by there was talk everywhere of 'too much starring', and next year, 1916, the poor recruiting figures made a measure of compulsion certain. A Compulsory Service Bill, applying to all men between eighteen and forty-one, was quickly made law, and in its toils Mr. Morley Blaize was neatly caught, because he was not quite forty-one. To his high indignation he was conscripted, but they didn't 'call him to the colours' till 1917, when they made him join the Royal Engineers. Why the Engineers no one ever

understood, for he had no experience in any manual trades, neither
as mason, smith, bridge-builder, carpenter, miner, mechanic, nor
electrical engineer, and, having been on the classical side at his
school, had no mathematics worthy of that name—but that was
the way things went in the boundless confusions of '17.

Now Stephen, his son, had volunteered, as we have told, in '15
and went with a commission to the Somme battlefield in '16, so
he had been an active soldier two years longer than his father.
And in '17, as a full lieutenant, he had taken his part in the
Passchendaele battle, while his father was no more than a new
sapper in a company of R.E.s at Slafham in Kent. This company
never left its camp in Kent, and for the next forty years ex-
Lieutenant Blaize could never imagine what Sapper Blaize had
been commanded to do in Kent. He must have been there from
the summer of '17 to the armistice of '18, and what on earth, or
in the earth, or over the earth, had occupied the sapper's energies?
Digging saps? Building fortifications? Laying mines? Gathering
them up again? Building bridges? Undoing them? The camp had
been bombed once or twice—that is to say a bomb or two had
fallen within a mile of it—and for the rest of his life Sapper Blaize
was so impressed with his months in the regular army, the dangers
he'd had to face, and the discomforts he'd had to endure, that he
was apt to brag about them, with the result that his son, remembering the horrors of the Salient, and certain honourable wounds,
was irritated by such talk and liked to say, 'How we could have won
the war, darling, without Sapper Blaize in Kent I simply can't
imagine,' or even, 'Now treat him with reverence. This is Sapper
Blaize who won the war. From Kent.'

The car was now at the door and Sapper Blaize was struggling
out of it, feet first. This little car, though second-hand and cheap,
always annoyed Stephen. Ever since his father's prep school failed
and died, leaving him with only a little capital and no pension,
Mr. Blaize, though none too well off himself, had helped the old
man with increasing sums—with no less than £300 a year as his
position in the Ministry improved—so he could never see this car

without thinking, '*I* can't afford even the smallest car, and it's thanks to the old devil that I've never been able to. Doesn't he realize this?' But Mr. Morley Blaize had insisted of late that now he was in his eighties a small runabout was a necessity. For the last thirteen years he'd received the State's old-age pension, and it greatly chafed Stephen that this was all devoted to new suits and cheroots and the car and other comforts instead of diminishing the demands on his son.

Having extracted himself from the car, he now stood on the pavement in a fine new grey suit, something Mr. Blaize had not seen before.

'Good God!' he grumbled to himself. And 'God help us!'

But old Mr. Morley Blaize, a much bigger and heavier man than his son and splendidly upright still, with a big dominant nose, a pink face and bright eyes—all in admirable condition for one approaching ninety—had always been a man of dress and obviously intended to go on being so, even if he was a pensioner on his son. Within the new two-piece grey suit, and over a merely reasonable paunch, was stretched a neat fawn waistcoat with pearl buttons. 'And I wonder what *that* cost him. That I should wonder sometimes about all these new and expensive garments never seems to worry him at all.'

One might say that the only thing in the senior Mr Blaize which suggested the nearness of ninety was his deafness, and this he declined to take seriously. He refused to make his well-groomed grey head, of which he was proud, look ridiculous 'with a hearing-aid in one ear and a cable festooned to the power house in my pocket. Not on your life, Stephen. And it isn't that I'm really *deaf*. Just a bit harder of hearing in the last year or two.'

Sidonie Diver followed him out of the car and said something in a voice too quiet for Mr. Blaize to hear through his window.

'*What?*' shouted his father in a way to be heard through half the windows in the street.

Sidonie started back at this bellow which had been directed full at her face. She always did start back when it was shot at her. A

37

small, thin, spare diffident spinster, she was all too clearly afraid of this bull-dozing old great-uncle whose housekeeper and chauffeur she now had to be. One of Mr. Blaize's little jokes was that Sidonie, having taken on the care of his father so as to escape into independence from a domineering mother, had plunged out of the frying-pan into the blaize.

Evidently she repeated what she had said, but Uncle Morley didn't answer her, for now Mrs. Diver, after making heaven knew what adjustments to her person in the car's back seat, got out and said something to him.

'*What?*' he shouted at her.

Mrs. Diver didn't start back; she was afraid of nobody. Small, spare, and lean like her daughter, even smaller and thinner in fact, she yet exuded an impression of power. Instead of an upturned nose and frightened eyes like Sidonie's she had a fine aquiline affair drooping over a firm mouth, and her eyes were alight with vitality and a hearty aggressiveness. Perhaps we may conclude that two explanations, the one of a lonely and retiring quality in Stephen Blaize, the other of a much greater diffidence and nervousness in Sidonie Diver, were now standing side by side on the pavement in the persons of Mr. Morley Blaize and Mrs. Peggy Diver, one big and heavy, the other small and thin. And both noisy.

While Peggy Diver and his father stood there talking, and Sidonie shut and locked the car, a woman, large, plump, and fifty, and not unlike Gwen in figure, passed them by. Mrs. Diver bowed to her.

'Who the devil's that cow?' shouted her uncle, unaware—or indifferent—how loud he had spoken; and this time even Mr. Blaize, behind his window, started back, horrified lest the woman had heard. Apparently she had not, because she didn't turn her face. His heart ceased its panic.

'*Ssh . . .!*' pleaded Peggy Diver to her uncle. 'That's Mrs. Rinehart. She's a friend of Gwen's.'

'Who's her husband?'

'Old Sam Rinehart, who used to be in the Indian Police.'

'Well, she's still quite a fine girl at fifty. Still bedworthy. Thoroughly bedworthy, I should say.'

'Oh, *do* be quiet, Uncle. She might hear.'

'Nonsense. She can't hear. And, anyhow, she'd be delighted if she did. You can't pay a great, fat, middle-aged cow a greater compliment.'

'Tssh . . .!'

Mr. Blaize ran into the passage, and nearly collided with Gwen, who was hurrying in with a plate of scones. 'For pity's sake, get them indoors, Gwen. Sapper Blaize is out there insulting every woman that passes. He's just insulted Mrs. Rinehart.'

'How do you mean, "insulted her"?'

'Called her a cow.'

'*No*, Stephen?'

'Yes, he did. And said she was bedworthy.'

'Oh, well, that's not so bad,' said Gwen, less worried.

'Fortunately I don't think the cow heard. But like the Battle of Waterloo it must have been a damned near thing. I'll get the old bounder in before he alienates any more of our neighbours.'

He hurried to the front door, opened it, and said to the three of them, now on the steps, 'Come in, children. We——'

But Gwen, who was in the passage behind him, now loosed one of her low and succulent jets of flattery over them. Nearly always she overwhelmed with some syrupy gush anything he had started to say, and usually he found this maddening because he had wanted to say something humorous.

'Come in, Peggy darling. And my darling Pop'—her affectionate name for her father-in-law—'come along in. . . . And Sidonie too . . . dear.' Sidonie was of the type that is usually an afterthought. 'Pop darling, so hardy you are! No overcoat or hat or anything. Isn't he magnificent, Peggy? Doesn't he look wonderful? If anyone has the secret of perpetual youth, it is he.'

'*What?*' demanded Uncle Morley, having gathered that they were talking about him. 'What did she say?'

Gwen shouted that he had the secret of perpetual youth. 'You look about fifty,' she explained archly.

'Fifty be damned. I feel thirty-nine. I don't care what I am arithmetically. Biologically I'm somewhere about thirty-nine.'

'I'm sure you are, Pop. But I'll tell you one thing—and it won't suit you at all—I was reading it today: if you want to live to be a hundred you've got to fast sometimes. At regular intervals.'

'You've got to *what*?' The three of them were still on the eight worn steps leading up to the threshold. They were stayed there by the talk; by Gwen's sprays of flattery. Gwen was now on the threshold, and Mr. Blaize in the narrow passage, having been by-passed not only by her words but by her thrusting body. 'I said, my dearest Pop, that you've got to fast at regular intervals.'

'Did you say——?' and Uncle Morley, who could be a coarse old man, even an obscene old man, priding himself on being above all pruderies, whether those of squeamish women or of men less male-blooded than himself, substituted a word for 'fast' that differed only in one letter. 'Oh, I do that at regular intervals all right,' he said loudly, because he enjoyed the joke. 'Don't you worry.'

'Really, Uncle!' protested Mrs. Diver.

'*What?*' demanded her uncle.

'Come inside, for God's sake,' called Mr. Blaize round the figure of Gwen; and when she was back in the passage with him, he muttered, 'Booming obscene jokes out there in the public highway!'

'Hush!' she rebuked.

'He can't hear.'

'He hears it if you don't want him to hear.'

When they were all seated in the drawing room Peggy turned to Uncle Morley and said, 'Uncle dear, did I tell you that I shall soon have Peter home for a little?' She was speaking of her son, who was an actor. 'He's nearly finished his season, and when it's over he's coming to stay with his old mother for a week or two. Won't that be lovely?'

'What's your boy doing now?' her uncle asked her, having clearly caught the word 'Peter'.

'I've just told you. He's nearly finished his season at Weston-super-Mare.'

'Nearly finished his thieving at Weston-super-Mare?'

'No, *no*.' Peggy laughed, straightened this difficulty out, and, abandoning hope of a successful talk about her boy, turned to Gwen. 'Now we want to hear all about Paris'; and Sidonie begged, 'Oh, *yes*,' dutifully echoing her mother, as she had done all her life on social occasions. Uncle Morley, having heard some of this, commanded, 'Yes. Come on! Paris.'

And immediately Mr. Blaize was hurt with them all because they had made no mention of Ypres. Hurt with Gwen because she immediately began to pour out stories of Paris as if he'd never stood by Bellewaarde Wood amid the ghosts of the past. A stretcher under the open sky. A shell-burst. A gun team dead. And forty years later a British call, the Last Post, sounded by Belgian youth at nightfall, in the Menin Gate.

Hurt, he kept silence, and the talk danced between Gwen, Peggy Diver, and Uncle Morley, who, when he'd heard something they were saying about Paris, intruded talk about his own visits there, thirty, forty, years ago, which interested him much more than this recent visit of Gwen's—which didn't really interest him at all.

When he had finished a single cup of tea he lit up a long cheroot, without any apology to those who were still eating their cakes; and, as ever, the cheroot annoyed Mr. Blaize, not because of its pungent smoke, drifting above his creamy éclair, but because he himself, years ago, had given up smoking, for economical reasons, among which was the need and, up to a point, the desire, to help his father.

Sidonie said nothing, having neither the courage nor the wish to compete in these fields of chatter with her over-bearing 'uncle' or her loud vivacious mother. Mr. Blaize, after doing his duty with teacups, and dishes maintained his dignified refusal to mention Ypres if they were not interested, and sat humpily on his chair, just listening sadly till, of a sudden, a new and pleasing thought took possession of his mind. This was that, while his father might be eighty-seven and Gwen and Peggy nearly sixty, none of them were adult, as he had been for two days now. None of them had ever had a Revelation, showing them that they must climb on to the bridges of their lives and be captains in control. They were still just drifting this way and that, tossed hither and yon by the waves that were merely self-regarding and therefore childish. Here was his father still indulging in self-display. Gwen pouring out flatteries that were largely mendacious, and Peggy Diver at the mercy of a compulsion to sacrifice anyone's character if thereby she could achieve a witticism. Not one of them was troubled by self-criticism. It was pleasant to feel the only adult in the room.

Striving to sit there as a proper adult, he set about controlling his impatience with Gwen's flatteries which were still gushing over the old man or over Peggy whenever an opening offered. He sat there trying not to be sickened by them. To accept them; to smile tolerantly at them; even affectionately at them; and forgive them. But they went on and on, one after another, all pitched in a low voice, soft and sweet, like a creamy milk too liberally sugared. Every modulation of her voice when she was speaking the creamy words, every softening of it, every lowering of it, was in excess. 'Really!' he thought. 'Given a visitor to the house, even if it's only the old man or Peggy, she changes from a woman talking naturally in her home into an exceedingly bad actress speaking insufferably sentimental lines. An amateur actress of the worst type who over-acts everything and thinks she's acting marvellously. 'Oh, Peggy, what a shame! After all you do for them. And all you do for every-body!' Sickening glucose nonsense about a pretty selfish woman —and in tones that were the very music of insincerity.

But stop it: this wasn't being tolerant and forgiving. No, come, come: it's just her kind of showmanship, and you have your kinds —or you did until two days ago. She's producing Gwendolyn Blaize, the Woman of Sympathy; the Woman whom one delights to be with because she warms you so with her blandishments; not to say The Lady with the Censer. In fact, Mrs. Blaize the Showgirl.

Let the show go on. Let the poor girl finish her performance for Sapper Blaize.

His father now, glad that the women were done with Paris, began on a subject of real interest to him: the new symptoms in his arteries. Indeed these were of sufficient interest to him just now to thrust aside his previous claim that he was biologically about thirty-nine. Sidonie had just managed to intrude her second —or perhaps third—remark of the afternoon, 'Uncle think's he's got hardening of the arteries,' and Gwen had instantly protested, 'Oh, but what nonsense!' though nothing could be more sensible about an old man nearing ninety. 'Oh *no*, Pop,' she said; and never was an 'Oh *no*,' more softly breathed.

'But oh, *yes*,' he answered, having heard her words, however softly breathed, for one is seldom so deaf as not to hear something about oneself that greatly interests one. 'Definitely yes. It's arteriosclerosis. Not a doubt about it. And why not? There's every reason why it should hit me at last. I've never paid the least attention to doctors. Always eaten and drunk and smoked exactly what I wanted, so the old arteries must be nicely pickled by now. Alcohol and nicotine *do* thicken the artery walls, but what the hell? It's taken 'em eighty-seven years to do it to me.'

Gwen breathed comfort over him like spray from a garden hose. (It's her Ministering Angel act, thought Mr. Blaize.) 'Oh but, Pop, you're so different from anyone else. You're so strong. I can never imagine any of these things happening to you. You haven't even got the bearing of an old man yet. He's remarkable, isn't he, Peggy?'

'Of course it may be atheroma,' he said. Though gratified with her flattery, which he'd heard properly because attending carefully, he was anxious to proceed with the clinical picture of his arteries, to which he'd been giving much book-study.

'But what's atheroma, *please*?' asked Peggy.

'Furring, my dear. Furring of the arteries, like what goes on in your kettle. Can't be helped. Comes at last to all us old boys who've led strenuous lives and denied ourselves nothing much

43

in the way of eats and drinks and smokes. I can assure you that
the pulse at my wrist —when I can find it; generally it's stopped
—feels hard as a bit of horn. That's high blood-pressure, brought
about by plenty of poisoning with whisky and tobacco. If I hadn't
the constitution of a bull it'd probably have killed me long ago.'
The cheroot dipped and danced beneath his lips as he bragged.

Listening to the braggadocio, Mr. Blaize was again happy to
think that he, unlike anyone else in the room, was now in pursuit
of (not to put too fine a point upon it) nobility; and he was thinking
this very happily when his father said, 'The old doc declares that
I'd be wise to give up alcohol and smoking, but I'm damned if I'm
going to. I'd much rather pop off suddenly and soon if I've got
to'; at which Mr. Blaize felt a big hope in his heart. A shocking
hope; as shaming as—as it was pleasing and thrilling; namely that
the old man was right and that he would 'pop off suddenly'.

And quickly.

It really did shock and shame Mr. Blaize. He had been con-
gratulating himself on an incipient nobility above that of most
men, and here he was—longing to end a father's life; ready, as you
might say, for a murder, a parricide; even eager for it.

Is it a small extenuating circumstance that he had a strong financial
interest in the old man's death? Alas, that is never an admissable
plea to rebut an accusation of murder. But the facts were that his
father's departure would not only release the £300 a year which his
son gave him, but would enable Mr. Blaize to add thousands to his
capital. A dozen years before this, having nowhere else to put his
father, he had bought for £1,500 the little house in Murry Walk
where the old man, then seventy-five, could live, with Sidonie to
care for him. There was filial piety of a sort in this, for he had
declined all rent, but there was some pomposity in it too—a small
cockiness about being a landlord. The mortgage was now paid off,
the little house was his, and in the present monstrous inflation of
house values he had only to dress it up with new paint, an antique
door-knocker, and sham Tudor ornaments (as had been done to
all its terraced neighbours) and call it a 'bijou residence', for it to

fetch anything up to eight or nine thousand. Others along the Walk had done as much. 'And the old man never seems to give a thought to this. It doesn't trouble him at all, and I've never had the heart to mention it to him. Been too damned decent. So there he sits with the whole house to himself, while Gwen and I . . . but *if* he——'

But, no, no! One mustn't sit here wishing an early death on an old man. Stop it for God's sake. . . . But eighty-seven is quite a good innings. No, *stop* it, I said. Death—think what it is. Extinction for a lively old devil who enjoys his roaring and booming about the world. Poor old——'

'Pop off? What rubbish,' Gwen was saying. 'I always maintain you'll live to be a hundred——'

(Oh, *no*—I mean, Oh, *yes*—or rather, I hope you'll live for some time yet. . . . God, I've a long way to go. You could hardly call me altruistic yet. In fact, I'm still rather unspeakable. And unspeakable's the word since one could never disclose such horrible thoughts to anyone.)

IV

'Only Happy When Being Good'

Mr. Blaize was so shocked by this murderous tendency in his mind that he went down into his study to think about it after the visitors had gone (including the proposed victim). Walking up and down in that little basement room, between closed door and garden window, he meditated at length on his natural depravity. Clearly this business of self-improvement must be looked into more deeply. Only two days ago he had imagined that his character was transformed, with nothing much more needing to be done to it; and here he was—guilty of the ultimate selfishness: to wit, requiring the death of another for his own advantage. Clearly Rome wasn't built within oneself—or perhaps it would be apter to call it Jerusalem —Jerusalem the Golden—in a day; nor yet in two.

He tried to get back to that moment of bright light in the Paris bedroom when he'd seen how all the infantile egotisms were still mighty in himself, and seen this, not in a dimness of worn-out words, but in all the brilliance of truth. And as he considered that illumination again, three familiar words suddenly stood before his mind. 'The Inward Light.' And, as before, he felt a thrill of pride that he should have been granted this Inward Light, not unlike St. Paul.

But 'Inward Light'—what were these words recalling to him? Quakers. Wasn't their whole religion based on something they called 'The Inward Light'? Mr. Blaize belonged to no church. He called himself an agnostic, and liked to do so. 'If you can't believe in the Christian dogmas,' he would say, 'then agnosticism is the only intelligent attitude, because atheism, denying everything, is just as uncompromisingly dogmatic as its opposite. When I say I don't believe in the dogmas of Christianity,' he would add happily, 'I'm not saying I deny them; I'm simply saying that I don't know; and that I'm not averse from trusting that in some way or other they may be true.'

So he was very fair soil for the seeds of the Quakers.

Quakers, he had heard or read, didn't enforce any dogmas on any member; they left each to his inner light. Then surely Quakerism was the religion for him. And he would like to have a religion because he had discovered, in the course of his recent efforts at a general amendment, the remarkable fact that he was 'only really happy now when he was trying to be good'. And so this evening he found himself saying, 'I've often thought I was a natural Quaker, and I feel more like it than ever now, because after all—I mean—I'm only happy when I'm being good.'

Extremely private thoughts, these.

In a fumed-oak bookcase he had an Encyclopaedia which he'd acquired years ago 'on easy terms' and complete with this special bookcase. He bent down and drew out Volume XX. He carried it to his desk, sat down before it, and opened it at 'Quakers'. And with his elbow at its side, his cheek resting in his hand and his spectacles pushed well back, he began to read.

'The Society of Friends.' For the moment he had forgotten that this was their real name. Each member was a 'friend'. Appealing word: he, a man all too given to loneliness, would like to be a friend. He read on happily. He read that, though a Christian society, they were without creeds, liturgies, priests or sacraments. The spiritual freedom of every member was absolute, his only guide to belief and behaviour being his inward light. In the beginning they had called themselves 'Children of Light' and they still believed themselves a body of people who had been granted a clearer insight into the deeps and simplicities of religion than those who took their doctrine from priests or pastors intervening between God and them.

'That suits me exactly.' Mr. Blaize heard these words in his mind. He didn't want anyone interfering with his dreams of private purification. In this business as in so many others he preferred to be alone. Secretive and alone.

The Inward Light, he read, would restrain him from anger, malice, ill-will, selfishness and from other disloyalties to his own insights into what was right and good, and would direct him towards gentleness, kindness, sacrifices and self-forgetfulness—why, this was exactly what he had seen for himself in his Paris revelation! The great mystics had always known God as a Voice speaking in times of quietness and withdrawal—reading which, Mr. Blaize was pleased to think that he was—in a small way—a mystic. And, reading farther that the Quakers in their first days were persecuted as heretics, he was no whit less pleased at the thought of being a heretic. A part of this pleasure, as he saw quite clearly, was the prospect of proclaiming the heresy before his father, for Sapper Blaize was a dogmatic and domineering Roman Catholic, without being a practising one. And Mr. Blaize looked forward to stirring up a fine storm of rudeness from his father.

Now he was reading how in their Meetings for Worship the Quakers sat, one and all, in a silence, waiting upon God; a silence which they called the Living Silence. And yet again he was pleased by this quietism in the Quakers for always, in his random reading, the word 'quietism' had appealed to him.

Read on. 'Organization and Discipline.' Discipline—not an appealing word. He was now aware of a recoil. 'Thought there was no discipline.' But the article said, 'The duty of watching over one another for good was insisted upon by the early Friends and has been embodied in a system of discipline. Its objects embrace exhortation and admonition to those who walk contrary to the standard of Quaker ethics——'

Oh, no; not at all sure that he wanted this. He always took a wound if someone admonished him; a wound which, as a rule, turned into a festering resentment. This hint at discipline was a rebuff, and he was sorry about it, because he'd been so pleased with all that had gone before; so happy in feeling that one aspect after another about these Quakers 'exactly suited him'.

But this sharp disappointment was not enough to arrest his reading. Too much of it had been too exciting and pleasing. So he read on about the philanthropic activities of the Friends 'to which their loving-kindness drove them'; their efforts to better the treatment of those in prison, in asylums, in the fetters of slavery—and to all this the heart of Mr. Blaize cried Yes. And because of this warmly approving Yes he decided that there must be much of this loving-kindness somewhere in him.

Thus everything that he had read—except that bit about discipline—had pleased him well—so well that, when he slowly and unwillingly shut the big volume, he was asking himself, 'Have I just been Called? Called to become a Quaker?' And he began to feel sure of it. Oh, yes; wonderful things were happening to him in these days. Revelations. Calls. The assurance, growing, produced in him a considerable elation of soul; an elation which, after further thought, became so considerable that he hurried up the basement stairs to tell Gwen all about it.

§

Gwen was in the drawing room, sitting by the fire, and busy with her long crochet needle upon a doiley for her dressing table. Mr. Blaize, on entering, walked to the window and looked out at the long grey monotonies of Denlow Road. With his back to her he began, 'Do you know, dear . . .?' in the tone of one who is going to introduce an interesting topic, 'I think I'm going to a Quaker meeting next Sunday.'

'But in heaven's name, why? You never go to church at all.'

'I don't know. I've been making a great study of Quakerism lately.' (He had, in fact, read only the Encyclopaedia article.) 'And I've a fancy to see it in action.'

'Well, I hope you don't expect me to come too.' Remarkable the difference between Gwen breathing unctuous sycophancies over her guests and talking naturally and without effort to him who was but a husband and a habit. Gwen went regularly and happily to the parish church of St. Mary Upbourne, unworried by doubts of any kind—to the shoulder-shrugging wonder of the agnostic, her husband. Privately he thought her ready Anglicanism facile and unintelligent, and felt superior to it.

'Oh, dear me, no,' he assented. 'I shall just wander along by myself.'

'But nothing ever happens in a Quaker service. It's all silence, isn't it?'

'Yes, I can see that wouldn't suit *you*,' he laughed. 'But a hell of a lot is supposed to happen inside one during the silence.' Still with his back to her he fiddled with the cord of the old-fashioned holland blind.

'But that can happen in a proper church service, can't it?'

'For those who are troubled by no doubt, perhaps. But, as you know, I can't begin to believe half the things an Anglican must accept. Among the Quakers there's absolute spiritual freedom. Absolute freedom,' he said, feeling now greatly superior to her because of this.

'Surely Quakers have to believe *something*?'

'There's no compulsion to believe anything except in God and Love and that there's a bit of God in us all. None of that presents the least difficulty to me. I believe most terrifically in love. I think it the answer to everything. Oh, yes.'

'And is that all Quakers believe?'

'All? It's a devil of a lot if you *really* believe it. And it's the very devil acting upon it, I can assure you,' he announced—was he not a recent expert in this activity? 'Most of them go farther than I can about Jesus of Nazareth. Still, one is not obliged to go with them the whole way over that. The Freedom is Absolute.'

This time he had said it, so to speak, in capital letters.

Now he came from the window and sat on a hard chair near her. He leaned forward with elbows on knees. 'A lot that I've read about them appeals to me very much. It seems to meet the difficulties of a really mature and adult mind. Sometimes it seems to me the one religion that a scholarly mind can wholeheartedly accept.'

'And yours is a scholarly mind?'

He didn't quite like this tone. No unctuous flattery here. Not for him. So he answered with some emphasis, 'In a small way, yes. In a small way, certainly,' and he rose and walked back to the blind cord and the window. 'I've always been a reader and a student. A seeker, as you might say. I have what I should call an unquiet intellect'—a pleasing phrase from the Encyclopaedia article—'but I cannot imagine any truly adult mind that can be anything else. So few people are adult; that's the trouble. They never develop their minds. The problem of the fully developed mind is to find some religion that is credible because it is acceptable to reason. Quakerism, as far as I have studied it,' he said to the window and to Denlow Road, 'seems to me such a religion because it springs from nothing but spiritual values and therefore needn't be worried by miracles and all the supernatural stuff in your Anglicanism or by any advances whatsoever in science. Science presents no difficulties. It can go on and on and do what it likes, without touching the heart of Quakerism. See what I mean? That's why you find so many people of high intellect and culture among the Quakers.'

And he came away from the window, well satisfied with the idea of being a person of high culture and a Quaker.

But Gwen, apparently, had not heard some of this exposition, having lost herself in some difficulties of her own with her crochet stitches.

V

Meeting

A WET November Sunday with a slicing cold wind that whistled the russet leaves along the pavement; and Mr. Blaize with coat collar turned up and shoulders held high (as if this helped to keep him warm) came slowly towards the little Quaker Meeting House in Woburn Lane.

Woburn Lane, a tilting side-road of small grey-brick houses, had this one grey meeting house in its midst. The road was empty because Mr. Blaize was approaching the place too early, so he now decided to postpone his entry for a little, not wishing to be too conspicuous a stranger; and he walked right past the doors, but not without giving a quick glance at their glazed windows. There were shadowy figures in the vestibule, which caused him to quicken his step and turn his eyes straight ahead, as if he were one of the least religious pedestrians in St. Mary Upbourne. Since Woburn Lane was not long it was still early when he reached its top so he turned at right-angles out of it and walked round the whole block of houses to come again at its foot. Still too early, but he was cold, and the embarrassment of being a conspicuous stranger now seemed a lesser evil than shivering in the wind. Pushing open the double doors, he entered.

Two persons in the vestibule. One was a man of his own age with large horn-rimmed spectacles framing large and serious eyes, and long drooping brown moustaches that made a down-turned chevron over his mouth and chin. He was a short, squarish figure, which made the much younger man at his side, who was tall, seem much too tall and too narrow, and to have shoulders that sloped like a steeple. This young man had a nose long and narrow to match the long narrow figure, and his pale eyes behind the rimless glasses were surely too earnest for his years; because while the shorter man might be fifty, he was probably still in his twenties.

The older man, recognizing a stranger, stepped forward at once. 'Good morning. You are a Friend from some other Meeting——?'

'Oh, no, no. I'm not one of you. Not yet. I——'

'Ah, you have just come to visit us?'

'Yes, I—I've been reading about Quakerism and I thought I'd like to come and see it in action—if you don't mind. Just as what you call a "seeker"—if I may put it like that.'

'Mind? No one could be more welcome. I am what we call an elder, and Evan Plaicey here is an overseer. Meet Evan Plaicey. He's a very earnest young man.'

He looks it, thought Mr. Blaize, while smiling in his friendliest way at the grave and lanky youth and thinking at the same time how different was the vocabulary of pious persons from his own. Never could he have described a friend before his face as an earnest young man.

'Now let us see what we can do for you,' said The Moustaches (so Mr. Blaize was calling him for want of any other name). 'Here, let me give you this leaflet. You see it's called "Your First Time in a Quaker Meeting" and it explains——'

'Oh, but I know a lot about what happens. Or doesn't happen,' laughed Mr. Blaize, thinking he'd said something funny.

'A great deal happens out of sight and hearing; deep down in the hearts of the worshippers,' said The Moustaches in full seriousness; and Mr. Blaize wished he hadn't tried to be funny.

'I'm sure it does,' he offered, as a quick *placebo.*

'My name is Amling. Maurice Amling.' Mr. Blaize was glad to learn this, feeling that to indulge the humour of calling him The

Moustaches was uncomfortably out of place within these sober walls. He nodded gratefully.

'You live in our borough?' asked Mr. Amling.

'Oh yes, in Denlow Road. For the last forty years.'

'Ah, then I hope we shall see more of you. Do write your name in our book here.'

'Certainly I will,' said the friendly Mr. Blaize, though feeling like a fly whose wing has touched the gossamer of a spider's web. The Visitors' Book had a column for the signatory's religion. Would these devout persons be horrified if he wrote 'agnostic'? Would Mr. Evan Plaicey? Mr. Evan Plaicey who was standing there with the round rimless spectacles in front of pale eyes that seemed to be dreaming of goodness and God? Mr. Blaize looked again at those eyes and said apologetically, 'I'm afraid I've always called myself an agnostic. But a sympathetic one,' he added, so as to lessen the blow for these good men and to be still welcome and loved.

'Leave it empty,' enjoined Mr. Amling. 'After all, agnosticism and emptiness are much the same thing.' Had The Moustaches actually made a joke?

'Oh, I don't know that I agree with that,' began Mr. Blaize who so far had been proud of his agnosticism.

But Mr. Amling wasn't listening. 'Evan, show our friend in.'

The long young man pushed open one of the inner doors and motioned to Mr. Blaize to enter. There was not a smile on his long face as he leaned back against the door he had opened. 'We are so happy to have you with us. Do sit anywhere you like. What we all try to do is to "centre down", as we put it, into that still heart of our being where we find "that of God" which is within us all.'

'I see,' said Mr. Blaize. 'Yes, I see. Thank you.'

'It's early yet, but there'll be more Friends soon. After Meeting do ask me anything you would like to know. That's part of my task as an overseer.'

'What is an overseer?'

'We try to watch over the interests of all members and to give advice and help to any earnest inquirers.'

'I see.' And Mr. Blaize smiled at the young man so as to assure him that he saw clearly.

'Shall you come often?'

'I rather hope so.'

'Then perhaps we shall be able to make you an "attender".'

What this word implied Mr. Blaize had no idea, and rather than get another wing caught in the gossamer he said hastily, 'I think for the present I'll just remain a "seeker",' and smiled again.

'A seeker now and a finder soon, I very much hope,' said Mr. Plaicey with never a smile. 'I must go back to Maurice Amling now. Do sit anywhere.'

Mr. Plaicey went back through the swinging doors, and Mr. Blaize found himself standing alone in a square bare room. Its only furnishing, within the bare cream walls and the brown wooden dado, was three concentric rings of chairs around a small table on which stood a water jug and a Bible. No organ, no prayer books, no hymn books, and certainly no altar. Only that little naked table. Mr. Blaize felt a certain pleasure in thinking that this room was the polar opposite of his father's R.C. church—not that Sapper Blaize had gone into that lavishly ornamental shrine for many a day.

The room was still empty of people because even now it was not a quarter to eleven. Mr. Blaize went humbly to a chair, not to one of those in the outer ring, but to one yet farther back, against the wall. Opening his overcoat he sat here in the emptiness. He was still unsure what he was doing here, seated quite still, like a limpet in a tank of silence.

He was alone here for some time though people had come into the vestibule and were standing there talking. Slowly in ones or twos or as families with children they entered this room and, taking their chairs, went into the silence. A clock ticked and ticked on the wall behind Mr. Blaize, its ticking the only sound. Soon there were some thirty persons placed sparsely on the chairs; old people and young. Mostly the older men sat with their arms folded across their breasts, the younger men and women with their hands joined on their laps. Nearly all had their eyes dropped; some with the lids lowered like blinds. Mr. Blaize noticed one tired and lined old woman whose eyes were tightly shut as if she was straining to 'centre down' into the deeps of her, as Mr. Plaicey had advised.

Eleven o'clock chimed from a 'steeple-house' near by (Mr. Blaize knew that the first Quakers so described all churches which sought a material splendour instead of a spiritual simplicity). With the last strokes of eleven Mr. Amling of the chevron moustaches came in with an older man whose silken white hair was stained with brown like a smoker's fingers. Presumably this was another elder, for these two went and sat side by side opposite the table. Like the other men they folded their arms across their breasts and drooped their heads. Evan Plaicey came in and sat by the doors, in one of which was a small square window at the height of a doorkeeper's eye, so that he could see any late-comers and silently, with a hanging rope, draw back a door for them.

The Meeting for Worship was begun, though nothing new had happened. Only the silence continued, and the clock ticked, and the noises from the street without seemed more audible than they had been—the silence of thirty being a deeper thing than the silence of one. A car hissed by on the newly wet road; footsteps passed, and voices; children's laughter sounded from somewhere; a drizzle beat faintly on the roof.

But—the Silence. What were all these people thinking behind their downcast eyes? Were they 'centred down' and believing themselves in touch—were they actually in touch—with the Author of all the stars? If so, should he be feeling some sort of community with them in their sense of that Awful Presence? He was feeling nothing of the kind. His thoughts persisted in roving. And every now and then he was priding himself, immodestly, on some idea that had come to him. Contrasting this silence with the sounds outside—cars, dogs, a motor-bicycle starting up, a milkman's bottles clinking—he thought of this room as a still centre in the midst of the world, like that within any one of these individual souls. He looked at the faces of young men in whom the natural male aggression had been happily overlaid, and at the faces of old people and young who hated nobody any more. This last seemed to him a beautiful statement of something, and it was *he* who had thought of it. Some had their hands linked on their laps as if just lowered from prayer; some made one palm into a couch for the other so that their hands seemed the very picture of rest. He looked at the wandering eyes of the smaller children and thought that they still had all to learn. He observed that nearly all the women allowed themselves the vanity of bright lipsticks, and this he found a relief. If made him feel less lonely, less hopelessly secular, less impious in this headquarters of piety.

Silence.

And the wall clock ticking . . . ticking.

Then loudly, and with a brusque indifference to this hollow cube of silence, the neighbouring steeple-house sounded the quarter. Instantly the few children slid from their chairs and went with their childish noise from the room, Mr. Plaicey's rope drawing open the door for them. Once on the door's other side—on the other side of the silence—they scampered noisily away. Mr. Plaicey let the door swing back. It shut in the silence again.

Mr. Blaize made his efforts to do as the others were doing, but he could get no picture of himself centred down into the last deep of himself, and talking with God there; rather did he feel as if he were standing on the edge of the known world and speaking into a blank Beyond. And words came not easily, nor did they seem worthy of any imagined Presence out there in the Unseen and the Unknown. 'Help me to conquer some of my ghastly selfishness. . . . Forgive me for my wickedness about Father. . . . Grant him a long life. . . . Help me to forgive him his—to forgive him as I need to be forgiven. . . .'

Strange the rapidity with which the second fifteen minutes of silence had gone by, for here was the church clock striking the half-hour. Had he been so lost in wonderings as to have been like a man asleep?

The chimes had hardly died when Mr. Amling rose from his chair by the table. At last, after thirty minutes, the Spirit, seemingly, had moved someone to speak. He spoke in a low voice as if the long previous silence commanded this.

'I have found myself thinking this morning again and again how often God will bring a soul to Himself at last, and perhaps after years and years of indifference, by some rude shock——'

Mr. Blaize was instantly gripped; he fixed his eyes on the speaker though noticing that he alone did this, none of the others lifting their heads. The leaflet which Mr. Amling had given him said that the 'messages' heard in the meeting might or might not, in Quaker phrasing, 'speak to his condition', but surely these words applied well enough to his shock in Paris.

Mr. Amling, however, spoke rather of men and women from whom God seemed to have struck everything away, by total loss of fortune, of fame, of wife, of loved one, and so forced them in their loneliness and emptiness to give themselves to Him; and Mr. Blaize began to feel restless beneath this doctrine, though wondering if it was true. It was only when the speaker suggested that the salutary loss might be the total loss of self-respect that he was back in that Paris room again.

Could it really be a fact that Mr. Amling with his moustaches was being instructed by the Spirit of the All-Highest to speak words for a Mr. Stephen Blaize's ear? In short, that words were being directed straight at him by the Author of all the stars?

A weird, unearthly thought, but oddly less disturbing than he would have imagined it.

Mr. Amling sat down, and the silence was back for Mr. Blaize's thoughts to wander about in. He began to weary of it and long for the church clock, striking the quarter, to break it again. He noticed one old man who appeared to be asleep—or was he in a trance? He noticed a gentleman's tie and thought, 'That tie'd go perfectly with my new brown pullover. I've often wondered what would be the right colour for a tie, but that's it; that's it exactly.' Growing uncomfortable on the hard chair, he ached to rearrange his buttocks, but when at last, after a courageous wait, he did so, it was with a feeling of guilt, so still, so motionless were all the others.

A very old lady rose from a chair across the room. Waiting for her to speak, he perceived that her face, which seemed made of crumpled grey parchment and could not stop its palsied shaking, must once have been that of a most beautiful young girl. Moments passed while she stood there in black dress and black bonnet and did not speak; only her head shaking. When she did speak the beauty of her low, soft voice was almost like a continuing but changed part of the silence. She began with a prayer. 'Our Father, we pray thee that this hour of quiet worship may cast its power over all the coming week, stilling our hearts to remember thy closeness and thy love through all the hours of what else must be only a vain and restless life. We thank thee for strengthening in this hour of silence our awareness of thee and our confidence in thy awareness of us.

'Friends, I would like to tell you two small stories. One is of an old Irish woman who was walking along with a heavy burden on her back. And along the road came a man in a cart. He stopped his horse at her side and said, "Oh, come, Mother, that burden is much too heavy for you. Get into my cart and I'll take you on your way." The old woman thanked him and climbed up into the cart with her burden; and they drove on. But after a time the man turned round and saw his old passenger was still carrying her burden on her back, so he said, "Oh, Mother, why are you doing that? Lay the burden down." But she said, "No. It was kind of you to offer to carry *me*, and I don't want your poor horse to carry my burden too."'

No laughter greeted this story, but a smile lit up the faces of most. Mr. Blaize, for his part, while the old lady pressed her point that the Saviour had come to carry the full weight of our sins, was thinking that, if the Holy Spirit had moved her to tell this story, then the Holy Spirit enjoyed a joke—perhaps especially about the Irish—and this seemed an encouraging thought.

'Also, friends, I feel moved to tell you another story about another burden,' continued the old lady, her face of ruined beauty still trembling ceaselessly. 'A small boy was walking along a road, bearing a much bigger and heavier boy pick-a-back on his shoulders. And a man came up with him and said, "My poor boy, that is much too heavy a burden for you to carry." But the boy, looking up at him, answered, "He is not a burden, sir; he is my brother."'

This time, with probably unconscious art, the old lady said no word more but sat down, leaving her point for those who could see it. Mr. Blaize saw it and adapted it instantly to himself. 'He is not a burden; he is my father.' But since his mind obstinately refused to think of the old man sitting in possession of that little house in Murry Walk as other than a burden, he told himself, 'Oh dear, oh dear, I'm miles away from the full Quaker love'; and he tried, against the resistance within him, to pray that the old man—'old devil' had been his actual words—might have a—a very long life. 'Oh God, give him ... years yet ... many years yet.'

Surely the time must be ticking on towards twelve when the meeting would end. Had he, in a dream, missed the striking of the third quarter? Mr. Blaize had a habit of jotting down in his pocket diary any good stories he had heard (some of them for male audiences only) and he now had a desire to get down the old lady's two excellent ones. For Gwen and the family. But he wondered if he ought to be seen by some of these heavenly-minded people writing notes in a worldly book. 'Hear ... brother Scots. ... A chiel's amang you takin' notes. And, faith, he'll prent it.' He decided to fix the stories on his memory instead.

He had begun to think of the silence as a still pool when the long figure of young Mr. Plaicey surfaced from the brink of the pool by the door. He now spoke in a low level voice, his rimless glasses seeking the ceiling as if to see Heaven and its wisdom through it.

'I feel I would like to add one or two words to what we have heard today from Maurice Amling, how God will sometimes bring a man to Himself by some terrible shock that reveals to him his hopelessness, his helplessness, and his need. And it has occurred to me, sitting here, that this thought could be applied, not only to an individual man but to the whole world just now. For we sit here in a time of tremendous crisis for the world—never such a crisis—a time for choice between death for the world and life for it. Inevitably I have felt forced to think again about the Quakers' traditional attitude to war.'

Resistance, like a swelling wave, rose at once in Mr. Blaize. In that Encyclopaedia article he had read of the Quakers' traditional pacifism, and he had reacted sharply against it with '*I'm* no pacifist'. He had recalled the conscientious objectors in the First War, the 'conchies' as they had been called in contempt by most of those who were doing the fighting, and he had no wish, even though his days for fighting were forty years past, to be likened to such as they. A conchy? Heavens, no! Somehow it would seem a disloyalty to those fifty thousand unburied dead whose names were nowhere but on the Menin Gate. 'I can't be a Quaker, if I've got to be a pacifist,' he had decided, not without disappointment, but, reading on, he had learned that the pacifist attitude was not compulsory and had felt relief. But an insecure relief. And now—were this young man's words directed again at him, at the command of the Lord?

'Before I say one word more about the pacifism which I profess, I would wish to say with Paul, in One Corinthians, Seven, "I *think* I have the Spirit of God." "Think" only, you see. Or again in the same chapter he feels compelled to say, "I have no commandment of the Lord, yet I give my judgment as one that hath obtained mercy. . . ." It is in that spirit only that I speak.'

Mr. Blaize was relieved by this modesty, for he had felt sure that Mr. Plaicey was going to insist on a complete pacifism as the only wear for a Quaker today.

'The Quaker doctrine of pacifism is based, most of us think, on the spirit and teaching of our Master, but it is against the whole of Quaker practice to impose a doctrine on anyone, not even their own members——'

Ah, good. . . .

'You will all remember the story of how William Penn, full of delight because he'd been converted and joined the Friends, asked of our founder, George Fox, in a sudden alarm, "But what am I to do about wearing my sword?" And George Fox answered, "Friend, wear it as long as thou canst."'

So fine seemed this answer that Mr. Blaize felt a thrust of George Fox's sword. A dread lest these people slipped their pacifism into his heart gripped him again.

'With an exactly similar wisdom Mahatma Gandhi said to an inquirer, "If you have a sword in your bosom take it out and use it like a man." He even enlisted Indians for service in the First War, saying, "I did not hesitate to advise them that so long as they believed in war and professed loyalty to Britain they were in duty bound to enlist."'

Mr. Plaicey's large rimless glasses became visible only when they reflected the light from window or skylight. They flashed now as he looked upward at the skylight in the roof, waiting for words. 'Another time, friends, that great Mahatma said, "I don't believe in the use of arms, nor in retaliation of any sort, but I once told the villagers of Bettiah that they who knew nothing of *Ahisma* were guilty of cowardice if they failed to defend their honour, their women, and their property by force of arms."

'So it is with our doctrine of pacifism. It is for each indivdual to adopt it as and when his conscience bids him. In our two wars there were Friends who refused to do anything towards furthering the fighting and went to prison in consequence; there were others who went into non-combatant branches of the Services; there were those who obtained exemption on condition that they served in the Friends' Ambulance unit or some similar body; and lastly there were those who went into the ranks and served in a combatant unit. All these were good Quakers——'

Ah, good, good, thought Mr. Blaize again. But this pleasure and relief were promptly disturbed when the speaker went on, 'There was, of course, a certain amount of sorrowful headshaking about those in this last category, but it was accepted by all, so I am told, that if they had acted according to their consciences they had done all that could be asked of them.'

Mr. Blaize felt very unsure again. Perhaps he had better escape from the splendid trap in this room—better keep far away from it. 'I don't want to be "shaken over" by any Quaker heads, but I'm quite sure I could never be a conchy.' Once again he saw the Salient and Bellewaarde Wood and the road to Zonnebeke and Passchendaele. His thoughts were now very far from 'centring down'; they were wandering in the Salient, over the duckboards and the mud of '17 and among the fertile fields and tall woods of today.

Meantime the young voice went on.

'So while being tender to all consciences I do feel moved this morning to state what is *my* judgment and leave it with any here who are troubled by the terrors of our time. I believe that it has never been more necessary for us to advocate everywhere the principle of pacifism, or non-resistance, not only between man and man, which is comparatively easy, but between our nation and any other——'

'No!' cried the heart of Mr. Blaize in an immense recoil, while his lips framed soundlessly. 'Impossible . . . impossible . . . impossible.'

But Mr Plairey, taking a sheet of paper from his breast pocket, continued, 'As a great philosopher has put it—I read this only yesterday and wrote it down: "Passive resistance, if it were adopted by the will of a whole nation with the same courage, discipline and self-sacrifice as they display in war, would achieve a far greater protection for what is good in the nation's life than armies and navies can ever achieve, and would do this with none of the carnage and waste and welter of brutality involved in modern war."' The paper went back into his pocket. 'I think it certain that after a time, a long time perhaps, the soldiers of a violent and invading army, meeting only a silent, dignified, disciplined and self-sacrificing non-resistance, would say, "We were enlisted to make war. This is not war; it is peace." I doubt if there are ten soldiers in a hundred, a thousand, who will get joy rather than dismay from using violence against non-resisters. These are not just Quaker truths; they are psychological and spiritual truths which can be brought home slowly but surely to all the more intelligent and spiritually minded people in the country.'

Hearing this, Mr. Blaize, while still in a fairly warm recoil from the idea of a whole nation standing about quietly while an enemy went ravaging everywhere, felt undoubtedly a desire, an ambition, almost a need, to be one of the more intelligent and spiritually minded people in the country.

And quietly, mercilessly, this extraordinary young man, with his earnest eyes staring into space and his rimless spectacles sometimes flashing the light from window or roof, drove on. 'Unlike some of you I, as a young man, have had no experience of war— I was only twelve when the Second War ended—but, like you all, I live every day beneath the dark threat of'—he shrugged— 'Heaven knows what. And I find myself thinking daily that pacifism is only a fruit or bloom of something deeper; it is not a root. I seem to see then that, if the great threat came upon us, not in the form of an annihilating bomb, but of an enemy invading us because he knew we'd offer no resistance, we should not be able to stand fast unless we had been training ourselves, day after day, year after year, in the root thing, which is love. It seems so clear that unless we are well practised in love for our enemies, and in the certainty that hostility can only be successfully resisted by love, then our pacifism will be but a halting, unsuccessful thing. Every day we must practise defeating anger in ourselves and allowing none of its fruit to ripen. It's just the ego rioting in us——'

'The ego,' thought Mr. Blaize. 'That's me. That's definitely me.

A rioting ego. He has a way with words, this remarkable young man. Do continue, sir.'

And the remarkable young man continued, 'Just as the soldier in war has to discipline his fear, so the pacifist must discipline his anger, and the one discipline is as hard as the other because both fear and anger are elemental instincts. If we are practised in using love to cast aside anger we shall see again and again that love is a creative force, sowing the seeds of itself even in the enemy attacking us. At the very least a response of wonder is stirred in the enemy, and maybe a first faint desire to imitate the wonderful thing. These seeds may fall only in the unconscious, but they fall. That is why I call it creative love. And "creative love" is the word I want to leave with you. With the further point that there can be no creative love in warfare, but only in the flat refusal to use the weapons of hate.'

Mr. Plaicey sank down on to his chair by the door; and nothing could have seemed more apt than that, ten seconds later, the church clock struck noon like a tocsin.

As the clock beat out its heavy notes Mr. Blaize was thinking several discordant things. He was thinking 'What an astonishing young man'; he was feeling some distaste for so much piety in one so young; he was wondering why his long, narrow, slope-shouldered figure should make him seem more of a prig; and he was telling himself that perhaps he ought to dismiss all such irrational antipathies and just sit and admire.

Mr. Amling allowed a few seconds to elapse after the last of the twelve strokes, then turned with a smile to the white-haired elder at his side and shook his hand. The white-haired man shook hands with a woman on his other side, exchanging smiles with her. Meeting for Worship was over.

§

All filed out into the vestibule, and Mr. Blaize followed behind. In the vestibule many talked together loudly—very loudly, as it seemed, for Quakers. There was much he would have liked to discuss with one or more of them, but no one was disengaged at the moment and he was too shy to wait for one. So he went alone to the street doors. Here a woman was trying to sell copies of *The Pacifist*, and he shied back from it like a startled horse. Nevertheless he smiled at her so as not to hurt her feelings and escaped into the street.

VI

Bearing Gwen's Burden

MR. BLAIZE, having repulsed, or at least kept at a distance, the pacifist exhortation of Mr. Plaicey, but wanting none the less to hold on to the picturesque idea of becoming a Quaker, was the more eager to accept the old lady's lesson: 'He is not a burden, sir; he is my brother.'

'Yes, I may not accept the one, but I do most wholeheartedly agree with the other. Of course one should bear one another's burdens. Granted I have not in the past done much about this, but I've always believed in it. I've seen the beauty of it. And I must begin now to really *do* something. A bit late, perhaps, but ...'

Manifestly the 'brother' nearest to him was Gwen, and an outcome of these secret thoughts was that he walked one morning with a pencil and a piece of paper into the kitchen where Gwen was putting a small ham to boil on the gas cooker. Sitting down at the table and tapping the pencil's top on it, he said, 'Here we are, Mrs. Gwendolyn. Now tell me what I've got to buy. Help me with the shopping list. It's only just occurred to me that, now I no longer go out to work, I might sometimes do your shopping for you. I admit the idea could well have occurred to me earlier. Still, let's act while the iron's hot. Come on: a loaf of bread, a flask of wine ...?'

Gwendolyn seized her hour; she certainly acted before the iron cooled; she left the ham and sat at the table to discharge this business thoroughly; she dictated a list of purchases at dairy, baker's, grocer's chemist's, fruiterer's—which he pencilled down with reiterated protests, such as 'Oh, *no!*' and 'Spare me' and 'Call a halt, *somewhere*' and 'Gracious saints, this is taking advantage of a good man. I'm not a packhorse. How can I carry all this?' And in a final despair, 'Oh *no*, woman, but this is death.'

'Nonsense. Of course you can carry it all—a strong man——'

'But old, dear, old. Sixty-four.'

'Sixty fiddlesticks. It's the sort of weight we poor wives carry home every morning.'

'Well, all I can say is, I wish I hadn't come in with this idea. Haven't we one of those wheeled shopping-baskets you pull behind you like a dog?'

'We have not. I've asked you to buy me one again and again, but you've never done it.'

'I've a suspicion I'll be buying one soon.'

'And about time too.'

'Look here—really!—I confess I expected a more grateful response when I came in with this handsome offer—not a slight hostility.'

She jumped up, kissed him, while he was murmuring with a shrug, 'Man is born to bear injustice,' and she declared as she returned to her chair, 'I'm awfully grateful, my pet. It's sweet of you. Will you do it regularly now? That'd be marvellous.'

'Oh, but I don't think that was quite my idea. Not every day.'

'Oh, yes, I think it was. You can be so sweet at times.' And she patted his head.

'But not when it's wet? You wouldn't wish me to go out shopping in the grievous wet?'

'Certainly. Then more than at any other time. You'll do it beautifully, I'm sure.'

'Lord help us, I wish I'd never come in,' he grumbled and stared down at that shopping list. After a while he picked it up. 'Well,' he said, 'this is extremely gentlemanlike. I take it that it will be accounted to me for righteousness.' And he went out.

To come at the High Street and the shops he had to pass through

Murry Walk where Sapper Blaize sat comfortably in his son's little house and on all his hopes of gain. It was ten o'clock, and this was the hour when Sapper Blaize often guided his ridiculous little Pekingese dog up and down the Walk from tree to tree, or lamp-post to lamp-post, for the duties of the morning. He was there now as Mr. Blaize came along with Gwen's big shopping-basket on his arm. There was a broad grass verge beneath the trees of the Walk, and Sapper Blaize paced along it with his after-break-fast cheroot at his lips and the busy little dog on its leash, all ruffle and falling 'feathers' and tufted tail and out-turned toes, waddl-ing in front of him like a large furry caterpillar in the grass. Sometimes he gave the preoccupied dog a gentle kick either to encourage it to begin the main operation or to steer it into a better course.

The dog's original Chinese name when bought was 'Yây Sih', which means, we are told (and who can deny it?) 'fawn', but Sapper Blaize had adapted this name, with every justification, so he maintained, into 'Ah Sin'. And perhaps the chief of the justifications was Ah Sin's resolute refusal to be speedy about the larger of his two morning duties. The smaller presented no difficulty; it was always performed promptly and enthusiastically; even repeatedly. (We may remember that Sancho Panza always spoke to Don Quixote of the greater and the lesser, whether referring to his own needs or those of Dapple, his ass.)

'Mr. Morley Blaize, I think,' said the younger Mr. Blaize coming up behind his father and seeking to be funny.

'Oh, *you*?' said his father. 'What are you doing out at this time?'

'I am helping poor Gwen with the shopping. I try to help her.' He spoke as if he'd been doing this for months.

'Well, that's right. I try to help poor Sidonie too, by taking out this little beast. We both help a bit. I with Ah Sin. You with the shopping.'

Mr. Blaize thought the differential here was just about the same as between a cushy camp in Kent and the Third Battle of Ypres.

'Well, don't let Ah Sin wear you out.'

Perhaps aware of a slight differential, his father stressed the difficulties of his present occupation. 'I can never persuade the little swine to get on with his Big Jobs. I tell him to, I kick him, I jerk his leash as a powerful reminder of what we're waiting for, but he's as obstinate as hell. As someone well said, nine out of ten pekes are obstinate and the tenth is deaf. Ah Sin is both, I think. Nothing induces him to fulfil the main purpose of this sentry-go one moment before he has a mind to. Obstinate? The word isn't strong enough. If I want him to come one way, and he wants to go another, he puts down all his four-wheel brakes and refuses to budge. He tried this strong-arm stuff just now, but it didn't work. I can be strong-arm too. But there! If I drag him along people say, Look at that cruel old man torturing that heavenly little dog. They little know. They little know Ah Sin. Come on, Sin! Get on with it.'

But Ah Sin paid no attention. With his flat black muzzle low in the grass he prospected here and there and over yonder, dragging his master after him. 'Oh, damn the dog,' said his master, jerking on the rein. 'Come along, Ah Sin. I can't wait all day. Get on with it.'

'I take it there's no question between you two about the smaller purpose,' Mr. Blazie submitted.

'Oh, good gracious, no. As I always say the little beast is well named as a pee king. But I shall go to my grave without understanding why a tree is necessary or a post or a wall, for the minor transaction. Why not the wide-open spaces which he invariably prefers for the senior affair?'

'Well, I must hurry on. It's nearly half past ten.'

'*What?* What did you say?

'I said it's getting late, father, and I must hurry on.'

'It's just on half past ten.'

'That's just what I've said.'

'What have I said? I said it was half past ten.'

This little obstacle having been ironed out between them, and since Ah Sin was straining to visit scents at the base of a

wall, or among the grasses or down in the gutter, before being
in a condition to return home, Mr Blaize raised a hand in farewell
to his father (Ah Sin was not interested) and walked on with his
big raffia shopping-basket towards the High Street.

And for some mornings thereafter he was to be seen in the High
Street with that basket piled high with household needs, and possibly, when it was the week's end, loaded so heavily that it dragged
his body down on one side. But not thus for many mornings. After
perhaps a score of visits to the shops he came home pulling a wheeled
shopping-basket behind him, rather as Sapper Blaize pulled Ah Sin
(or Ah Sin pulled Sapper Blaize), and nowadays, if he encountered
a woman friend when he was dragging it along, he might say,
'I trust you make your husband do this sort of thing sometimes';
or, if it was a man friend, 'Look what Mrs. B. makes me do. Are
you treated like this? I sincerely hope so.'

§

A further fruit of his attendance at Quaker meetings, and of his
new leisure on weekdays, was that he started to read the Bible
from the beginning with some idea of reading it to the end. There
is, however, a powerful lot of it, and this enterprise did not last
many days. He enjoyed the pastoral stories of Genesis, though he
was greatly shocked by some of the incidents. But this did nothing
to arrest his reading, and he pushed on, not a little impressed to be
studying the Bible thoroughly like this. It gave him a feeling of
superiority to Gwen who had certainly never set herself down to
any such task. The early Exodus was entertaining enough but he
began to weary with the furnishings of the Tabernacle and still
more with the garments of Aaron, the ephod, the robe, the mitre,
the girdle, the breastplate of judgment, the Urim and Thummim.
These ended the enterprise. It was not resumed.

Two stories of Genesis remained always in his mind because of
their strange hidden mystery. One was the appearance of three men
at Abraham's tent door, before whom he bowed, addressing them
as if they were one. 'My Lord, if now I have found favour in thy

sight, pass not away.' Sometimes the story spoke of them as 'they', sometimes as 'he', and sometimes simply as 'the Lord'. Very strange. Thrilling in its mystery. The other story, in the next chapter, had a like mystery; *two* men appearing to Lot as he sat in the gate of the city; two men, seemingly angels, come to announce the destruction of Sodom; and yet Lot addressed them as if they were one. 'And Lot said unto them, "Oh not so, my Lord: behold now thy servant hath found grace in thy sight. . . ."'

With his habit of private humour he remembered this second story one evening when, wandering about the living room, he came to the window and saw two men coming along the pavement, one short and one too tall; one with long chevron moustaches and the other with a young grave face behind large rimless spectacles. He recognized them at once, saying, 'Ah! The Moustaches and Plaicey.' They came up his steps; his bell rang; and as he went to the door he quoted to himself the opening of the second Genesis story, 'There came two angels to Sodom.'

Mr. Amling on the threshold greeted him merrily. 'Good evening, sir. You appear to have borne with our meetings a second and a third time, so we thought—it was young Evan Plaicey's idea—that we might come and see if we could perhaps advise and help you in any way.'

Mr. Blaize stared at them in a slight alarm. He had wanted to approach Quakerism more cautiously than this. But his ever kindly consideration for others forbade him to show the alarm, so he said, 'It's most kind of you. Do come in.' And he preceded them into the living room, unobtrusively tidying away anything that was best out of view or disorderly. In the flurry of leading them in and hiding anything unseemly he had left the front door ajar. Remembering this, and running into the passage to shut it, he saw Gwen on a basement stair peering into the hall to learn what was afoot. 'What is it? Who are they?' she asked in a whisper.

'Angels,' said Mr. Blaize. 'Come to Sodom.' And he waved her back down her stairs with an anxious palm, after a hasty interpretation of his words lest she were too bewildered. 'Quakers. Quakers, my dear. Come to save my soul.'

Then he went back to the Quakers where they sat in the two armchairs on either side of the fire. He drew up a straight-backed chair and sat between them. 'It's most kind of you,' he said again. And Mr. Amling repeated with a laugh, 'It was Evan Plaicey's idea, as a good overseer.'

Which Mr. Plaicey, an unsmiling young man, enlarged upon without laughter. 'Yes, we make it a custom to visit new Friends between meetings so as to get to know each other and perhaps offer advice and encouragement.'

'Most kind of you. Very kind. But you mustn't think of me yet as a Friend fully——'

'Oh no—we don't. But Maurice Amling is particularly well founded in the Quaker faith, so if you are in any difficulty he will be well able to speak to your condition.'

Well founded . . . speak to your condition. . . . Once again, Mr. Blaize thought, 'The extraordinary young man! Talking to me like this, who must be nearly forty years older. Still, it's always interesting, even enthralling, to have one's condition discussed (if that's what "speaking to" means) so let's go to it. So long as it's not admonition. I don't care for admonition. I'm not taking admonition from either of these chaps. Certainly not from the puppy.'

To start them off on his condition, and to hear all that they would say about it, he laid before them such religion as he could honestly profess. He was no atheist, he said; no, no; atheism could be nothing but a blind guess and was therefore wholly unintellectual. Agnosticism was at least an intelligent attitude; and he was an agnostic. He wanted simplicity in his religion, he explained; he didn't want to be burdened with difficult and perplexing dogmas. 'I must say that your Quakerism appeals to me as a religion that offers none of these difficulties and strains to the adult mind. The —what I might call, the *developed* mind the scholarly and questioning mind, if you see what I mean.'

As he spoke, suggesting to them that *he* was adult and of a developed mind and scholarly, he was very conscious that Mr. Blaize the Showman sat on his chair.

'It may be easy for the mind,' objected Mr. Plaicey with his earnest eyes behind the large rimless lenses seeking some far distance. 'But it's by no means an easy religion to practise. It's an extremely strenuous business. It involves the most exacting self-discipline. We feel that we can scarcely be too hard on ourselves when we are applying Quaker principles to our lives.'

At which Mr. Blaize thought 'Oh dear!' and sat discouraged.

Mr. Amling chimed in with 'Yes. Evan's right that the difficulty of Quakerism is less for the mind than for the soul. As we sometimes put it, every day for a Quaker has to be a Lord's day and every hour a Lord's hour.'

Mr. Blaize's thoughts now ran, 'You can count me out, my dear chaps.'

'We make it our business,' continued Mr. Amling, 'to be constantly reminding one another of the Gospel's exacting demands on every department of our lives. We have our so-called Advices and Queries which are read often at our meetings so that we can ponder them.'

'Indeed?' inquired Mr. Blaize. 'And with what do they deal?'

'With everything.' Mr. Amling said it with a laugh. 'The Queries ask us to ponder on our condition in every way. Our love and forgiveness for our neighbours, for instance. Our honesty with one another. With the Government. Have we perhaps done something, however small, that defrauds the public revenue?'

'God!' said the thought of Mr. Blaize, as he remembered a few small pieces of contraband which he and Gwen had kept from the view of Her Majesty's Customs when they were returning from Paris, and a few Income Tax returns in the past which were a trifle below this Quaker standard.

Fortunately Mr. Amling left this uneasy topic so as to deal with another which obviously raised in him a peculiar fervour: Quakerism's indifference to class distinctions. Here Mr. Blaize was happier; here he had no doubts about himself. 'Oh, yes,' he agreed. 'I shouldn't fail you there. I don't think I have a trace of class-consciousness left in me. I didn't feel it in the First War when I was a young officer. I couldn't feel all that superior to my men, and some of the other chaps used to say I was too familiar with them. But I just liked them—and there it was. I feel the same now when I do my wife's shopping—I make a practice of doing her shopping, you see—and I feel an absolute drive to have a little joke with every assistant behind the counters. I just like them, you see. Love them.'

'Yes, but I'm not sure I didn't mean more than that,' said Mr. Amling. 'Much more. I am one who thinks we should abandon the last shreds of privilege——'

'I too,' interposed Mr. Plaicey emphatically.

'In what way?' asked Mr. Blaize, his anxiety returning.

'In every way. In education, for example. I did not hesitate to send my children to a state school. People told me they'd acquire some horrible Cockney accent there, to which I replied that I'd rather they lost the accent of the privileged classes if it was a barrier between them and their working-class fellows.'

This didn't suit Mr. Blaize at all. He wanted to keep the distinction of being an old public-schoolboy, small though his school had been, and the accent of a gentleman, which he didn't doubt he possessed. He kept silent.

'But not all Quakers think with me in this,' confessed Mr. Amling. 'Others maintain it's best to accept the present order of classes and ranks, and just to infiltrate it everywhere with Christian love.'

Mr. Blaize was much relieved: he felt he could do this. In fact, he thought it was what he usually did. So he turned to the matter which presented for him the greatest difficulty and the greatest interest. 'I feel I can accept most of that, but my greatest trouble, is your pacifism.'

'Ah, *quite!*' exclaimed Mr. Plaicey enthusiastically, as one who sees before him a topic with which he is eager to deal. 'Exactly! Now listen——'

But Mr. Blaize wanted to expound his own case. He poured out all those thoughts which had been his, as he stood, two months ago, by the craters in Bellewaarde Wood: how—say what you like—Ypres and '17 had been the peak of his life; how there had been drama then, and excitement, and escape from the pavements into green open spaces, and a secret pride that one was sharing hardships and dangers and that one was even ready—very secret this—to give one's life for something. 'Perhaps having been wounded so soon,' he said, 'I didn't experience enough of all the horrors and terrors and discomforts which we're always reading about, but the fact remains that all the old boys I meet who endured far more than I did *all* say the same. It was the one great time of their lives, and their lives have never had the same quality since——'

'Quite,' the eager Mr. Plaicey attempted again, but it was no good. Mr. Blaize was on his finest and fastest horse.

'And it all comes down to this for me—I was thinking this in your meeting a few Sunday ago when you spoke—I was thinking, Suppose I was young again, and the lads had to go again as they did in '14 and '39, I couldn't stay behind. I just couldn't.'

'Quite.' The way was at last clear for Mr. Plaicey. 'I quite understand all that. This idea of pacifism is very difficult to accept at first. As a rule the acceptance of it comes very, very slowly. But do let me say that all these thrills and excitements, and all these military virtues can be there for the pacifist too: all of them: devotion to a cause—suffering for it—risking all for it. It's just the same——'

'But it's *not* the same,' interrupted Mr. Blaize. 'I don't know why, but it isn't. Now listen. I was at the Menin Gate some weeks ago when, at nightfall, they stopped all traffic through the arch and in the silence sounded our British Last Post for our fifty-six thousand dead whose names are inscribed on its walls. And I tell you ...' Here Mr. Blaize the Raconteur took over, unseating the Showman, so that he 'wrote up' the scene, lying just a little to make it even more beautiful, exaggerating his emotions that day, till the choke was in his throat now, and the tears behind his eyes. Mr. Blaize was always the listener most easily moved by his own stories and most liable to tears. When he had got on top of the choke and had thrust back the tears, he asked, in a voice that tripped, 'Can pacifism give you any emotions like those?'

'Yes,' insisted Mr. Plaicey. 'Of course it can. And they are nobler emotions. If war comes again and it's at all like '39, it'll be a great hour for us pacifists; a peak hour, as you call it; the hour when we stand by the cause, not of our country alone, but of all humanity, ready for contempt and persecution if necessary; happy in the knowledge that it's in the hour of persecution that we shall demonstrate as never before, and to the whole world, our belief that hate and violence and murder can create nothing anywhere but themselves. Our action will be a cry to all men everywhere; a cry to them to be one.'

'Yes, yes.' Mr Amling put in a word here. 'And we Quakers believe that there is something in every man, no matter how poor his intelligence or how evil his past, which can hear this cry. The divine essence is in every man.'

'But what you don't see,' objected Mr. Blaize, struggling to defend his cause, though disordered and discomfited by much that they said because it sounded so true and fine, 'what you don't see is that you are refusing to accept that some things are more important than life and one must be ready to die for them.'

'And what *you're* not seeing,' countered Mr. Plaicey, 'is that while you may be justified in sacrificing yourself for an idea, it doesn't follow that you are justified in sacrificing others. The essence of war, my dear sir, is not dying but killing.'

This was the sentence that, more than any other—and even though he didn't like 'my dear sir' from anyone so young and lank as Mr. Plaicey—pierced the unwilling heart of Mr. Blaize. May I not wear my sword, asked William Penn of the founder of the Quakers, whose latter-day children these two visitants were. Wear it as long as thou canst, George Fox replied. And what a sword that answer was.

Mr. Amling was now supporting the arguments of his young lank partner with a picture of what he called 'a wholly pacifist nation'. Such a nation was likely, he held, to be left on one side and in peace by the warring nations, so that it would ultimately surpass them all in creative power. Its wealth, its arts, its sciences, its quality of living would all transcend theirs. But even if this was not so, even if it was enslaved, the defence of one's country was a lesser duty than a striving for the salvation of all mankind.

Mr. Blaize frowned and frowned, but in cerebration, not in anger, over these thoughts.

Soon after this exhortation the two men rose to go. 'I do hope we haven't intruded on you,' said Mr. Amling, shaking hands and smiling, just as he did when he closed a Meeting for Worship.

'Oh, not at all. Most kind of you,' assured Mr. Blaize as he walked with them towards the house door. 'Very valuable. Very valuable.'

He did not shut the door on them till they were both at the foot of his stone steps. Then he smiled again at them and shut them out.

'Golly!' he said to himself when he was in the passage alone.

§

Down in the kitchen he could hear Gwen clinking about with saucepans. Might God keep her thus occupied because he wanted to be alone in the living room with an awful conviction. The unwanted conviction that his two angelic visitors were right.

He put himself in the deep armchair which Mr. Amling had filled; and with his fingers fiddling in front of him went over all that they had said.

No doubt that they were right in all that they had said about the Quaker life being a strenuous business, a matter of exacting self-discipline day after day . . . every day a Lord's day . . . strictest honesty . . . no defrauding the Government.

The strain of it! Still, in that Paris bedroom he had vowed to himself that he'd overcome himself, and he'd been happy ever since trying to do this. 'Only happy when I'm being good.' If he withdrew from the happy contest, he'd be disheartened and wretched, after placing himself in a line of descent from St. Paul . . . and Buddha . . .

And right—oh, all too right—in their pacifist arguments. Ever and ever he recalled and re-examined these arguments he saw the trees of Bellewaarde Wood, and the Menin Gate with its stone lion on the apex gazing out over the Salient. The Salient where in their hundreds of thousands the sons of Britain had died—and fifty-six thousand had disappeared.

'Wear it as long as thou canst.'

The acceptance of their position could be a long, slow process, or sudden. And suddenly Mr. Blaize chose that it should be sudden. Suddenly, with excitement and delight, and an uprush of pride, he accepted it, leaning forward in his chair. Perhaps he was not as confident that he would continue in this acceptance as he could wish, but leave that ... push that aside. Yes, the Inward Light! Loyalty to the ghosts of the Salient would now take this form. It was thrilling. Trying to do things that would help forward something which they, surely, if blindly, had died for. And disappeared for. An end to war. He must do something for this cause while there was still time. Sixty-five now; only five short of three-score-and-ten ... but this thought reminded him that his father was eighty-seven, and then he was no longer thinking of saving humanity, but of how good it would be to tell Sapper Blaize, the intolerant (if unpractising) Catholic, that he was now a Quaker, and Sapper Blaize, the hotly militant Tory, that he was a pacifist. Yes, telling his father this—tomorrow or as soon as possible—should prove an invigorating episode. Mr. Blaize, who could see the truths of himself very well, was always interested in the fact that, while he hated quarrels with other people, and suffered after them, he enjoyed quite heartily a row with Sapper Blaize. He would report it to Gwen as 'another "blaizing" row, dear'.

§

But first there was Gwen. Downstairs quickly to tell Gwen. On the stairs it gave him pleasure to think that, even though nearly all marriages were less than perfect, it was always to Gwen that he hastened with news—good or exciting or bad.

Especially if it was bad.

The news this evening he conceived as drama. The story of a conversion. To Quakerism. And more remarkably to pacifism. The lifelong agnostic (and intellectual) to become a Quaker; the veteran and proud remembrancer of Third Ypres a pacifist. A pacifist ready to go to prison if desirable. Not that at sixty-five he was likely to be called up for military service, but there might be some other compulsory service which he could defy. And certainly would. Even as far as prison.

Gwen, in a flowered and frilled apron which seemed too small on her big square body, stood before the gas cooker stirring a cheese mixture in a milk saucepan, between lifting the lid from the potatoes to see how they were progressing and glancing at the bread slices toasting under the grill. She was also muttering to herself.

'Gwen dear, I've something to tell——'

'Oh, damn, damn! Oh *God*! Oh *look!*' The toast, left too long, was in flame. 'That's only the third piece I've burnt.' She snatched at the handle of the gridiron which scorched her fingers. 'Oh my God, is anything ever going right? I simply can't do everything. Will nobody come to help me? I'm sick of it all.'

Then Gwen was in one of her glooms. These were of frequent occurrence: 'One or two a day, as required,' Mr. Blaize used to say. They irritated him, these glooms, they chafed and wearied him—'They make me long to escape from the house,' he would say, 'to a pub or somewhere, where *someone's* jolly'—which was extremely unfair, as he could see, because he never failed to come to her seeking comfort for *his* glooms, which were less frequent than hers, but by no means sparse; and always he got it. She would listen at length to them. In fact, she seemed interested in them, whereas he found it difficult to be interested in hers.

'I thought you came and helped me when it was welsh rabbit. I told you it was welsh rabbit.'

This was a rebuke, it was admonition, and it lifted a flame from him, like the toast under the grill. 'How in the name of God could

I come and help you when I had two men—Mr. Amling and Mr. Plaicey——'

'It's quite impossible to do toast under the grill at the same time as anything else. One's blind to what's happening down there under the grill. One doesn't know till the whole place reeks of burning. Three times the bread's been burnt to a cinder.'

'I had these two men—Mr. Amling and Mr. Plaicey— discussing——'

'All the washing and ironing and cooking and sweeping—I don't know how I cope with everything. Or how I shall be able to go on coping——'

'I tell you I had these two men upstairs. Two of them. Mr. Amling and Mr. Plaicey. I have great gifts but I can't be upstairs in the drawing room entertaining Quakers and downstairs cooking toast at the same time. That's beyond even my capacity.'

'I heard them go hours ago. I heard them go down the front door steps.'

'They went perhaps ten minutes ago.'

Both were lying now to justify themselves.

'Well, that was the longest ten minutes *I've* ever known. I've too much to do with these huge old-fashioned rooms, and no help ever. It's killing me. A kitchen about as big as a Town Hall. Those horrible dark basement stairs. This kitchen floor alone—its walls——'

'I don't want you to have no help. I tell you to get a woman in.'

'You know we can't afford a woman. What's the good of talking about a woman? The money they expect now! Two or three mornings a week'd cost me pounds. I'd rather spend such money as we've got on other things——'

'Well then, if it's a deliberate choice on your part——'

But it was no good: she'd listen to nothing that'd undo the gloom which for the present was her enjoyment, her balm, her peace. 'I sometimes think that if I see this cooker again or that sink I shall scream. I shall sit down on a chair and scream. These never-ending meals. Four a day. And a man now in the house for every one of them——'

'I can't help being in the house. It *is* my home. Can't help being always around.'

'If I were alone I'd be content with an egg. But a man needs a proper meal. And everything in this old house is out of date, not a labour-saving device anywhere.'

'I bought you a fridge. I spent seventy pounds on it.'

'Other women have washing machines, dish-washing machines, garbage extractors, electric food mixers—I've nothing. I sometimes think I'm at the end of my tether and shall have a nervous breakdown. I'm worn out by money worries as well as housework. The price of everything in the shops! I never go out but what I spend a pound on food alone. It's all too much. I can't cope.'

'I try to help. I do the shopping. I usually help with welsh rabbit but I can't if Quakers come to visit me. They're important people, Mr. Amling and Mr. Plaicey——'

'Oh!' she protested impatiently, flinging her head to one side.

'And let me tell you I don't want to be oh'd. I've only talked the simplest sense, and a don't see why I should be oh'd.'

He was now in a dark pit of disappointment and, because so disappointed, ready, spoiling, to be rude. To come charged with the drama of a great decision and to be met only with a string of household frets! So trivial and transient they seemed compared with the great statement he had come to offer her, a statement about the Inward Light, the need to save mankind, the nightmare peril in which the world stood even as they spoke, with the Last Thing ready to fall at any moment. She was, as you might say, opposing her potty little temporal matters against these Immensities. Women! Always she was ready to shift the talk from international politics or deep spiritual matters because she had no interest in them. Women! Did they never see anything *sub specie aeternitatis*? That he should be occupied with Immensities rather than with toast made him feel greatly superior to her; which sense of superiority increased his anger by justifying it. A desire to say words that would wound seized him and was not to be resisted.

'Well, I'm sorry if your life's not been happy with me. I'm sorry if I've never had the money to give you the comforts you would like. I'm sure I've tried always to do my best.' ('Alas, not true,' he thought. 'It's only of late, only since Paris, that I've tried always to do my best. And I'm not at all confident that I'm doing it now.') 'But if it's all such a failure, I'm afraid there's nothing much we can do about it as late as this. I'm sixty-five now and can't very well make any more money.'

All she did on hearing this was to feel in the flowered and frilled pocket of her apron for her handkerchief and to dab with it at her eyes. He, for his part, had no intention of being moved and softened by tears. Or of seeing them—officially. Sadly and a little sourly he put his hand on the gridiron and swore as no Quaker should because it was hot. Laying two new slices of bread on it, he pushed it under the grill and stood waiting. So they now stood side by side at the cooker, one on duty with the saucepans, the other with the grill, she bigger and squarer than he, and neither speaking to the other. His great statement would have to wait; it was worth a happier occasion.

VII

The Blaizing Row

'WE ought to see something of the old man. We seem to see so little of him now,' said Mr. Blaize to Gwen next evening (all quarrels forgotten) and he deplored the deceit of pretending a dutiful visit when all he wanted was to provoke the old man with powerful arguments for Quakerism and Pacifism. Sapper Blaize, the non-practising Catholic, had been so shocked years ago when his son lapsed into agnosticism. He would be just as intolerant now of Quakerism. And as for Pacifism! 'When do we go and see him?'

'See who?' asked Gwen, lifting her eyes from the book which had got between her and his words. 'Go and see who?'

'Sapper Blaize. The gentleman who won the war from Kent. It must be lonely for him sometimes with nobody in the house but Sidonie. And, if you remember, he said he wasn't fit. Rheumatoid arthritis or something. It'd be a kindness to Sidonie too. Poor child, it can't be much fun for her, always alone in that house with that ghast— that old man.' Once launched in a little private skiff of deceit, one can only go sculling gently on. 'Shall we go and see them both?'

'Oh, yes.' Gwen seldom disputed any proposal for a social visit which offered chances of gossip with another woman. 'And you can tell him all about your Quakers.'

'Oh, well ... perhaps. ...' Mr. Blaize allowed, as if that were an idea which had hardly occurred to him.

So two afternoons later they came into Murry Walk. And there, conspicuous among the score of houses in the terrace behind the trees, was No. 10, his own house, bought so proudly for his old father when it was cheap. It was conspicuous because, while standing almost in the middle of the row, it was the only one which was not, in Mr. Blaize's phrase, 'tarted up' with brilliant paint on the door, green tiles on the steps, and decorative railings before the front garden. 'Tarted up' seemed the perfect phrase because they were painted and dressed to lure large money out of persons hungry for accommodation. Decorative bijou accommodation. Only a few days ago one had gone for nine thousand. And there at No. 10, in unworrying comfort, sat——

But there *was* the old man among the farther trees, being dragged along by Ah Sin. There he strolled, as carefully dressed as ever, in neat biege trousers with a knife-edge crease and a neat beige cardigan instead of a jacket, buttoned closely around the rotundity of his paunch. Beneath the taut cardigan you could detect his handsome waistcoat with the pearl buttons. Shirt and collar were beige too, to match the suitings, and a brown cheroot at his lips completed the picture of a well-dressed and apparently prosperous old gentleman. Since beige is not far from fawn, and since the little creeping dog was extremely well dressed too, with a full coat of falling fawn feathers and a tail like an ostrich feather or the plume of a dragoon, they made, suggested Mr. Blaize to Gwen, a fine matching pair. 'Does he dress to match the dog, darling, or did he get a dog to match his favourite colours?'

'I don't know,' Gwen answered, gazing at that little cylinder of fur waddling through the grass on the verge, 'but will you tell me why, wherever one goes, it's always a case of the larger the man the smaller the dog?'

Man and dog, having reached the end of the Walk, turned about —at least Sapper Blaize turned about and with a violent pull induced Ah Sin to do likewise. He recognized at once his approaching visitors.

'Ah,' he said, as they drew nearer. 'Yes. . . . Sidonie said you were coming. You'd better go in, and I'll follow. Sin entirely refused to do his Big Jobs this morning, and I fully intend to keep him out here till the point is settled between us—if it takes all night. He knows perfectly well what I've brought him out for, and here we wait—here we walk—till he realizes who's master.'

'The darling!' said Gwen in her fruitiest voice, brought along for this social occasion. 'He *is* the sweetest thing.'

Ah Sin chose this exact moment, while they stood talking, to achieve the purpose of this afternoon outing. As he did so he stared up at them from big round wistful eyes set almost in line with his small black punched-in nose. Gwen exclaimed approvingly, 'There! The pet!' and Sapper Blaize promptly picked up the pet to carry it home. He laid it on its back along his right arm, from which resting place it looked out at the persons passing by, at the occasional car, at a dog issuing from a house; and indeed at life in general. Apparently it had no objection to being carried baby-wise like this, though its small pink tongue slanted out at any passers-by.

Sapper Blaize led them up the steps of No. 10 to the door which was ajar. He called out commandingly, 'Sidonie. Come on. Steve and Gwen. Steve and Gwen.'

'What did you say, Uncle Morley?' called the always frightened voice of Sidonie from some doorway downstairs.

'*What?*' he shouted back at her, and Mr. Blaize could imagine her starting back, as she always did, at that bellowed '*What?*', even when he was not firing it into her face, even when there was a wall, or a flight of stairs, between her and it.

'Did you say something, Uncle Morley?'

'*What?* What *is* the girl talking about?'

'She asked if you said something,' his son explained.

'Of course I said something. Sidonie,' he bellowed down the stairs, 'I said your Uncle Steve and your Auntie Gwen.'

With which he turned and went ahead of them into the little front room. They followed in time to see him throw himself into his own big upholstered chair—being big it was the only com-

fortable chair in so small a room—and, tossing off one brown
slipper after another, stretch his legs on to a leather-bound pouffe,
that his feet in their ribbed beige socks could enjoy the fire.

'Sit down,' he commanded, not very graciously; almost as if he
would say, 'Well, since you're here, we'd better make the best
of a not very exciting business.'

Mr. Blaize and Gwen sat on a settee in the window. Sidonie
came in and without a word to anyone sat humbly near the door.

Mr. Blaize began, 'Our real reason for coming, father, was to
learn how you were.' (Mr. Blaize the Liar, he thought.) 'Gwen
hasn't seen you since you told us you were suffering from——'

But Gwen immediately took this matter out of his charge, and
left him silenced. Silenced and alone. Speaking with the soft, sugared
drawl which she kept ready for solace, her head going to one side
as if weighted with interest in the person she was addressing, her
whole face changing as she assumed a social duty and becoming
that of an actress registering daughterly love, she began, 'Yes, my
poor darling Pop, how's the arthritis? You said it hurt a lot sometimes. What can we do for you? Sidonie, what can we all do for
him, poor sweet?'

The Ministering Angel act, thought Mr. Blaize. Her business
isn't to speak any truth, but to be a ministering angel. And as the
sympathy and solace poured on, low and slow and loving, he
chose musical terms for the performance. '*Pianissimo . . . rallentando
. . . con espressione, with a vengeance.* Why does the woman never
understand that an act can be so overplayed as to sound insincere?
. . . *con amore now . . . con overwhelming amore.*'

'What are you all talking about?' demanded Sapper Blaize.
'Arthritis? Oh, I don't worry about that. A little stiffness at times,
but I've forgotten about that. I'm no invalid.'

As he said this, the old wicked thought, in the shape of a disappointment, appeared, pat on its cue, in Mr. Blaize's mind. No,
no, put that shocking thought away——

'I never felt better in my life,' continued his father, and therewith
gave the disappointment several more seconds of life.

'Isn't he wonderful, Sidonie?' commented Gwen, modulating easily into flattery. The voice was not quite so low and soft for flattery, but it was still low and soft and measured. And very irritating to Mr. Blaize. Amongst other things, why didn't the woman see how much less financially worried he'd be if his father —no, put that thought away.

Pleased to be called wonderful, his father said, 'Yes, I only really feel it when the weather's damp.'

'Well, then, you needn't worry for a bit, Pop darling. The report says it's going to be fine and sunny. But cold.'

'The porter says what?'

Sidonie explained. 'The weather report, Uncle. It says it's going to be fine and sunny but cold.'

'Fine in Sunny Cove? Where the hell's that? And what do I care about Sunny Cove? I don't know where it is.'

To clear this difficulty out of the way Mr. Blaize said loudly and, as it were, with capitals, '*Sunny*, father. Sunshine. But *Cold*.'

'Oh, I see. Good. Then Sidonie shall drive me a little way into the country. I love the country in winter-time. Sidonie, have the car ready for a nice little drive tomorrow.'

'Yes, Uncle,' said Sidonie, ever unquestioning in her obedience.

That little car which was something Mr. Blaize had never been able to afford! He glanced through the window behind him and saw it standing against the kerb on the far side of the Walk.

'Yes, Sidonie,' said Gwen, agreeing with them both. 'You must certainly take him out. A really nice drive. It'll do him good.'

And Mr. Blaize thought, 'Yes, you may well encourage him like that. It's not you who have to foot the bill.' But even as he was resenting this, a new and strange phenomenon in his father's deportment began to irritate him. Those two feet on the pouffe in their ribbed beige socks were standing upright on their heels (so to say) and bending their toes in simultaneous movement towards a leaping flame in the fireplace, like two disciples of Zoroaster bowing repeatedly before a symbol of the Divine. Side by side they bent their toes up and down, up and down, till Mr. Blaize, after watching them fascinated, wanted to shout in protest. He sank his body lower on the settee in the effort not to shout.

'Stephen's going to be a Quaker,' announced Gwen cheerfully.

'*Quaker?*' The two feet stopped all bowing and stood upright, as if they'd heard something that required all their thought—angry thought. 'Did you say Quaker?'

'Yes.' Gwen was pleased with the sensation her words had plainly caused.

'Oh, no. You can't be serious. I'm sure no Blaize has ever been a Quaker. I hope we've too much red blood in us for that. I should be horrified if any son of mine became a Quaker. Milk-and-water conchies, most of them.'

'Then I'm afraid you'll have to be horrified because I certainly *am* going to become one.' Angry with his father for his puerile contempt of men far better than he, and with Gwen for having introduced the subject before he was ready to play it properly, he now fired both barrels of his shotgun in immediate succession. 'And not only a Quaker, my dear father, but an out-and-out pacifist.'

'*Pacifist?* You mean a *conchie?* Like the ones we had in the war?' Ex-Sapper Morley Blaize was always apt to forget that there'd been a second war.

'Precisely. Certainly. I'm through with all wars.'

'Well, I never expected to hear anything like that from a son of mine; I didn't really. I never had any use for the conchies; I despised them. I infinitely preferred the enemy in front of me. He at least was ready to fight for his country.'

'Well, of course, in Kent you had the Channel between you and him, or he might not have seemed so lovable.'

Either his father had not heard these words (for he seldom listened to arguments he didn't want to hear) or they didn't seem as rude to him as Mr. Blaize thought they were, partly with pride and partly with a faint alarm. 'Oh no, my dear chap,' was all his father said, with offensive geniality, 'you're no Quaker. You're just talking nonsense.'

'I'm talking no nonsense. I've given the matter enormous thought and have made up my mind to be both Quaker and pacifist.'

'Well, look'—the elder Mr. Blaize's underlip came forward, thrusting down his mouth at the corners, like the underlip of a bulldog—'I'm afraid I'm the sort that speaks my mind and I must ask you, if you really do anything so extraordinary, not to publish it abroad. I don't particularly want any friends of mine to hear about it.'

This was rude enough to have set the row properly alight but Mr. Blaize's indignation was momentarily abated by the fascinating, if horrifying, behaviour of those two feet on their stage. They were bending their toes towards the fire again and again like a pair of simultaneous dancers making their curtain bows to prolonged applause. They even swung on their heels to bow to left and to right, as if to one and then another fount of applause. You could almost imagine the smile of good troupers on their faces.

'Conchies!' Ex-Sapper Blaize repeated the word in disgust while the toes bowed. 'I thought them unspeakable in '14. And I think them unspeakable still.'

'Then I'm unspeakable because I shall certainly be a conchie in the next war—if there's any chance of anybody being anything but dead.'

'Now then, Steve!' This was a warning and a rebuke from Gwen.

But her Uncle Morley hadn't listened. 'They pretended it was conscience but in nine-tenths of them it was just cowardice.'

'And that's a wicked thing to say,' declared Mr. Blaize, now dangerously heated. 'How can you know? Could you see into their consciences? They went to prison for their beliefs.'

'And it happened to be much safer in prison than at the Front.'

'But somewhat less comfortable in prison than in a camp in Kent.'

'What-do-you-mean?' This was roared. 'Are you suggesting that I had a cushy time in Kent? I'd have you know that we were worked like coolies and in constant danger day and night.'

'Danger from what?'

'From? From bombs of course. And ... and heaven knows what——'

'Exactly.'

'From sabotage. There were traitors all round us. One was shot in a farmyard, or so we heard. Just as all your conchies should have been. If they'd known they'd be shot for refusing to fight they'd have toddled off to the Front double quick. My God, it'd have done them good to be put through some military discipline. I'm all for military discipline. It's the one and only thing that trains men to forget themselves and be ready to sacrifice their lives for the good of their fellows.'

'Were many of you killed in Kent?'

'Not killed; no; but——'

'Wounded?'

'What are you trying to suggest? That I didn't do my bit in the war? I served in the ranks, I'd remind you—no officer—no living in comfort in the Officers' Mess—and I was over forty.'

'The Officers' Mess at Ypres wasn't exactly comfortable.'

'Now, stop it, Steve. What's the sense in riling your father?'

'What's the sense in his riling me?'

All this time Sidonie had sat upright and staring from one disputant to the other in discomfort and fear. She started back in fear whenever her Uncle Morley's voice, lifted in anger, bruised her hearing and her nerves.

Whatever Uncle Morley's career as a soldier had been, he had tactical sense enough to perceive that in this matter of combatant service in Kent he was not operating from strength. It would be better to launch his assault at the religious centre of the Quakers' position rather than at their political flank. As a lifelong Catholic he could command heavier guns than as a late arrival among the Sappers. Wisely he withdrew from this engagement and attacked the centre in force.

'I must confess that I am greatly shocked by this news—if you really mean it. To one who's been a Catholic all his life it's no small blow, after eighty years, to be told that his son has become a Quaker. No small blow at all. As I've said, I'm one who speaks his mind——'

(And God save us from all who say that, thought Mr. Blaize. Cocky hectoring bullies, most of them.)

'And to my mind all Protestants are by definition parasites on the Church. I've no use for any of them. And clearly the Quakers are the extreme of Protestantism. They've cast overboard everything the Church teaches—ministry, sacraments, *de fide* dogmas—and what are they left with? Nothing but a little ethical muck. Don't ask me to approve of your astonishing step. Ethical muck. My Catholicity means too much to me for that. I've sacrificed everything to it, right through my life. If I'd hidden it or turned Anglican I've no doubt I'd have been offered a headmastership sooner or later. But I wasn't hiding it from any man. And in the end it hanged me. It finished off my own little school because other schools were started up by Anglicans around me, and I refused—absolutely refused—to conceal that I was a Catholic. All my life I've preferred principles to money. That's why I'm not a rich man now.' The toes, satisfied with this spirited laudation of himself, bowed.

(Not rich! thought Mr. Blaize. That's a pretty way of saying it. But he forbore from providing a crueller description.)

'I took up schoolmastering because I was interested in service, not money. I had a fancy to live a life devoted to something higher than acquisitiveness.' More bows from the pouffe.

(My dear father, what a thoroughgoing old fraud you are—so Mr. Blaize thought as his father steamed on. Do you really suppose I haven't eyes to see through all your shams? That I didn't see thirty years ago how you started your own school because you had no hope any more of a headmastership and were too much of an old coxcomb to go on being ordered about by other men? And that I don't know the gamble failed in the end, not because of your Catholicity but because parents preferred younger and politer men. And don't I know that your Catholicity is only a dress like that fawn waistcoat with the pearl buttons? I don't believe you've been to Confession for fifty years or to Mass for thirty. You may remember I asked you about this once, long ago, and you snapped, 'That's *my* business.' An answer which told me all.)

A pity one couldn't say all this to him, but one hadn't the heart to strike such blows. And in any case it was late in the day for them now. So he just said, but not aloud, 'You silly old man.'

Still, Mr. Blaize was not displeased with the way his religious demonstration had gone. Just as he wished, it had stirred up the old man till the brew was all hot and a-splutter in his pot. So he was content to call it off when Gwendolyn said, 'Now shall we all stop talking politics and religion? We didn't come here to antagonize poor darling Pop——'

(Not so sure about that, thought Mr. Blaize. In fact that was rather my idea.)

'—so, Sidonie, go and make us our tea. I'm starving for my tea.'

Sidonie got up and ran out with her usual wordless obedience.

§

'If ever,' said Mr. Blaize, as they walked home, 'I'm inclined to shout you down when we talk, and to be a domineering old bully —I probably have a little of the old man in me—if I show any signs of never listening to what you say but just steamrollering you out of the picture in the rudest possible way, don't argue with me, just say quietly, "Sapper B." That's all: "Sapper B." Just like that. My God, I shall understand! The last thing I want to be is like that rude old man.'

'I certainly will, dear. I must remember that. "Sapper B."' She rehearsed it to herself, rather as if it would come in useful, quite often.

'Yes. I must take myself in hand if there are any traces of the old man in me. I don't think there are many, but there may be some.'

'Just a few,' Gwen agreed.

'*What?*'

'A few.'

'*What do you mean?* That I'm like him?'

'No, but just what you've said—that inevitably you have tendencies that are like his. You do get hot sometimes and try to bulldoze me out of——'

'*I* do? I simply don't! I've never heard such——'

'Oh yes, you do. Sometimes, my dear. As Mrs. Parkhurst was saying to me only yesterday, most husbands, even the nicest, have traces of the bully in——'

'I never heard such wicked and arrant nonsense.'

'Ask Peggy Diver and see what *she* says.'

'Peggy Diver's a cow.'

'Oh come! She's——'

'I won't listen to what Peggy Diver says. She's the one who's always been the bully. Look at the way she's bullied poor Sidonie all her life. I'm not taking any talk from Peggy Diver.'

'"Sapper B."'

'*What?* No, no; that's ridiculous. That wasn't justified. I was only defending myself. One must be allowed to defend oneself.'

'You hardly let me complete one sentence——'

'Oh yes, I did. Oh yes, I have. But you implied that I was a bully and I'm blowed if I'm going to allow that to pass. I'm certainly not that, whatever else I am.'

'All right dear, you're not. But do you think this "Sapper B." idea is going to work?'

VIII

Mr. Blaize Dreams Again

MR. BLAIZE is about to die. He who had been Stephen Blaize. Gwendolyn is at one side of his bed, holding his hand and looking down on him; Sidonie at the other side. No one is speaking. Sidonie is weeping, and, so far as his terror will allow him, he is touched by this. His father is not there, and is not missed. Indeed, for some reason or other, Mr. Blaize has not observed his absence and is not worrying about it. The whole world outside this room seems to be without existence any more.

The room is strange; it is not his familiar bedroom in Denlow Road; it is a large place furnished with huge brown Victorian pieces on which stand large Victorian ornaments. Heavy plush window-curtains droop from a knobbed brass rail to the floor. His bed is a wide field with a metal rail at its foot; each upright bar crowned with a shining brass knob.

And he is dying. To be dying, *dying*—it is terror. Through all the days of one's life, one has given so little thought to death. Death may have been admitted into the chamber where one's thoughts and hopes and loves moved and danced incessantly, but only for a minute. A brief minute, and that unwanted grim-faced caller is shown the door. The door shuts and stays shut. But now —to be dying is to know what death is. It is to be done for ever with all one's hopes, one's loves, one's friendships, one's aims, one's jokes; it is to be cast out for ever from the lively, noisy, sky-lit

95

world where alone these things have any meaning; it is to be alone somewhere, and never to see Gwendolyn again. Probably never—*never*. He looks at her. Never able any more to run and tell her of a triumph. Of good words spoken about him. Of an exciting decision come to. She is looking down upon him as he goes, and pressing his hand as if she would struggle to keep him—Sidonie seems to have faded out of the room like some shy ectoplasm that may not stay—he is not thinking of her any more than of his father; he is seeing only Gwen as he goes, and a voice in his head is telling him, 'You are dreaming, dreaming, dreaming. It's only a dream. Wake . . . wake out of it . . . *wake*'—he struggles and wakes.

He wakes, sweat running on his brows, heart beating at its cell walls like some captive crazed at last; but he is back in his familiar room as he can see by the slivers of light bordering the closed curtains. Quickly he switches on the bedside lamp that he may be yet more safely in the world of the living.

He tosses over and throws away the bedclothes to be rid of sweat. And remembering what it was to be dying, he remembers that he is in his sixties; that he is coming all too close to what happened in the dream, to the reality of what his death will be —and instantly comes a sudden vision, own sister to that in the Paris room: *you can only face death if you have built a character equal to it*. A character, that is to say, which is not wholly selfish; which can remember kindnesses done; which had other aims than one's glory and one's own comfort—in other words, a character of some greatness.

And he lies there now, resolving to begin building this very fine character tomorrow. And hoping that he still has time, at sixty-five, to do it.

It is the same experience, in gentler form, as that in Paris. Heartbeat and horror, tossing and sweat, are gradually succeeded by a warm pleasing glow at the thought that he has been obviously chosen by the Powers on High for illumination. A chosen vessel. Elect, as you might say. Like . . . in a small way . . .

like Gautama Buddha . . . St. Paul . . . Ramakrishna . . . Blaise
Pascal.

Blaise! Stephen Blaize. . . . Stephen Blaize the illuminated.
The Seer . . . the enlightened . . .

And so to sleep again.

IX

The Restless Ones

Sɪᴅᴏɴɪᴇ, shopping in the High Street with a loaded basket on her
arm, saw Mr. Blaize coming towards her with his wheeled shopping-
basket following behind. 'Uncle Steve! Uncle Steve!' she called,
for he was in a daydream; he was thinking, after that terrible night-
dream, how glad he was to be doing Gwen's shopping, something
unselfish; and had not noticed Sidonie. 'Uncle Steve!'

He saw her and exclaimed with a smile as they met, 'Sidonie,
my dear! What a load you've got there. I must buy you a pull-me-
round like this. And look at the load *I've* got. That's one day's
shopping only. How they make us work, you and I. I'm trying
my hardest to lose this job. I thought smashing the eggs or getting
the wrong bacon or forgetting the potatoes would do it—but no,
I can't get myself fired. Stuck with the beastly job.'

'Oh. I'm so glad to see you, Uncle. There's something I want
to say.'

'Well, walk on with me and say it. I've many more things to
buy yet. I'm not sure it wasn't a mistake to retire. I never had to
do this sort of thing before.'

Side by side they walked back up the High Street, Mr. Blaize
dragging the wheeled basket behind him like a big brown dog
on a taut leash. And Sidonie told him what she wanted to say.

In his recent demonstration of Quakerism before his father (which
had been more of a performance by Mr. Blaize the Showman than

the profession of a convinced devotee) he had made no convert of
Sapper Blaize or of Gwen. Sapper Blaize had argued against him
at the boil, and Gwen less hotly but at the simmer, her steam being
less of a jet but clearly issuing. It now appeared, however, that he
had stirred the interest of Sidonie though she had never once
opened her mouth to join in the battles but had just sat by the door.
Neither Sidonie nor Peggy Diver, her mother, were Catholics like
their Uncle Morley, Peggy's mother having been his sister-in-law
and an Anglican.

'Uncle, I was so interested in all you were telling us about the
Quakers, and I——'

'Can't be of any interest to you at all. You never go to church.
A lapsed Anglican, that's what you are. And so's your mum. Out-
and-out heathens, both of you.'

'I was so interested that I thought I'd love to go with you to
one of their services.'

'Services? They don't have services. You just sit there and do
nothing for an hour. But I'm glad *someone* was interested. My
impression was that the whole audience was shouting me down.
Of course it might be restful for you after a week of the Sapper.
You have a point there.'

'Well, can I come with you?'

'I'd love to have you with me. It'd be fun. Though perhaps
that's not exactly the word.'

'But, Uncle, I don't want Uncle Morley to know I'm going
with you. You know what he is.'

'I have some small knowledge of him, yes. And my private
estimate.'

'So do you mind if we keep it quiet? I'll just say I'm going to
church. It's kind-of church, isn't it?'

'Kind-of, yes.'

'So it won't be a lie.'

'Not at all. But I think it's a pity he shouldn't know. It'd do
him good.'

'Oh no, Uncle. There'd be the most frightful row.'

'Well, can I tell Gwen? It'd do *her* good.'

'Oh no, she'd go and tell Uncle.'

'Not if I sternly forbade her. Though I'm not sure that that's true. Nobody obeys me.'

'I think I'd rather you didn't.'

'Okay, my dear. It's a conspiracy between you and me. We'll sneak off together. It'll be bound to come out in the end, I suppose, and they'll blame me, but I don't mind in the least if they say I led you astray. You'll make a much better Quaker than I ever will. But you'll have to give up fighting the Sapper. They don't allow fighting.'

'I never fight him. I'm much too frightened of him.'

'Well now you'll have to refrain from fighting, not because you're frightened of him but because you forgive him everything. And that, my child, is the most difficult row of all to hoe.'

§

The next Sunday he stood waiting for her outside the Friends' Meeting House, and when he saw her coming up the tilt of Woburn Lane he gave her a grin. On the threshold he took her by the hand and led her into the vestibule.

There, before the table of pamphlets and Quaker books, stood the long figure of Evan Plaicey, and Mr. Blaize presented Sidonie to him. 'Evan, this is my young cousin. She's interested just as I was. But, like me, she's no more, at present, than a seeker after truth.'

'We are most pleased to have her.'

'Yes, but look, Evan, you mustn't go with Comrade Amling and visit her in her home, as you did me, because you'd get a distinctly unamiable reception from her uncle who happens to be my father. It might even be a rude reception. He's eighty-seven and the very opposite of a pacifist. In fact, he's rather a bad old man.'

'Oh, we mustn't say that of anyone.'

As so often with Mr. Plaicey a joke had missed its target because there was no target to receive it; there was only the empty air; and any nicely directed arrow went on and on into the mists to be lost for ever. Mr. Plaicey with the solemn eyes behind the big round rimless lenses was not interested in jokes. So Mr. Blaize decided it would be useless to explain 'he'd been trying to be funny' and said only, 'Well, we'll go in.' He rather wished, at the same time, that he hadn't said 'Comrade Amling'.

'Yes, you go in and sit wherever you like. So pleased to have you both.'

They went together into the bare chamber and sat where Mr. Blaize usually sat, in the back row of chairs against the wall. It was nearly eleven and the Silence was already in the room. At Sidonie's side he could feel her interest as the people came quietly in and sat down, lowering their eyes or closing them, while their hands lay clasped on their laps. Soon the elders entered and took their places near the table, Mr. Amling (yes, certainly it was unwise to have said 'Comrade Amling') and two women, one grey-haired, one white-haired. (What had 'Comrade' to do with Quakers? Just silly.) The clock of the neighbouring church struck the hour, and now the silence was unbroken by any newcomers.

Mr. Blaize tried to send his thoughts down into the deeps of him, but they surfaced almost at once and wandered about the room. They came to rest on a very small girl in a pink dress sitting on a low child's chair by her father. A little pink flower of a child she seemed, and if one thing was certain about her, it was that *she* wasn't 'centring down'; she was far too interested in everything around her. With a finger between her teeth she studied one silent figure or another, not omitting Mr. Blaize, at whom she stared for a long minute. Then she wearied of all these motionless humans and found more interest in the electric fixtures hanging from the ceiling. She counted how many lamps hung from each fixture, using the finger which had been in her mouth to point at them as an aid to calculation. One ... two ... three ... her lips formed the numerals as she pointed and counted.

'Never anybody less occupied with the Eternal and the Invisible,' thought Mr. Blaize. 'The temporal and sensuous world for her.'

But as he thought this he perceived that it was true of him too —for the moment, at any rate—so he turned his eyes from her with a view to losing the sensuous world, and they were immediately caught by another restless figure. This was a figure away to the right in the front ring of chairs. One whom he'd never seen at Meeting before, but almost certainly the old husband of Elizabeth Bletcher who came regularly and by whose side he now sat. Mrs. Bletcher, a working-class woman of about forty, had been a cleaner at the Hospital, but now made rather better money by 'obliging' many different ladies with an hour or two of charring. She always sat in the silence with her eyes so tightly shut that they gathered wrinkles above them, and her lips so pressed together that they forced her mouth upward and her lower lip outward. Mr. Blaize had exchanged friendly words with her sometimes and knew that she had married, when a widow, a man much older than herself. Here undoubtedly was he. A man of sixty and more, his lean face was weather-reddened, his long neck a series of pleats, his long fingers work-twisted. Most remarkable was his moustache; it was waxed at the ends so as to give a horizontal black stiletto on either side of his face, a fashion which had surely died out with the military of Victorian times. His hair was still dark, and it had been clearly oiled and spread across his forehead for this religious occasion. His clothes were old and old-fashioned, the white collar uncomfortably high and stiff, in honour, one guessed, of his Quaker hosts; one suspected that the lean pleated throat was more accustomed to a muffler.

Presumably Mrs. Bletcher had brought him along much as Mr. Blaize had brought Sidonie. Not that he was anything like as interested as Sidonie. Like the little girl he was looking about him —at walls, at windows, at this silent person and at that—in search of interest; in hope of it as a relief from boredom. More restless than the little girl, he slid his haunches back on the hard chair every time they slipped in their weariness forward. He yawned, beating at the yawn with the back of his hand. He blew forth a sigh, a visible sigh if not an audible. His elbows dropped forward on to his knees and his joined hands fell between the parted legs, a position probably never seen before in Meeting.

But then, to his pleasure, he caught sight of the other restless figure, the little girl, and was delighted to have discovered a fellow victim.

He sat up, laid an arm along the back of the vacant chair beside him, and gave himself to entertaining her, as a ministration to her boredom. He held up a finger to match hers that was doing the round of the electric lamps again. His finger went the round with hers, counting 'One ... two ... three ...' after he'd given her a wink to show that he was in this business with her. As an expression of sympathy he then enacted a huge sigh which sank his shoulders down and seemed to pitch his chest into his stomach. Next he spread his two palms for her in a recognized gesture of despair. With a shrug and a lifting of sad eyebrows he registered for her their common helplessness. He laid his finger beside his nose and then held it up in front of his face as a mischievous warning that silence, alas, was the order of the hour.

The little girl watched at first in astonishment and wonder, but then responded to his smile with one of her own. And since no one (except Mr. Blaize) was likely to perceive these happy exchanges, their eyes being cast down or closed, Mr. Bletcher (as he surely was) thought it safe to bring his right hand to the side of his ear and from this position, the thumb touching the lobe of the ear, to contrive a small wave to his new friend across the room. Whether such behaviour was in accord with a Quaker Meeting for Worship Mr. Blaize doubted, but he had a happy moment of thought when he decided that it accorded well enough with 'that of God' in both of them; for what was this mutual goodwill but a flowering of neighbourly love? There they were, the two of them, one at either end of the gamut of age; one five perhaps, the other, in his own terms, 'rising seventy'; but both of them united now as brother and sister in boredom, sympathy, and fun.

The church clock struck the first quarter, and at its opening note all the children, including the little pink girl, rose to go, their eager rising disclosing their boredom. Mr. Bletcher, not less pleased by this unexpected stir, rose to escape too, but Mrs. Fletcher, without opening her eyes, shook her head, whispered 'Sh'ush!', and stretched out a finger to guide his tall worried figure back on to its seat.

Mr. Bletcher looked at her but did not dare in the silence to ask, 'Hey! What the devil?' so he just sat down again. And now he had no little friend with whom to lighten the slow monotony. And there he was obliged to sit for another three-quarters of an hour during which the silence was broken only twice, once by Mr. Amling who spoke of God's long patience, saying that he didn't expect to put the world to rights, or even a soul to rights, in a single night (which comforted Mr. Blaize), and once by an old lady who was moved to rise and pray.

Twelve o'clock and it was over; the elders shook hands; the people rose to file out; and Mr. Blaize took a last look at the retreating Mr. Bletcher, feeling sure he'd never see *him* again. In the vestibule, however, Mrs. Bletcher stood chatting with other women and her husband was compelled to stand waiting near by, not without an aura of impatience forming itself around him like a thickening cloud. You could almost see the words struggling to get past his lips, 'Oh, *come* on, Liz! For the Lord's sake——' only the imprisoned words were probably a trifle more blasphemous. Catching Mr. Blaize's glance, and assuming that any normal man would share his distaste for gossiping women, he manifested it with a wink and a shrug of helplessness like the one he'd provided for his little pink friend. This being cordial, Mr. Blaize, with Sidonie at his side, stopped to speak to him.

'Mr. Bletcher, isn't it? This your first visit?'

'*I* should say so,' he affirmed with an emphasis which suggested it would be his last. 'Liz brought me. She's got it badly. And she's been getting at me for weeks past to come, so, Gawd love us, I come this morning. I said I would for once if only to see what goes on. And Lor' bless you, *nothing* goes on. What you might call, absolutely damn-all. For an hour.'

'What goes on is supposed to go on inside you.'

'Pardon, guv?'

Mr. Blaize repeated the explanation.

'Nothing went on inside me,' Mr. Bletcher assured him.

'The idea is that good thoughts come to you in the silence.'

'The only good thought which come to me was that it was slowly getting towards twelve o'clock when the Brown Tankard'd open. Which was a good thought, yes, but 'ardly what *you* mean, guv.'

'I'm not a full-fledged Friend yet. Just what they call an attender.'

'Well, I guess I've attended once too often. S'not my idea of religion. I'm not a religious chap, but I was a choirboy once, and *that's* my idea of religion. It suits Liz though. Seems to suit 'er like one o'clock. She's got it badly.'

'Yes, I can see it means a lot to her.'

'A lot? She don't talk of nothing else. But I *will* say it makes her a helluva lot nicer; I will say that for it. No longer throws half the kitchen at me when she's riled. Still loses her wool, o' course, occasionally—who don't—and when she wants to, she can't half create—what woman doesn't?—but it don't last long now. We're gassing again in no time.'

'Well, that's fine.'

'Oh yes, Liz is all right. Always 'as been, really. Never one of those nagging, bellering, 'ollering types. And now she's—well, I mean to say—really nice. Not but what there isn't room still ... So the more she goes quakering the better for me.... Yes ... on the whole ... but, crikey, after that gen'l'man got up and spoke, I was afraid *she* might get up and argue the toss. As she does at home, with me. It fair put the wind up me. And not only because I'd've wanted to go through the floor with shame, but because when our Liz starts chewin' the fat, she's apt to go on and on and on and on ... and then some more.... She's my second, you realize that, don't you? Yes, I lost my first, come seventeen years ago, and Liz, who'd lost her first too, took me on, even though I was twenty-eight years older than what she was. Twenty-bloody-eight.' Mr. Blaize shivered at the adjective, not for its own sake but for its appearance in this place. 'She lost her first in the last war. My war was the 1914–18 do. But everyone's forgotten about that.'

'1914–18 was my war too.'

'Gawn! Was it? Why, you 'ardly look old enough.' This pleased Mr. Blaize.

'I'm sixty-five,' he said.

'Yes, well, I suppose you could be.' Mr. Blaize was less pleased.

'Actually I'm not sixty-five till October,' he felt driven to say.

'I'm sixty-seven.' Now Mr. Blaize was shocked to learn that this lean and wrinkled old man was only two years older than he; shocked while the lean old man continued, 'That means I was nineteen in '14, and I enlisted straight away. No bloody conscription for me.'

'I joined up when I was eighteen—the next year.'

'What were you? P.B.I.?'

'Yes. Poor Bloody Infantry,' said Mr. Blaize, using the adjective himself now, to show that he knew what P.B.I. stood for.

'I was a gunner. Two-Five-O Siege Battery, R.G.A., Royal Garrison Artillery.' He gave the words in full, proudly. 'In this second business I was only in the Home Guard. Gor-crikey, that was a fair old Fred Karno scream, wa'nt it?'

'*Come* on, Wally!' commanded his wife impatiently, having concluded her gossip and lost her friends.

'Well, I like that,' he complained with a grin. 'You been talking your head off for donkeys' years, till at last I had to start a crack with this gen'l'man for something to do. He was in the Old War with me, I'd like you to know. The Poor Bloody——'

'Oh, *quiet*, Wally!'

'The P.B.I., while I with the bloody gunners was shooting him from be'ind. It's probably no thanks to me that he's standing 'ere now. This is Liz, guv; called Liz after the Queen Mother. *Gor-*

blimey, she was only born in '23 just when the Queen Mother married the Duke, so they called her Liz too. That's right, a'nt it, Liz?'

'That's right. Are you liking our Meeting, sir?' she asked Mr. Blaize, but before he could answer, went on, 'Isn't it lovely? Oh, I do enjoy it. Mr. Amling—he's a lovely man, isn't he? And that young Mr. Plaicey. They both talk lovely. It's all so restful, like, after my week's work, washing and scrubbing and suchlike.'

'Yes, she works 'ard, Liz does. Has to keep me. Keep the old man.'

'Is this young lady your daughter?' asked Mrs Bletcher, having noticed Sidonie, who'd been standing in silence and patience beside the two men.

'No, my niece. Or so I call her. Actually a cousin once removed.'

'Ah,' said Mrs. Bletcher, not clear about this.

And Mr. Bletcher came in with, 'Well, what about a pint? Could the young lady sink a pint? Or a gin, perhaps. That's what the ladies like. Till they're married, when their 'usbands learn 'em double-quick to drink beer at 'alf the price. But I'll be glad to stand the young lady a gin, seeing she ain't my wife.'

Mr. Blaize wondered if such an invitation had ever been heard in this Meeting House before, and Liz was clearly thinking the same for she rebuked him. 'Wally! Do be quiet! These people are practically all teetotallers.'

'Crikey!' said Wally. 'Well, Gawd 'elp 'em.'

The women declined the invitation but the four of them walked together to the foot of Woburn Lane. Here Mrs. Bletcher said to Sidonie, 'We'll go along together, shall we, dearie? And leave these gentlemen to their drinking? Unless, of course, you'd like to go with them?'

'Oh, no,' said Sidonie with a frightened conviction that was barely polite.

So the women went one way and the men another, heading for the Brown Tankard in the High Street. Outside the Brown Tankard

Mr. Bletcher hesitated a second and then turned towards the Saloon Bar door. Mr. Blaize guessed his thought at once and said, 'The Public Bar's all right for me.'

'Nah!' Mr. Bletcher objected. 'Nah, nah! Public Bar's no place for gentlemen like you. All right for common chaps like me. This way, sir.'

In the Saloon Bar Mr. Blaize made an effort to get first to the counter and buy the drinks, but Mr. Bletcher would have none of this. 'Nah, nah! S'my invite. Two pints, please, miss. Two pints o' bitter.'

'*Best* bitter?' inquired the flaxen barmaid.

'What? . . . Best . . .?' Again that moment of hesitation which Mr. Blaize perceived, understood and sympathized with. 'Yeah, of course. . . . Two pints of best bitter.'

They took their pint mugs through the Sunday press of chattering drinkers, through a smoke-clouding atmosphere smelling of strong tobaccos, flat beer and human sweat, to a table against the wall; but here they remained standing. Like the rest of this crowd Mr. Bletcher preferred to drink standing.

'Well, here's to it, mate.' He lifted his mug to Mr. Blaize. 'And here's to the old P.B.I. Most of them dead now, I suppose—them that got out of it alive. I've nothing against the Infantry in this last show, but, lord help us, they travelled like gentlemen. They didn't have to march twenty miles a day with ninety pounds of kit on their backs and then spend a week or two in front of Eepriss with nothing but mud and water in sight anywhere.'

'Were *you* at Ypres?'

'*Me* at Eepriss? I like that! I was at Eepriss One in '14, Eepriss Two in '15, and back again, sure as fate, for Eepriss Three in '17. Some of the old boys used to call it Wipers, but I soon learned that its proper pronounciation was Eepriss.'

'I was in Third Ypres.'

'*You* were? And in the P.B.I.? And we're both standing here alive! Drinking beer. Funny. O'course, being a gunner with our six-inch how's I was a bit behind you, but I was out in the mud all right in front of Eepriss. Didn't have to go over the top like you, naturally, but mind you——'

'"Over the top and the best of luck",' Mr. Blaize quoted. He was happy to be at last with an elderly man who, like him, obviously rejoiced when he was with someone before whom he could unpack his tales of the old war. He looked at the waxed stiletto ends to Mr. Bletcher's moustache and realized that they were his pleased and permanent statement to himself that he'd been a soldier forty-odd years ago. Here was just such another as Mr. Blaize himself, one who'd been shut in by the unending streets before the old war, and who never left them now, though life was flowing faster and faster; and for whom therefore Ypres was a peak of his life.

'Mind you, guv, I often had to come up alongside of you poor buggers when I went with my officer to an O. Pip we had in the ruins of a farmhouse near a place called Frezenhoek—though there was nothing freezin' about it just then, I can tell you.'

'Frezenhoek? I was——' He was about to say, 'I was wounded near there,' but, on hearing that signallers' shorthand, 'O. Pip' for 'Observation Post', he too wanted to speak the old language, and he altered his words to, 'I stopped my packet not far from there.'

'You did? A Blighty one?'

'As it turned out, yes. Just wounds in the head and leg.'

But Mr. Bletcher was anxious to get back to his own memories. 'I always hoped for a nice cushy Blighty but—no such luck, not even when our No. 3 gun got red-hot and burst, killing three lads and one officer. I stopped nothing. I just helped to carry the wounded away. We were firing all sorts of shells then: high explosive, shrapnel, gas. The bloody batteries were practically wheel to wheel——'

'I know. I was there. Look, Mr. Bletcher, don't you think——'

'Bletcher be damned. Wally's my name.'

'Well, look, Wally. Don't you think Ypres is the great name of the war? The Somme was over in a month, but Ypres! Year after year of it; Ypres One, Ypres Two, Ypres Three; '14,' 15, '17, and it never fell, not even in the Huns' great push of 1918. Nothing much left of it then, but we were still around what was left. Have another pint on me.'

'Don't mind if I do, sir.' They walked back through the noisy press to the counter and the flaxen barmaid. 'Yes, we hung on to it all right but at the cost of three hundred thousand men. Nearly half a million, that. Nothing like that in this last business.'

'No. And that's why Ypres is a name alone. Two more pints please, miss.'

'Ta, sir,' said Wally, picking up his pint. 'Gaw, it's a treat to meet someone who knows what it was like and is ready to talk about it. "What did you do in the Great War, Daddy?" Christ, that was a fast one the recruiting boys pulled on us, wasn't it? Did your kids or any others ever care a bloody damn what you done in the Great War, or if you done anything, come to that? Nah! Just bored if you tell 'em.'

'I was back in Ypres last year,' said Mr. Blaize.

'You *were*?'

'Yes, and I walked straight on to Bellewaarde Wood which I wanted to find again. In '17 it was just a hump of wet mud and a few sticks. It's a huge thick wood again now.'

'Gaw! I've always longed to go back. I've always felt I could walk straight on to our gun sites, even though the Salient is all green fields now—or so they tell me. And I believe I'd find the site of that O. Pip. But I've never had the money. I'm only a builder's labourer, see; and I was out o' work most of the thirties. Plenty of work in this last war, but they didn't want me over in Eepriss just then, looking for an old O. Pip.'

'Are you working now, Wally?'

'Me? Nah! Who gives work to an old boy of sixty-seven? Just sitting on me bum, doing nothing. Only got me pension now—two-seventeen-six—and, strike me pink, if I did any work they'd dock me of that! It's Liz who earns the lolly now, obliging the ladies. I'd say she was keeping both of us if I 'adn't me two-seventeen-six. A good girl, and a lot softer with her old man, as I told you, since she got mixed up with these 'ere Quakers. Quite a lot softer. And it's catching, you know. I'm nicer than I was. Not much, but a shade nicer. Fancy a mere kid like that, just coming up forty, taking to an old codger like me. Why do they do it? But they do, you know. Between you and me, I'm quite clear I ain't really worthy of her, though I don't tell her that; yeah, quite clear about it, except when she's mad at me and ticking me off. Not so clear then. . . . No, I shall never get back to old Eepriss. Never. Too late. And no money. But I'd like to have found that O. Pip.'

It was as he said this that a very pleasing but foolish desire stirred in Mr. Blaize; nothing less than the desire to take this brother veteran back to Ypres as a 'treat'. He was already longing to return there himself, and it was always pleasant to be generous, to play the part of a Mr. Bountiful. If only he had the money for this! But . . . he began to think of the cost and of his narrow budgeting; and the pleasant if foolish idea faded and died there in the Saloon Bar. Or lay down like one dead.

X

The Overseer Calls

SIDONIE came again and again with Mr. Blaize to Meetings, and each time she told her Uncle Morley that she was going to church. And after each meeting Mr. Evan Plaicey came and talked earnestly with her, obviously hoping to gather her in as a Friend. That she enjoyed his earnest expositions was clear to Mr. Blaize. Sidonie was not small for a young woman but she seemed small and short, standing in front of the up-ended strip which was Mr. Plaicey, and her eyes, looking into his rimless spectacles so high above her, were bright with interest. Mr. Blaize, studying the two of them, began to suspect that Mr. Plaicey would soon make a full-flavoured Quaker of Sidonie—partly because he would be aided by an unconscious desire in her (as unconscious in her as it had been conscious in him) to announce to her Uncle Morley a religion that was the opposite of his own. And since Mr. Blaize had a strong desire that she should do this he left her regularly to the vigilant and dangerous attentions of Mr. Plaicey, chatting merrily with other Friends till she was ready to come away.

It was after their sixth visit to the Meeting House that Mr. Plaicey, forgetting his instruction not to call on her in Murry Walk, remembering only his duty as an Overseer and her palpable interest in his tutelage, sought her address in the Visitors' Book, and one evening, impelled by his Inward Light, brought his large rimless discs along the Walk with the mild earnest eyes behind them seeking, all innocently, Uncle Morley's steps and front door.

The front door bell rang through the house. But since Sidonie could not come at once, being in her bedroom upstairs and between one dress and the next, and since Uncle Morley, at eighty-eight, had as much curiosity in him as any one of six or seven, and a like irrational hope that a ring on the front door bell might portend something good, he rose from his deep chair and walked to the door in his beige socks (he'd just been warming and comforting his toes). Ah Sin, not less curious and hopeful, came waddling hastily after him.

Being himself heavy, square-shouldered and deep-chested, Uncle Morley saw on his threshold a young man whom he thought despicably lanky and slope-shouldered. The young man's eyes too, behind the round lenses, he thought earnest, unsmiling, and rather contemptible. Staring at this vision with more of amazement than hospitality, he asked himself, 'Who on earth or what on earth is this over-earnest telegraph pole?'

'Miss Sidonie Diver, sir?' the pole inquired in a tone soft and courteous.

'*What?*' bellowed Uncle Morley, never aware how loudly he spoke. This was so loud that Ah Sin barked too, and more than once. If his master seemed to disapprove of someone on the doorstep, Ah Sin disapproved too, with barks. Unprepared for a 'what?' of such volume, the telegraph pole leant back from it, just as Sidonie usually did.

'Miss Sidonie Diver, sir? She lives here, does she not?'

'Yes, she lives here.' Uncle Morley allowed this but offered no further help. He was, in fact, annoyed that this strange apparition had only come to see Sidonie and could not be construed as anything of interest to him.

'Could I speak with her then, sir?'

Uncle Morley stared at him—stared as if this were the most surprising question he'd heard for several years, and it was only after a discouraging pause that he said, 'Yes. I suppose so. Who is it?'

This had been spoken softly because unwillingly, so Mr. Plaicey had to ask apologetically, 'Pardon, sir?'

'I said *Who is it?*' explained Uncle Morley, anything but softly. 'What—who—what shall I say is your business?'

'My name is Evan Plaicey. She will know it.'

'Heaven *who?*' Mr. Morley frowned over the unheard syllables.

'Plaicey, sir. I said my name was Evan Plaicey.'

'It is, is it?'

'Yes, sir. And she knows me well. I come from the Society of Friends.'

'Psychiatry *what?* What did you say?'

'Society of Friends.'

'Psychiatry offends?' Now Uncle Morley could sometimes direct a joke at a person he was liking not at all, if for the moment the joke seemed better worth while than the dislike. And in such moments of jocularity he didn't mind if the joke had its root in his deafness, even though in cantankerous times he denied the deafness. So he demanded now, 'Psychiatry offends, did you say? I quite agree. Always said so. Lot of damned nonsense.'

'No, sir. I said the Society of Friends.'

'Friends?'

'Yes, sir. Society of Friends.'

'Who on earth are they?'

'The Quakers, sir.'

'Oh, of course. Quakers. They call themselves Friends, don't they? Are you collecting for them?'

'No, sir, I——'

'Because if it's for some peace meeting or other I'm not giving a penny. I don't agree with it. Quite frankly I hold that all people who won't fight for their country are traitors and nothing else. I'm sorry, but I can't stand pacifists at any price. You're talking to an old soldier, let me tell you. One who was in the Great War, even though I was over-age at the time. And in the ranks too. Come back, Sin! Come *back*, I tell you! You Quakers are all pacifists, aren't you? Well, it's just as well that you should know

what some of us think about young men who'll take everything
their country does for them but refuse to lift a hand in her defence.
Without mincing matters—I was never one to mince matters—
some of us feel that they should just be put up against a wall and
shot.'

'But, sir, I haven't come to——'

'What are they but traitors? A traitor is one who gives active
and recognizable assistance to the King's enemies, and that is precisely what they do. Precisely.'

'My visit is nothing to do with that, sir,' said Mr. Plaicey, his
answer an admirably quiet example of non-resistance to violent
attack. 'It's just that Miss Sidonie comes frequently to Meeting on
Sundays.'

'She doesn't. What are you talking about? You've got something
wrong.'

'But this is Miss Sidonie Diver's home, isn't it?'

'As a matter of fact, it isn't, it's mine. But she lives with me and
goes to church every Sunday.'

'But—sir—the last six Sundays she's come to our Meeting.'

'My God! Your Meeting? And she told me she was going to
church! My God!'

Momentarily stupefied, he could only gape at the visitor. He did
not know that Sidonie was now standing at the twist in the stairs
and looking down at them both, and trembling.

'I thought I'd come along and discuss our principles further with
her. She is greatly interested, so I felt that, as an overseer, it was my
task and privilege to come along and speak to "that of God" within
her.'

'To the *What* of *Which* within her?'

Mr. Plaicey did not care to shout the sacred phrase along the
corridor of Murry Walk, so he was silent for a moment while
Uncle Morley swung round to yell 'Sidonie!' up the stairs, but saw
her standing there, half in view and half hidden round the bend.
'What the hell's all this about? Here's someone says he's a
Quaker——'

'Mr. Evan Plaicey.' The bruised young man provided his name again.

'Oh, I don't know anything about that. If what you say is true, the girl's been lying to me. Sidonie, what's it all about? He says he wants to talk to you.'

'It's all right, Uncle. I——'

'But it's not all right. He says you've been going regularly to his—whatever they call it—his chapel or tabernacle or Holy-of-Holies—*I* don't know what they call it.'

'It's quite true, Uncle.' Sidonie came down the stairs, frightened and shaking but defiant as never before. Perhaps it was the tall presence of Mr. Plaicey on the step that gave her courage, but this was the moment in Sidonie's life when the spirit of the worm beneath the sod lifted it out of its comfortable security and into the upper air.

'But you told me you were going to church.'

'Yes, well ... all right ... I told a lie. ... Unless a meeting for worship is "church" just as much as your Mass is. Come in, Mr. Plaicey.'

'I don't like being told lies to. And where, pray, is he coming to?' Uncle Morley had no desire to vacate his chair by the fire or have a pacifist sitting in his living room.

'It's all right, Uncle. We'll go downstairs to the dining room.'

'But I don't want—I'm not sure that I've any intention of letting them turn you into a Quaker. I'm not at all sure.'

'I'm afraid you haven't any say in the matter, Uncle.' Probably Sidonie was not less amazed at this answer than her Uncle Morley was. 'Come in, Mr. Plaicey.'

'No, I'll go, Miss Diver. I quite understand.'

'No, you won't go; you'll come in. I shall enjoy hearing all you have to say. I apologize for what has happened, but my Uncle Stephen did warn you that there might be rudeness if you came here.'

'I'm so sorry, Miss Diver.'

'Nothing to be sorry about. I'm glad it's all come out into the open. Come downstairs.'

'But *good God!*' exclaimed Uncle Morley, standing in the hall and seeing the pair of them pass by him so as to descend the basement stairs. 'Good God, am I nobody? Is this my house or someone else's? People taken past my nose, downstairs. Quakers coming into my house and going downstairs. Apologized for—to Quakers—on my own doorstep.' Downstairs the door of the little dining room shut—shut loud enough for him to hear. 'Going down my stairs and slamming the door. That tapeworm going downstairs and without so much as a by-your-leave closeting himself with a young woman in my charge. Not that he's likely to get up to any games with her. Doesn't look more than half a man. Looks more like a lamp-post with spectacles walking past my nose and going downstairs.'

Since he couldn't very well follow them downstairs and initiate a further scene he went back into his sitting room, but he was so furious, so inflamed, that he could no longer get into his chair and give himself to the business of warming his unshod feet. He became seized of the notion that he wouldn't sit down till that lamp-post had come up the stairs and passed out of the house, leaving him free to say a few things to Sidonie. Violent insulting words formed in his heated brain. 'Now perhaps you'll tell me what that upright and walking clothes-line has been doing with you down there. And perhaps you'll tell me what right you have to bring anyone into my home, past my nose, when I was not at all certain that I was prepared to let him in. A filthy pacifist type. I feel like having the sanitary inspector in, now he's gone, and having the place fumigated.'

But Mr. Plaicey did not come up for half an hour, for three-quarters, for an hour, and Uncle Morley, resolutely refusing to sit down, had to stride his room till the swelling impatience and fury made his head feel like some kettle left on a flame too long and ready to burn and burst. Sometimes he walked to the top of the basement stairs to learn if there were any symptoms of the visitor's departure, any hope of relief from this ache of fury. Of late any exasperation, even much smaller ones than this, turned his head into a single massive ache. It was one great ache now, and his breaths began to shorten, his lower lip to protrude.

§

That same evening, an hour or so after Mr. Plaicey had gone, Sidonie was on the step of the Blaizes' home in Denlow Road, knocking impatiently on the door, pressing impatiently on the bell. At that moment Mr. Blazie was in his study below, sympathizing seriously with himself, because of a heavy cold and a notable head-ache. He was wanting to take three aspirins at least, but not wanting to take them till Gwen was there to see. She would surely enter the room soon, and it seemed a waste to do anything so dramatic in solitude. Besides he had a little joke all ready for her, in response to her gushing condolences. 'Bad? Yes, it's bad, but not too bad. I don't feel I shall have to be destroyed.' For the present all he could do was to leave his study door ajar, despite a draught, so that she in the kitchen could hear him sneezing. And blowing.

But now this bell! That knocking! They dispelled all thoughts of his cold and drew him up his basement stairs at speed. Surely the bell had borne a note of haste, of alarm. Before he got to the door the bell rang again, its ringing prolonged.

He snatched the door open. Sidonie, pale. Pale as if with fright. 'Sidonie ... *dear* ...?'

'Oh, Uncle. Something awful's happened. It's Uncle Morley. He's had a stroke or something. Mr. Plaicey came to see me in spite of all you said, and Uncle Morley——'

'Tell me. What—what's happened?'

'He's—he's——' But first she told him how, after seeing Mr. Plaicey out of the house, she had not gone at once into the sitting room because she was frightened of what Uncle Morley was going to say; instead she had hurried down to the basement again, leaving it to him to seek her. But he did not come. And there was only silence. A silence that grew stronger. Not a cough. Never that loud and guttural phlegmy clearing of an old man's throat. Never the creak of his chair. At last she crept up the stairs and peeped round the open door of the sitting room. He was lying on the floor, 'straight out and still', with his little dog, which had not barked, nor whined loud enough for her to hear, pressing its nose in curiosity against its master's hip. She rushed to kneel beside him but he was unconscious, his face purple, his mouth dragged to one side.

'Come in. Come in, dear. Don't just stand out there.'

Sidonie stepped two paces into the passage; two paces only, while he shut the door gently, as in the presence of grief and fear.

'Didn't you hear him fall?'

'I wasn't in the kitchen underneath,' she said breathlessly. 'I was in the dining room behind with Mr. Plaicey, and I fancy now I did hear something, but I was lost in all Mr. Plaicey was saying. It was interesting me so much.'

There in the passage, just standing there, she continued the story. She had rushed to the Pearsons next door who had a telephone; they summoned Dr. Blythe and then came in to help. They were being splendid, she said. The doctor seemed satisfied that it was an apoplectic stroke, and something he had often feared for Uncle Morley. Between them they had got Uncle Morley to bed. He was still unconscious with one side paralysed—'but he can get better of that,' she comforted him. 'The doctor says it's often only temporary. It may all pass in a week or two, and he'll be himself again.'

It must unfortunately be set down that Mr. Blaize's first response to this sudden alarm had been one of pleasure—not because there was a chance that his father might die; he was not thinking of that —at least not yet— but because all excitement is pleasure; because the prospect of having to assume the chief role in a considerable drama was an accompanying pleasure; and because the sense of being about to behave admirably, skilfully, with authority but without panic, an example to excitable women, was perhaps the most gratifying of all.

'Gwen,' he called. 'Gwen.' But even as Sidonie had been at the bend of the stairs when Uncle Morley turned to call her, so now

Gwen was just appearing round the top of the basement stairs to learn what strange affairs were astir in the passage.

'Father's had a stroke, Gwen!'

'Oh! My poor Pop!'

'Yes. Sidonie found him lying on the floor. Straight out. And unconscious. Absolutely unconscious.' Let the drama be strong for Gwen. The stronger the drama, the better one's calm, sympathetic, capable behaviour would appear. The darker the background, the brighter the—but never mind these thoughts just now. 'I'll go at once and see to everything. Sidonie mustn't be left alone there. Maybe I'll sleep in the house for the next few nights. On the sofa in the sitting room.'

'Yes, you'd better do that, Steve.'

He thought that perhaps Gwen was taking this unselfish offer too lightly. 'It won't be comfortable, but we can't help that. We mustn't leave Sidonie all alone.'

'*I'll* go and sleep there sometimes.'

'Yes ... well ... perhaps we'll take it in turns.' Undeniable that he had been slightly disappointed by her suggestion. Could it be that the thought of a week or two's holiday from Gwen and his home, with Sidonie to look after him—and look *up* to him as her strong male support—was something he didn't want interrupted by a take-over from Gwen? Such a take-over would return him to lonely, undistinguished nights in his familiar home, with the necessity of making his own breakfast in the morning. And whether or not he would enjoy a spell in the Murry Walk house with only Sidonie, he was never happy alone in his own house without Gwen. 'Now, don't you worry, Sidonie dear. Gwen and I are here to help you in every way. Poor old man. Let's hope Dr. Blythe is right, and he'll be well again soon.'

But here it was that the old wicked thought came uninvited and stood in the chamber of his mind. Was the old man going to die? If so, hundreds would be released for his own income and thousands realized by the sale of the house. Hundreds. Even thousands. But one *must not* wish him to die. No, no. In the conviction that he mustn't he shook his head as if to shake the thought out of his brain and on to the ground. He would *not* be a murderer in thought. Stop it! Stop it! *Stop it!* His mind varied for him an old text: 'Whosoever looketh on a man to lust after his death has committed murder already in his heart.' And worse than murder. Parricide. He must battle and battle against this desire which appeared and reappeared so readily. A most secret battle, of course. One couldn't mention it to Gwen or to Sidonie. And still less to the old man. 'Gwen darling'—here he noticed that when one was doing battle against a native selfishness one's words became loving to everyone—'Gwen darling, I'll go back with Sidonie now. Poor old man. I'll stay in the house and perhaps you'll very kindly put together a few night things for me. And come along later. Come as soon as you can. Poor old man.'

'Oh yes, I shan't be long,' said Gwen who in her own way, but without his self-knowledge, was enjoying the drama too. 'My poor beloved old Pop.'

'Well, don't worry too much, Gwen dearest. The doctor said he can get better, and if I know my poor old father all right, he'll be the man to do it. He's as tough as they make them, thank God. . . . Yes, thank God for that.'

He did sincerely try to thank God for it, while Sidonie was saying, 'Yes, the doctor told us some people have recovered from as many as ten strokes'; which produced an immediate disappointment. And he was disappointed by this immediate disappointment. This secret battle was going to be difficult and long, and perhaps never wholly won. 'Come, Sidonie dear,' he said sadly. 'We'll go back together and do all we can.'

§

Gwen arrived at the little house in Murry Walk less than fifteen minutes later, so keen her interest and her longing to be in the midst of everything with Sidonie and Steve. These were enjoyments but along with them went all her feminine compassion for a stricken old man. The house door was ajar—which was impressive, and she could hear the voices of Sidonie, Steve, and the doctor in the bedroom at the back. So she went into the sitting room and there waited, wishing they would finish their talk and emerge. It was chafing that they should stay in there so long and she be left outside. At last they went along the passage, still talking, and the doctor said some last words on the steps.

Then the front door shut and Steve came into the sitting room.

'What? Gwen here already? How splendid. The old boy is conscious now. Such a relief. The doctor said they were always in grave danger unless consciousness re-established itself, so you can imagine how worried I was. I was terrified when he admitted quite frankly that a first stroke could often be fatal.' This was not the exact truth: Mr. Blaize's first reaction, on hearing these words, had been a summary fight to drive away the old evil hope which had instantly reappeared in his mind. 'The doctor says that if they don't recover consciousness they can pass away in a few hours. So you can gather how great was my relief.'

'How is he now, Steve darling?' (Everybody was being affectionate to everyone else in this hour of anxiety.)

'Somewhat bewildered, Gwen dear, but able to recognize us. He said. "Hallo, Stevie"—just like that—almost lovingly. And "Hallo, Sidonie" quite gently. Fortunately he'd forgotten all about Mr. Plaicey, and long may Mr. Plaicey remain out of sight in the shadows. Of course he's quite helpless down the whole of one side, but the doctor assured him that the paralysis would probably pass and his recovery could be complete. The poor old boy just asked, "How long, doctor?" rather sadly; and the doctor said, "In a few weeks, I hope," but he only smiled and said, "I'm an old man now, doctor."' It was at this stage that Mr. Blaize the Raconteur took over. His story was appealing to him now as so pathetic that it might as well be improved upon. Besides, an elaboration of the pathos would suggest his own pity and effectively hide that shocking hope which *would* come and sit in his mind. 'The poor old boy was quite different from what he usually is. So gentle and so soft. You'd have hardly known him for our tough old Sapper Blaize

He looked at me and asked—just as if he were meeting me in the street—"How is Gwen?" I said you were fine and were coming round to give all the help you could, and he just answered gently, "I shall be so glad to see her." He said "I'm——"' But here Mr. Blaize's voice was halted by his struggle with tears, so moved he was by the Raconteur's story. 'He said . . . he said . . . "I . . . I don't want to be a trouble to anyone——"' Gwen was in tears now—'he said "Poor little Sidonie. What's *she* going to do?" And of course I said we'd all be there to help Sidonie. I joked—joked'—Mr. Blaize had to repeat this because he had gulped—'saying that I had retired just in time to give up all day to looking after him——'

Further speech was now impossible for a few moments, so Gwen, after padding at her eyes with her handkerchief and brushing at her nose, asked, 'Can I go into him now? I'd like him to see I'm here.'

'Yes . . . yes, of course go in,' said Mr. Blaize, not easily because of the smothered sobs. 'You go in. Go in.'

§

Left in the sitting room, he was so shocked by the strength of the evil hope, which, to tell the truth, was now actively resuming possession of his mind—even dancing with delight there—that he decided he must pray for help. He began to pray, walking up and down the little room; but the prayer was difficult because he seemed to be praying against himself; his head praying with insufficient help from his heart. It was not easy, he found, to pray 'against one's income' and against the hope of some thousands of pounds. But he went on praying as he walked up and down. 'Oh God, make him get better. Make him get better.' Because of the difficulty and because of his desire to defeat his selfishness he wanted at one point to force himself on to his knees and pray thus, but he decided that it would be embarrassing to explain what he was up to, if Gwen or Sidonie came in. Of course it might make an impressive exhibition of filial solicitude; quite a good performance for Mr. Blaize the Showman; but in his present mood of striving after virtue he didn't want to be hypocritical: a ration of hypocrisy might be inevitable in this life, but he recoiled tonight from putting on quite such a good show as that.

Three weeks, and it was clear that his prayer had been answered. Sapper Blaize was up and about again, with only a small weakness on that left side. He was as vigorous, as loud in voice, and as ready with rudeness as ever when he felt in the humour for it. The memory of Mr. Plaicey was back in residence and a frequent incitement to rudeness or coarse jesting. It was a festering sore, and he eased it with harsh jibes at the young man's expense, deliberately designed to hurt Sidonie who had dared bring him into the house. He rejoiced in piling up grotesque descriptions of him. He would say 'Where's that milk-pudding Quaker of yours? I trust we've seen the last of him.' Or 'God in his heaven, I never recall that apparition without thinking of tapioca. Or worse: semolina.' He was particularly pleased when he thought of the phrase, 'That unripe stick of rhubarb of yours.' Sidonie did not argue with him for fear of another seizure; she just ensured that he'd seen the last of the stick of rhubarb.

Within a month he was walking up and down Murry Walk taking Ah Sin to his duties from tree to tree, as robust, broad-chested, bright-eyed—one had almost said 'as bonny'—as ever. All the neighbours in the street said what a wonderful recovery it was, and what a wonderful old gentleman (or, alternatively, 'old devil') was Mr. Morley Blaize at No. 10. They also said how wonderful Young Mr. Blaize had been. Young Mr. Blaize, sixty-five, said the same flattering things about his father's vitality to many inquirers, and always with a show of pleasure. And all the time he was trying to believe that he really was pleased, and not disappointed, to have had his prayer so quickly and efficiently answered. But whether he was pleased or not, the show must go on.

XI

Noblesse Oblige

An idea, in the course of his struggle to be a better man, arose one day among the secret thoughts of Mr. Blaize. It was not immediately welcome because it involved expenditure, but the more he considered it, and walked with it, the more engaging, even compelling, he found it. This was the usual process among the thoughts of Mr. Blaize when he was visited by a desire to do something generous.

The inspiring idea was as follows. Gwen was for ever complaining about the endless work in their old-fashioned house and he was all too often impatient with this 'non-stop bellyaching'. Had he not given her all the house-keeping money he could afford, and did she not always declare that she didn't want to spend any of it on a 'woman'? And had he not tried to help her with the work? Shopping? Doing the shopping? Washing up? Often washing up and wiping—*both*? Laying the table? Cooking breakfast? But . . . *had* he done all he could to help her? *Had* he, because always financially timid, and more financially timid than ever now when he was in his sixties and might have a stroke like his father at any time, never really given her enough? Mrs. Bletcher. Liz Bletcher. A charwoman. A religious charwoman. It would be rather wonderful to arrange, at his own charges, for Liz to come, say two whole mornings a week, and help poor Gwen who was certainly not as young and limber now as she used to be.

Yes, surely this new idea, shining before him, was a gift of his Inward Light.

He began to long for next Sunday when he could speak after Meeting with Liz. More than once in the friendly exchanges after Meeting he had talked pleasantly with Liz, both because his desire was to be jolly with people of every class and because he wanted to be liked by people of every class and described by them as 'a man with absolutely no side'.

So next Sunday, when many were chatting together in the vestibule, he walked towards Liz and, as soon as she was free to listen to him, began by asking after her husband who, as he had foreseen, had not appeared at Meeting a second time.

'Oh, Wally!' she laughed. 'He's no good, sir. He's hopeless. He come that once but never again. He says the silence fair got him down. Says it was worse than me talking.'

'I'm sorry if we shan't see him again. I enjoyed my chat with him.'

'He says the most he can do is to come and meet me sometimes.'

'Well, tell him to come and meet me too, and we'll have another pint together.'

'Yurse, I'd like you to talk to him. You might persuade him to come again, like.'

This had not been in Mr. Blaize's mind at all. He didn't want, as he put it, 'to do a Plaicey on poor Wally'. Wally, he conjectured, would be a much tougher subject than little Sidonie. But he agreed to the extent of saying, 'Yes, there's a lot he and I can talk about together. Our old war, for instance.'

'Oh, yes, you're much of an age, aren't yer?'

Never pleasing to Mr. Blaize, this. True he was only two years younger than Wally, but surely he looked ten years younger. Her words drove him to say, 'Actually I'm a bit younger. But we were both at Ypres.'

'Oh, was you? Well, he'll talk for hours about Eepree.' Why she should pronounce it 'Eepree' and her husband 'Eepriss' he did not understand. Possibly it was a genteelism adopted after listening to the ladies she obliged. 'He can't get over that I wasn't born or thought of when he was at Eepree. Not by four or five years I wasn't.'

'Mrs. Bletcher, may I ask you something?'

She looked surprised at this abrupt question. 'O' course, sir.'

'Wally told me you often obliged ladies by helping them in the house.'

'Oh, yes, that's what I do now. I preferred it to the 'Ospital. More free, like, and better money on the whole. They only give me three-and-sevenpence-'ay-penny an hour at the 'Ospital.'

This figure raised dismay in the heart of Mr. Blaize but he was too much in love with his idea to be able to leave it, and he drove on, even though a brake was now pressing on his wheels. 'I suppose all your time is taken up. You're greatly in demand, eh?'

'I do quite a lot of ladies, yes. But what had you in mind, sir?'

'I was wondering if you could help my wife sometimes. Two mornings a week, perhaps. But probably you're too busy?'

'I should like to oblige her. But I could only manage one afternoon. I tell you what, though. If there's a lot of messy work, not suitable to a lady like your wife—I mean cleaning floors and stoves, and washing down walls that she can't reach, why not have Wally one morning? He'd be glad to do it for you, I'm shaw. He's got no work, you see, and he'd do it cheaper than what I could.'

These last words, meant kindly, stirred conflicting emotions in her hearer. He liked the idea of paying less but disliked being thought poor and only able to pay for cheaper work. 'Why, what are your usual charges, Mrs. Bletcher?'

'Wurl ...' she drawled apologetically, 'I generally ask ... in these days ... you see ... kind of five shillings an hour. Not but what I get six sometimes.'

Mr. Blaize's inward comment on this was a horrified 'Crikey!' borrowed from her husband. Aloud he said only, 'I see. ...'

'But I wouldn't arst more than five from you, being as how you're one of Us, like. And Wally'd do the messy work for you at, say, three-and-six an hour, I'm shaw.'

A spring of comfort, here. 'Well, that'd be kind of him.'

'Yurse . . . and he'd do it well. He cleans a floor lovely. And he'd beat your carpets for you if you arst him. He beats 'em lovely. Clean your winders too, if they're not on too high a floor. He'd save you money there because it's something chronic what winder-cleaners charge today.'

'Our flat is just ground floor and basement.'

'Oh, wurl . . . he'd do them winders for you on his head. And if we each gave you kind of three hours, it'd only come to fifteen bob and ten-and-six. Twenty-five-and-a-tanner, all told. That wouldn't break you, would it?'

'No,' he agreed with a smile, though not happy that she should be apparently placing him so near the breaking line.

'Well, I promise you that what Wally does, he does well, even if he does talk in his old army languidge all the time. Saying everything's got to be ready for the C.O.'s inspection—me being the C.O., you see—and all the kit laid out properly for the Orderly Officer—that's me again, you see. Did yer ever hear the like? And I tell you what: he'll mend anything for you. He's quite a plumber. Says anything comes easy after them guns.'

So it was settled between them: Liz on Thursday afternoons and Wally on Tuesday mornings. And Mr. Blaize, excited and happy about what he was buying, hurried home to Gwen. It was appropriate that he should find her labouring at the gas cooker in the kitchen.

'Mrs. B.,' he said. 'I have a small announcement to make.'

'Have you?' she asked, as if less than interested, and not turning round from the cooker.

'A slightly chilly reception.'

No answer came from her. Nor did she turn round.

'Sour, in fact,' he submitted.

Her head only tossed.

'Is it that I'm in bad odour? Perhaps that is it.'

'Of course not! Don't be silly.' But very snappily said.

'Well, I may not be in bad odour but everything suggests that

I'm not in delightful odour. Do I conceive that you are being short with me? Because I must confess I strongly dislike being been short with.'

To these pleasantries she gave no response and apparently no heed.

'May I suggest,' he said, standing behind her, 'that I could be talked to with advantage, and turned round at.'

She turned round, looked at him for one moment, and, saying nothing, returned to her cooker.

'Could it be understood, please, that I take strong exception to being looked at with displeasure or, may I say, with contumely?'

Still no heed.

'I'm sure I have many faults. I'm always willing to admit I have faults. I . . . I can't think of one at the moment. . . . No . . . but doubtless you can help me.'

'*Oh, do stop this ridiculous joking!*' She fired this at him. 'I don't find it funny. I'm tired of this sink, tired of everlasting meals, tired of the unending work in this house. I'm in no mood for silly joking.'

Here all humour rushed from him, as a sickening disappointment and a temper on fire replaced it. Hot, scalding words leaped for immediate use—but his late joy in what he had come to say inhibited their utterance. He so wanted them to be happy together when he told her. He mastered the temper, accepted the disappointment, and called the humour home again.

'Well, God forbid that I should incommode you in any way. I realize that I'm not loved, but I had none the less come to tell you of two small prezzies I have bought for you.' As with many married couples or lovers they had an idiotic baby-language for use between themselves. A present was always a 'prezzy'.

She did swing round now. Her face was quite different. The hostility had given place to surprise and gratitude. 'For me? But why?'

'Well, after giving profound thought to the great strain I must be to you, I've bought a little something to cheer you up. It's a sprize.' (Surprise.) 'In fact, it's two sprizes.'

'Oh, tell me, tell me. *Two* presents? What are they?'

'Now don't hurry me. One is Wally Bletcher.'

'Wally . . .?'

'I told you about Wally at the Meeting. The other present, believe it or not, is Liz Bletcher, his lady. She is what we now call a domestic help. In less egalitarian days, a char.'

Her face was now one great question-mark. 'What in the name of pity are you talking about?'

'It's simple. Wally's coming every Tuesday morning to do all your dirty work, and Liz every Thursday afternoon to do other chores. There's no argument, please. It's my prezzy.'

'Steve!'

'Yes, and I may tell you it's quite an expensive one. Costing me the best part of thirty bob a week.'

She came and put her arms around his neck. 'Steve darling, it's sweet of you to think of it—so sweet, and oh, did I say nasty things about his little jokes? It would be wonderful, but you mustn't do it. You mustn't. We can't afford it.'

'Oh yes, we can. I've worked it all out.'

'One of them, perhaps. One only. Not the man as well.'

'Didn't I tell you, woman, that there was to be no argument? I think it's going to be fun. I like Wally. He's another old forgotten boy of the First War, like me, and I shall enjoy talking to him while he's washing down your walls. And you can gossip to your heart's content with Liz. As far as I can see, she's a real old rattle like—well, she's a rattle, except at Meeting when she obviously has to hold her face terribly tight if she's to stay silent. You and she'll get on fine. You know how you like a nice long girls' talk.'

And that was that. Henceforward Liz Bletcher arrived regularly at two o'clock on Thursdays and worked for three hours at a famous speed while, as often as not, and just as Mr. Blaize had foretold, she chattered fluently and verbosely with Gwen. Gwen would sometimes follow her from room to room as she swept or dusted or scrubbed on her knees, Gwen sustaining a full part in the gossip from one pace behind her or from a convenient stance at her side.

Liz was certainly in the first flight of professional charwomen. Years of practice had made her scoured hands as swift as those of an international pianist in a concerto when a bravura is at its fastest. There were no slow movements in her three hours' symphony. And because of this, and despite the accompanying chatter, she got through twice the work of artists less practised and skilled. But this remarkable expedition was not achieved without loss. Velocity is often accompanied by its sister Vehemence and its daughter Violence; and the velocity of Liz all too often cracked dishes, chipped plates, demolished glasses, and disabled the legs of chairs. A few weeks of this, and Mr. Blaize had but one name for her —her *nom de guerre*, as he aptly called it, for her operations resembled a war: 'Smasher Bletcher'. He liked the onomatopoeic sound of these four syllables. 'Smasher Bletcher.' They *sounded* like one of his handsomer dishes crashing to the floor. There were times, however, when he simply referred to her as 'The Smasher'. 'Has the Smasher gone? What are the survivors of the tea service?' Followed by an old army phrase 'Bring me a return of effectives, please.' This weekly despoiling and destruction slightly blotted their happy picture of her as a help, but both Gwen and Mr. Blaize agreed that, even so, she was worth this extra price—even though Mr. Blaize would shiver and shut distressful eyes in his study, when he heard a glass go down to death on the scullery floor, or the leg of a chair give vent to a cracking report. Before opening his eyes again, and while he heard her gathering up fragments, he would plead, 'God give me patience. God give me understanding. . . .'

Still, he couldn't doubt that Gwen looked forward to these Thursday afternoons, whatever their cost, and he was happy to have built them for her. Confined too much to the house, she enjoyed the presence of Smasher Bletcher; she relished the feminine talks conducted from room to room and along the intervening passages. Sometimes he stood at the door of his little basement study and listened to the two of them 'hard at it' in kitchen or scullery or on the stairs. Once he heard the Smasher talking about Wally.

'Oh, Wally ... he's all right in his way. ... I might'a done much worse after Mr. Humes passed on.' Mr. Humes was her first husband. 'But you know what it is, Mrs. Blaize, with these gentlemen that are *yurs* older than what you are.' This sentence started an alarm in Mr. Blaize and he came a little farther out of his room to hear. Was she going to put ideas into Gwen's head, because he was damned if he was paying her for that. And, damn it, he was only nine years older than Gwen; not twenty-eight like Wally; she couldn't be referring to him. 'They don't want to do anything or go anywhere, do they? They just want to sit on their shoulder-blades in a chair with an old newspaper. I say "Oh, *come* on!" when I want to go to the pictures and he just sighs and says, "Must I? Hell!" because his languidge is chronic sometimes, but I *will* say he usually gets up and comes. And he never wants to talk, really. Not, anyhow, about anything I want to talk about. He just says "Yes" and "No" and "That's right, Liz" when he ain't really heard a thing. 'S often as not he says "Yes" when the proper answer was "No". But I suppose all men are much the same. Mr. Humes wasn't all that different. Never listened really, after the first month with me.' As she spoke one could hear her brush clattering and guessed that she was on her knees sweeping the grate before the Ideal boiler with Gwen standing beside her listening. Clatter now as of Liz rising from her knees; they were coming out of the kitchen into the passage, and Mr. Blaize swung quickly back into his study. He noticed that when he was in danger of being caught in some sly activity the old deceit took rapid command, even though he was 'only happy when being good'.

There was no such feminine entertainment for Gwen when Wally came on Tuesday mornings, though she did sometimes stand and talk to him as he scrubbed or swept or came erect for what he called a 'breather' or a 'stand-easy for a bit'. Mostly it was Mr. Blaize who found himself standing behind Wally, or walking behind him, as he swept his way from room to room.

And not seldom their talk was once again about comedies or tragedies they'd had their part in during their great years from '14 to '17.

Wally came at nine and worked till twelve 'for ten-and-a-tanner if that suits you, sir' and Mr. Blaize accepted this arrangement rather quickly, glad to be saving four-and-sixpence on the three hours; but after a time his conscience worried him, not to the extent of making him say, 'No, Wally; five bob is the rate for the job'; he could not force himself as far as that; but he did take to saying, 'Twelve o'clock, Wally, and what about that pint with me? Come on! Knock off!' To which Wally would reply, 'A pint? Well, don't mind if I do,' or 'Yes, a pint would go down very sweetly. Come on, Bombardier Bletcher! Right turn! Dismiss.' And off they went to the Brown Tankard. Pints for two cost Mr. Blaize three-and-fourpence, but he was still saving one-and-twopence out of the five shillings.

There was a morning when the mantel clock in his study, tinkling twelve, lifted him from his chair, and he went out to Wally who was trimming turf edges in the garden. Using the old language which was so often their common tongue, he said, 'Come on, Wally. A visit, I think, to our little estaminet. A small binge, don't you think?'

'Aye, aye, sir,' said Wally, discomfiting Mr. Blaize by becoming a sailor for a change instead of a soldier. 'Aye, aye, sir.' And after putting his tools in the tiny shed, he fell in behind Mr. Blaize who was waiting by the garden door. As they walked off together towards the front of the house, he behind his employer, he was a soldier again and said, 'Cap orf! Belt orf! Prisoner and escort, quick march! Up the stairs! Halt!'—this was when Mr. Blaize was opening the front door and his prisoner marking time—'Mark time! Left wheel!' and so got them out into the street.

In the Saloon Bar of the Tankard, he accepted his pint, raised the mug, said, 'Here's mud in your eye, sir,' and after a deep quaff which necessitated a wiping of his lips with an edge of his hand, and a touching up with a knuckle of both stiletto moustache-ends, he announced, 'Brought something to show you, sir. Yes. Thought it'd interest you. Belongs to them old days.'

'What is it, Wally?' The smoke-befogged bar-room was full of drinking men but they were the only two whose ages were over sixty, and therefore the only two who'd known the Salient's mud, trodden its duckboards with Death beside them, and lived fifteen feet below it. 'Something to do with Ypres?'

Instead of answering him, Wally drew a wallet out of a breast pocket and produced two faded photographs mounted on yellowing, stained, and perishing cardboard. He proffered the first of them. 'Have a dekko at that.'

Mr. Blaize took it. It showed a tall, clean-cheeked, handsome young soldier in a sheepskin jacket and steel helmet. How those breeches and puttees under the sheepskin said nothing but '1914–18'. Mr. Blaize could see no resemblance to the tall old man with the horizontal waxed moustaches, but supposed it was he.

'You, Wally?'

'That's right. Me. When I was first given a sheepskin. Taken by a French bint in Pop. Was you ever in Poperinghe?'

'Was I *not*? Who wasn't who ever went to Ypres?'

'Well, the French girls were doing good biz in Pop when I was there. Trade was fair booming. And why not? Last town this side of Eepriss. Last chance of civilization. A mile or two out of Pop and Hell began.'

'You're telling *me*!' Mr. Blaize agreed. He was remembering billets behind ruined walls in Brandhoek and Vlamertinghe on the long straight road to Ypres.

'Nice kids they were. Wonder what they're like now. Rickety old mums, I suppose. Or dead. I clicked with the little piece what took that there photo; and now, do you know, I can't even remember her name. A poor lumbering old woman now, I dare say, and she was such a nice little piece then. I wonder if she ever comes across this old photo among the muck in a drawer and can't remember who the devil it was. And it was me—here! I had it enlarged when I got home and it hangs in our parlour now.'

Mr. Blaize could imagine it hanging there, perhaps in the place of honour over the mantelpiece: Wally as he was at the beginning of his few great, signal years.

Wally now handed him the other photograph. It was a group picture of his Siege Battery, the officers seated along a wide row in front of all the N.C.O.s and men on tier above tier behind. There looked to be many more than a hundred of them: every man dressed and arrayed to perfection for the eye of the camera.

'That was us,' said Wally. 'That was our full crowd taken in England in '14 just before we embarked for the Front and, Gawd help us, First Ypres. Have a good look at 'em, sir. Nice-looking lads, weren't we? All clean and poshed up. And, d'you know, when I got my ticket in '19, the officer said to me, "Well, Bletcher, you're lucky. I been through the records and there are only six of the gunners left who first came out of England. You're one of 'em. And, what's more, two of them six was officers' servants, and not on the guns like you." So there it is: I suppose the rest of the first-outs were killed or too badly wounded ever to come back.'

'God!' murmured Mr. Blaize.

'Well, give us the ole picture back—and back into bed it goes. Yeah, that's what the officer said to me. But never mind. Your poor old P.B.I. fared worse. *We* didn't have to go over the top, praise the lord.' The picture had now been carefully replaced and Wally emptied the last of his pint down his throat, wiped the back of his hand across his lips, said 'That's the stuff to give the troops', and put out his hand for Mr. Blaize's mug. 'Now, sir, mop that little lot up and have another. Same again?'

'No, no, Wally. This was my treat.'

'Oh, nuts to that, sir. Fair doos. This is on me. And after that I must vamoose. I've a pretty strong notion that my sergeant cook's just about ready for me now. And if I don't bloody well jump to it, she'll be taking my name and number.'

XII

Sleepless Night

MR. BLAIZE had been asleep only a little while when he realized he was awake again. And widely awake. Woodenly awake. He protested, '*Tst! Tst!*' and 'Damn!' because he'd been doing this for nights past. Waking at three or four and staying awake till morning. He flung out a hand and snatched his watch from the bedside table. Twenty minutes to three, said the luminous dial.

'Damn!' He tried auto-hypnotism. 'I've only had about three hours' sleep. I'm bound to get off again. Bound to get off. Bound to get off. Bed beautiful and warm; I love it. Cosy and warm. Cosy and warm. Bound . . .'

But he was not getting off. He was warm and comfortable but never more fully awake. The auto-hypnotism was working the wrong way. By repeating endlessly these hypnotic suggestions he was only providing a powerful suggestion that he needed them because he couldn't sleep. The Law of Reversed Effort.

So he stopped them and just lay there telling himself, 'I don't care if I sleep or not. I am cosy and warm. My bed is beautiful and I love it. I can stay awake for all I care. Stay awake. . . .' But somehow the Law of Reversed Effort didn't work this time. This time the suggestion that he'd 'stay awake for all he cared' declined to reverse its effort. It remained positive and potent, and he stayed awake. He tossed from one side to the other; he said, 'Boring. . . .

Boring, boring, boring.... Sad....' but the indifferent hours marched on, their footsteps silent in the dark. It must be four o'clock ... half past four.... With sick anger he snatched at the watch again. Ten minutes past five. Even later than he thought. Could it be that he had slept for a little?—no, that he would never admit. He'd been wide awake since before three. Of that he was certain—or he was certain that this was what he would tell Gwen.

Past five. Another hour or so and he would see the room paling grey with morning light. And now he wasn't sure that he wanted to sleep because to do so would spoil his story to Gwen. 'Stayed awake for three hours' would be but a poor story compared with 'Been awake all night'.

In the old days he would have lied to make the story fine, but not now; not since his Revelation; not when he was 'only happy being good'.

But, oh, dear, he longed to sleep—good story or not—and the more he longed, the less likely it seemed that he would do so. Once he tossed over to the other side so impatiently that the angry, violent move started an odd little pain above his heart. A stab and ache. Cause for worry? Age? Heart disease? He pictured himself dying in his sleep. Gwen coming in the morning and finding him dead—lying there dead. And it was splendid that his first thought, on creating this picture, was not pity for himself but pity for Gwen —Gwen who could never manage the business side of their lives —Gwen who hated loneliness—Gwen standing at the bedside and knowing herself alone. He must not die; he must remain with her because, whatever his failings, she needed him. He was delighted that, without effort, his first thought had been unselfish; it showed, did it not, that he was a better man than he had supposed. Pleasing indeed: a real unselfish love for Gwen; a love that sought her need before his own.

This sharp proof, so unexpected, of one unselfish ingredient in an otherwise unsavoury compound turned his thoughts to the night in Paris and his happy resolution then to clean himself up a bit, however late it might be.

In this very private business of achieving a self-mastery that would defeat the habits of a lifetime he would often make use of auto-hypnotism in his bed at night. Obeying the advice of the experts he would try to drop off to sleep while repeating positive and power-ful suggestions of improvement. One monotonously repeated suggestion (not to be told to anyone) was 'With all my heart and soul I aim at triumphs of character. Against whatever odds. Triumphs of character.'

So now, encouraged by this fine unselfishness in his love for Gwen, he crowded the bedclothes about him and gave himself to the pleasing business of improving his character yet further with this habitual suggestion. 'I aim at triumphs of character. Against whatever odds. Triumphs of character. Triumphs of character, whatever the age. Sixty-five now. Ageing. I aim at triumphs of ageing—I mean, character. Triumphs of ... Seventy, now. Only two choices before one: to become a testy, exacting, peppery old man—Sapper Blaize—or a nice old man, what they called old Ed Wilkins at eighty-five, "that dear old man".... Sixty-five ... seventy-five or eighty.... Universally loved. Rather like Pope John ... "Papa John" ... "Papa Blaize" ... Holy night ... Sleep-less night ... Heilige Nacht ... Papa Stephen.... Only happy when good....' Somewhere here he slept.

And dreamt that he was lying in this same bed with a lovely young girl in his embrace whose long naked limbs he was stroking, stroking. Who she was he had no idea, except that she was certainly not Gwen. She was a stranger, and very charming. So charming, so lovable, that it was a pity to wake from the dream, but he did so just when it was at its best.

He awoke less to a feeling of guilt than to one of irritation with Fate and its tricks. He even addressed Fate as if it were a living power with a sense of mischief; he protested, 'That wasn't funny at all. It was just cheap.' And to himself he explained, 'One's not responsible for one's dreams. One really can't be responsible for what happens in sleep. It's no discredit, really.' But the fact remained that it was not something he would care to describe to anyone. To

Mr. Plaicey, for instance; or to Mr. Amling; or, least of all, to Gwen. So perhaps he *was* a little ashamed of it. A little ashamed, but also a little pleased that at sixty-five . . .

Oh well . . . if only he could get to sleep again after these hours of wakefulness . . . and . . . perhaps resume . . .

XIII

The Liberal

SIDONIE went regularly now to the Quaker Meeting. Uncle Morley might grumble and grunt and be rude about it, but it seemed that Sidonie's hour of defiance when she drew Mr. Plaicey into the house had given her an appetite for more rebellion. There had always been an intermittent tendency in her to revolt; it had appeared when she broke the prison of her mother's house and escaped into Uncle Morley's; and now, after three years' submission to Uncle Morley, it was appearing again. Together with this occasional defiance there went an opposite tendency and a more constant one: a readiness to be someone's disciple. Uncle Steve used to call her 'a congenital disciple'. In childhood she had been the unquestioning disciple of her dominant mother; at school the devotee of an adored mistress; and in her twenties she had found an inspiring friend in a woman psychiatrist and given all her discipleship to her. After this learned friend's departure to a high appointment in Edinburgh, and after three years in the Uncle Morley Obedience, she had probably been too long without a teacher to follow, so that she was willing to be a disciple of Mr. Plaicey. That earnest young man might be some years younger than she, but he seemed two feet taller, and perhaps that helped. Also, no doubt, his serious eyes and his slow quiet voice were an agreeable change from Uncle Morley.

So Mr. Blaize when he went to the Meeting House would see

Sidonie already in her chair with her eyes cast down properly and her hands at rest on her lap. Sometimes after Meeting he and she came homeward together, but more often he left her drinking deep from the copious wellspring of Mr. Plaicey.

One day as he was making his way out alone, having decided that those two talkers, the pupil and her tutor, didn't want him, Mr. Amling laid a gentle hand on his shoulder near the door and said, 'Wait a minute, Blaize. You're a Liberal, aren't you?'

'A what?' demanded Mr. Blaize, surprised by such an assertion.

'A Liberal. I have heard so.'

'A Liberal?' In truth Mr. Blaize had only a vague idea what his politics were, his one clear notion being that he 'was certainly not a Tory'; a conviction which had long been reinforced by the hot, loud, brow-beating Toryism of his father. He had never called himself a Liberal when arguing with Conservative friends, but he was flattered, here by the door, to be spoken of as a well-known Liberal, and accordingly he answered, 'Yes ... well, I—I am. Yes, of course.' (And from that moment he *was* a Liberal because he had to abide by his own unexpected statement. But he was as pleased to be a Liberal as he had been to become a Quaker; it should be much easier, much less exacting, to be a Liberal than a Quaker.)

'Yes, I thought so,' said Mr. Amling. 'Someone told me so. Well now: I am on our West Ward Committee and they've asked me to be its chairman——'

'Good,' Mr. Blaize interrupted, as a congratulation.

'No. Wait. I don't want to be. I couldn't do the job properly. There are too many demands on my time. My office work is heavy just now because I can't get staff, and there's my service on my hospital committees, to say nothing of what I try to do as an elder here. These tasks are all that I feel I can honestly undertake; and it occurred to me suddenly that this particular job could best be done by someone who had retired and enjoyed more leisure than most of us. And I immediately thought of you. We could put you on our committee and make you chairman very soon. Why not?'

Mr. Blaize's surprise at this suggestion was great, but his hidden pleasure in it was greater. Greater than he desired to show. He must make a show of demurring at first though with a hope that this hesitation wouldn't be taken seriously. 'Oh no, surely not!' he protested. 'I am honoured by the suggestion, but surely you must have someone else who's been on the committee some time. I'm a good Liberal, of course, but so far I've done no active work for the party. Taken no active part at all.' Hearing his own words, he perceived that his polite reluctance didn't sound very convincing, and was glad of this.

'Nonsense,' said the unconvinced Mr. Amling. 'None of the others are available for the post. Some, like me, have too many commitments; others are too young, and we all feel that the position must be filled by a man of some substance.'

Well pleased to be thought a man of substance, he was more than ever ready to assume the dignified position, but he felt that the decent shrinking should be enacted for a little longer. 'But look, Amling: the Liberal Party today is a Young People's party. I'm too old. They don't want old boys like me.'

'Rubbish. Nobody thinks of you as old.'

(From beginning to end a delightful conversation, this.)

'But could I as a—as a pacifist'—he did not speak the word with great conviction—'honestly be chairman?'

'Certainly. Just as our Society of Friends is wholly permissive in this matter, so there is the same freedom of conscience in the Liberal Party. The very heart of Liberalism is freedom of conscience.'

'Yes . . . of course . . . I understand that. Well, if you really think I'll be of use——'

'I most certainly think so. And so do we all.'

'You have mentioned me then, have you?'

'Indeed yes. And they all agreed that I should invite you. They agreed with acclamation.'

'Well . . . I can only say it's an honour I've never dreamed of.'

(True. How dream of yourself as a Liberal chairman before you've been told you are a Liberal?)

And so home to tell Gwen: hurriedly at first because eager to report the flattering invitation, but then more slowly because of the difficulty of explaining to her that he was—well, a Liberal. He could not remember that in all their married life he had once discussed Liberalism with her. He was walking homeward alone because he had seen Sidonie in laughing conversation with Mr. Plaicey. Yes, that grave young man had been throwing back his head and laughing heartily—a phenomenon which Mr. Blaize could not recall having witnessed before. He had looked again to make sure that he was seeing correctly.

As he went up his steps towards Gwen within, he decided that it would be best to carry this citadel at a rush; it might be compassed around by difficult breastworks. In his hallway he heard her down in the kitchen below, but it was not at a rush that he descended the basement stairs. He went down them slowly because he was assembling his armament.

'Hallo, darling,' he began. Did one always speak more affectionately when uncertain of one's position? 'How was church?'

'All right,' said Gwen, and no more. She was seated at the long kitchen table with her eyes on the potatoes which she was peeling for the Sunday meal.

'Did the Vicar preach well?'

'He didn't preach. It was a stranger. A good-looking young man from Australia.'

Mr. Blaize, not being really interested in who had preached, or what the sermon was about, asked no more about the good-looking young man. 'I had rather a compliment paid to me after Meeting today,' he said, walking to the window and looking out at their narrow area below the pavement of Denlow Road.

'What was that?' asked Gwen, but only formally as she added another peeled potato to those in the basin. She seemed hardly more interested in the compliment than he in the sermon.

'Mr. Amling asked me to be chairman of the Liberal Party here.' So long as one knew in one's mind that 'here' covered only the West Ward, one of seven wards in the parliamentary borough of

St. Mary Upbourne, this rendering was not an exaggeration. Not a lie. 'He invited me on behalf of all the members. He even said they had carried the proposal with acclamation.'

'But are you a Liberal?' asked Gwen, simply.

'A Liberal? Yes ... yes, certainly.' He came back from the window to assure her of this.

'But you voted Labour last time. Much to my horror.'

'I did, but there was no Liberal around then. I am naturally a Liberal. I could never be anything else. Liberalism is an attitude of mind. Basically it is a belief in the maximum freedom for every individual. Freedom from all despotisms whether of powerful people on the right or the left; whether from the exploitations of Big Business or the tyrannies of Trade Unions. Yes ... yes, just as it was the spiritual freedom among the Quakers that drew me to them, so it was the political freedom that has—that has always made me a good Liberal.' He was astonished at the fluency with which the Case for Liberalism was gushing from him, and he was comforted and established by it as a Liberal. He was almost as pleased with this new ardour for Liberalism as he had been with his sudden conversion to—well, Goodness—in that Paris room. 'Personally I always find it difficult to see how a man of intellect can be anything but a Liberal.'

'Oh, but that's nonsense,' argued Gwen, peeling away at her potatoes. 'Heaps of intellectual people are Conservatives. And heaps more are Socialists—though I can never see how.'

'I can understand their becoming Socialists,' he conceded, 'but never how they can remain Tories. Of course I'm far more to the left than to the right—what you might call a Left-Wing Liberal.'

'Well, I suppose I'm not intellectual at all because I'm a Conservative. A good Conservative like my father before me,' said Gwen proudly.

'That's what defeats me about women,' he objected, impatiently. 'Why don't they think things out for themselves instead of being content to reflect some man or other, their father or their husband?

Your very tone showed that you were quite proud of not being intellectual, and not troubling to think it out, but leaving it all to your father.' And just as he had contrasted her facile Anglicanism with the fine vision, the profound thought, the fruits of much reading, in his Quakerism, so now he was contrasting her facile Toryism with his intelligent Liberalism. Here in the kitchen, watching her finish those potatoes, he was feeling immeasurably superior to her intellectually. And while he was feeling this she wounded him not lightly by inquiring, 'Is it an important job they've asked you to do?'

'Of course it's important. Doesn't it amount to being a leader locally? What else do you think a chairman of the Liberals is?'

'Well, I shouldn't tell your father anything about it. We don't want another row like the time you told him you were a pacifist. He hates Liberals even worse than Socialists. For pity's sake keep it to yourself. The doctor said another stroke might be the end of him.'

Immediately the evil thought was there, standing in his mind, having come, as it were, through a closed door. He tried to thrust it from the room, but even as he was doing this, it whispered darkly something about the possibility of deliberately inducing this second stroke; a worse thought than ever, because it amounted, not merely to desiring a death, but to considering how to bring it about. . . .

Force the thought away—keep it out—try to hold the door tight against it—talk of other things and forget it.

§

Greatly flattered, he lived now with a longing to be known as 'the finest chairman of them all'. Such was his ambition, and nothing less. A fascinating occupation for his retirement. It had been a disappointment, after his trumpeting in the kitchen, to find that his Ward Committee (which in moments of crude humour he called by its initials) mustered no more than eight or nine active loyalists, some of them elderly women, and two of them youngsters

from the Young Liberals, 'one rose-lipped maiden and one light-
foot lad', as he said to Mr. Amling, who didn't know what he was
talking about, not being a student of poetry. He did not speak
of this disappointment to Gwen, but one effect of it was to make
him set about enlarging the membership of the party in his
ward and strengthening his committee, so as to render his position
more like what he had conceived it to be when offered it by
Mr. Amling. A happy new broom, he launched a campaign to
double the enrolled and paid-up membership of the Party in his
ward; this he did not succeed in achieving, but he did add many
new members, partly by a letter urging every known member
to find one more, and partly by sending personal letters to all
new voters arriving in the ward. By personal visits he persuaded a
Presbyterian minister, a Scottish wine-merchant and two Jewish
solicitors to come on to the committee (all Scots, it seemed, and
nearly all good Jewish lawyers, were Liberals). In less than a
year his ward had the largest subscribing membership in the
borough, and he had his name as the most active of the ward
chairmen.

So much so that when Mr. David Emmanuel Leon expressed his
wish to retire from the chairmanship of the Executive Committee
(that is to say the ruling committee of the whole Liberal Association
in St. Mary Upbourne) they put the chairman of the West Ward
into his seat. And was the new chairman exalted by this election?
It really meant, he explained to Gwen, that apart from Sir Arthur
Ronnell Cust, the President, who was little more than an absentee
figurehead, he was the leading Liberal in the borough. 'You must
say it's rather a compliment, this appointment after less than a
year's service on the Ward Committee,' he suggested to Gwen;
and she answered, 'Yes, it's quite remarkable to me because I didn't
even know you were a Liberal.'

'Oh, yes, I've always been a Liberal,' he said, walking to the
window, less to look out at Denlow Road than to walk away from
this argument.

After being the best ward chairman he was now resolved to be the most remarkable Chairman of the Executive that they'd had for years; but he did not know that the local prominence which this would bring him was going to lead him into a black and heart-searing experience, the memory of which shivered and sickened him for ever after.

XIV

The Speech Heroic

THE Mayor this year bore a famous name. He was Lord Wetherloe, still Lord of the Manor of St. Mary Upbourne and the owner of its land. A man of great wealth, he was famous for his benefactions to hospitals, universities, schools and national appeals, and sometimes to his own manor of Upbourne. This last was a tradition in his family. Wetherloe Park on its green height, with its groves, parterres and carpet gardens, was his grandfather's gift to the Borough when he was its Charter Mayor in the year of its becoming a London Borough. That was more than half a century ago, and this was only the second time that the noble lord of the manor sat on the chief citizen's throne.

Soon after Mr. Blaize's election to his much humbler throne in the Liberal Executive, Lord Wetherloe decided to mark his mayoralty by a big dinner, offered not only to the borough's chief officers and committee chairmen with their ladies, and to the leading representatives of all the local associations, institutes, chambers and charities, whether political, literary, scientific, commercial or religious, with their ladies, but also to the mayors, deputy mayors and town clerks of the adjoining boroughs with *their* ladies. When he and his dinner committee discussed what form the speeches should take, and who should deliver them, they resolved on a 'Topic for the Evening' under the title 'Our Borough in the Future' and that after the Mayor had spoken on the borough of today, the leaders of the three political parties should speak to their ideas for the future, being as controversial as they wished, so that the speech-making, all too often a succession of dreary formalities, should carry a real interest and probably provide occasions for not a little fun.

When Mr. Blaize received an invitation to this sumptuous affair he was surprised and pleased, and ran to show it to Gwen; he was less pleased when after a prompt acceptance for Gwen and himself, he received from the Town Hall an invitation to speak 'for ten minutes' on behalf of the Liberal Executive, their president being abroad.

The letter produced a sickly palpitation. As he read it on his doormat, his heart seemed to be sinking, deflating, and throbbing —not to say, thundering—all at the same time. One part of him desired strongly to do this highly distinguished thing; another part desired most strongly not to. Gwen was still at the breakfast table in the kitchen, and he went in to her with the letter. He went slowly, but at least he would enjoy displaying this honour before her. 'Look, love,' he said, 'I'm invited to be one of the speakers at that Mayoral dinner, and there are only five of them. It's rather an honour, I *must* say.'

'But, darling, how wonderful! I'm sure you'll do it beautifully.'

The lack of understanding! The facile, unconscious lack of under-standing and sympathy. 'I don't know that I shall do it at all.'

'Of course you will. Why ever not?'

Not even to Gwen did he ever admit that when he was obliged to speak in public, no matter how small the audience, his heart became a small quaking lump in his breast. He tried always to conceal this condition from the whole world. So now he said only, 'I'm so new to this Liberal business—I don't mean as a Liberal —been a Liberal all my life—but new to a high position in the party, because it *is* high, you must allow. I don't feel that I can find enough to say For me, you see, Liberalism is an attitude more than anything else, and, to tell the truth, I'm not even sure what our present policies are.'

'You know enough to speak for ten minutes.'

'Do I? I don't think I do. It'd have to be in very general terms.'

'But that's all they want, isn't it?'

'Do you think so?' he asked sadly.

'Yes, and you must do it. Of course you must. You mustn't let them down. They obviously think a lot of you.'

So easily did women urge you to do something they'd never do themselves.

'The Conservative and Labour leaders will certainly accept,' she went on, 'and you can't be the only one to refuse.'

No—the finest chairman the Executive had ever had—no, he couldn't refuse, but perhaps he could accept now and 'go sick' on the eve of the party. Standing there by Gwen and thinking, he seemed to remember that in the army, if a man desired strongly not to 'go over the top', he sometimes chewed cordite extracted from one of his cartridges, which conveniently sent his temperature into the hundreds. Or he avoided a peril in the near future by an 'S.I.'—a self-inflicted wound, which earned him enormous condemnation, but probably saved his life for the days when the war and sergeants and officers would be no more. Something like that, perhaps. Not an 'S.I.' ... but where could he get hold of some cordite? Would Wally Bletcher perhaps have a clip of cartridges among his souvenirs? Some such trick as this would give one all the honour of being on the list of speakers and none of the miseries of having to speak. But would all the virtue have gone out of the cordite after some fifty years?

'I suppose I'd better accept,' he said, while still wondering what he would do.

'Yes, you accept; and I shall be so proud hearing you speak,' she said—a sentence which dropped his heart and left it shaking. She sitting in the audience with eyes fixed on him as he spoke! Noticing probably the trembling of the notes in his hand, the quaver in his voice, the sweat on his forehead. Why must she say such things? Turning his heart into palpitating blubber.

And in the next weeks he had a feeling that Gwen had taken

command and was joyously steering him towards this alarming tryst with fate. It was in some way a fear of Gwen which forced him to write—with a shaking hand—and accept 'the honour of being asked to speak'.

What was he to say when he spoke? Liberalism. What was Liberalism about? Tory and Socialist would have spoken before him, and he mustn't be an anti-climax after them. Simply mustn't. No, no; he must try to surpass them. But how and about what? What?

'Our Borough in the Future!' Suddenly a thought! Would this large London borough have any future? Might not the near future see it as a wilderness of rubble in a wide silence—something like Zonnebeke and Passchendaele in their vast desolation under the skies of '17. And not, like them, laid waste by hail-storms of shells, but by a single bomb.

Great God, had his subject appeared before him? Had the Inward Light shown it to him? His breath came fast. Here was a subject that could surpass anything Tory or Socialist would say. And it *was* the supreme question of the day to which politicians of any party should address themselves. It now seemed possible that all the guests at the dinner would acclaim him as the one really profound speaker of the evening. If he were to say, 'We must not leave this most urgent of all questions to *Them*, the people in power; it is life-and-death for *Us*', how they would sit up and listen. Unfortunately he had sense enough to see that, if he were to advocate a conscientious refusal to have part or lot with hydrogen bombs, he would have to propound the total pacifist line, since there was not a doubt but that any war, however started, would end in the use of nuclear weapons. Up to this moment, to be sure, and whatever he had pretended to his father, he had found it difficult to *feel* a complete pacifist; some deep and surging instinct fought against any such idea. But he was half-way there, and now, for the purpose of being held the profoundest speaker of the evening—he was ready to convince himself (temporarily anyhow) that he was the uncompromising pacifist.

Had he *really* a great and startling subject? He began to fill with excitement. He rose from his study chair and paced about while words for the speech wrote themselves in his mind. He would purloin plenty that Mr. Amling and Mr. Plaicey had said in Meeting (neither would be present). For example: that no persecution which a pacifist and unarmed nation might have to endure could equal the burning and blinding extermination that hydrogen bombs would wreak; that the example of a nation refusing at any cost to handle a world-murdering weapon would draw other nations to its side—splendid!—and that while this example of a great nation willing to risk all for the sake of humanity as a whole might not produce all its fruit at once or for some time, this must not deter us, because 'Man's spiritual and intellectual growth has ever been a matter of a few men proclaiming at all costs new truths that are hotly rejected at first but accepted as commonplaces in the end.' (Mr. Amling.) 'The blood of the martyrs. . . . The more you mow us down the stronger we root and the stouter we grow.' Splendid again! Why not the Latin itself which he remembered from school-days: *'semen est sanguis Christianorum'*—that would impress the people. . . .

After these surely convincing statements he would proceed—his blood rose and his heart expanded as he thought of it—to the daring, possibly unpopular, but certainly true statement that the defence of one's country was *not* the most important thing in the world; there was a greater thing: the defence of humanity.

What a speech. . .! Up and down his room he walked with it.

Mr. Blaize was ever a man subject to sudden inspirations. There had been that sudden vision in the Paris room; his sudden and happy plunge into Quakerism; and now there was this sudden ambition to do a heroic thing.

Also, less nobly, to do a sensational thing.

Surely it would be heroic. If the topic of the evening was the Future, then this was the one thing someone ought to have the courage to say (he began to be worried lest the Labour boy said it first). If the speakers were to be, as the Mayor's Secretary had told him, as controversial as they wished, what more likely to raise controversy than this; what more likely to introduce sensation? And before such an audience of the prosperous and the high-placed, an audience therefore preponderantly Tory and nationalistic, what more heroic?

Here were two sides of Mr. Blaize, two ill-matched sides, working excitedly together: the one his new selfless desire to be good and, if necessary, heroic; the other an exceedingly selfish desire to attract all the limelight to himself and all the best applause. In the next weeks it was, we fear, this less noble half which was most often in his mind as he composed his speech. Morning after morning he was happy as he gave himself to creation. Excitement crowded the nervousness into a dark corner. Only ten minutes the speech must last; he could endure nerves and palpitations and sweat for ten minutes. Ten minutes only, and yet he gave morning after morning to labouring on it with masses of books and pamphlets to help him. And morning after morning to dreaming of it. They would listen spellbound—with hostility at first, perhaps, but spellbound all the same; and so convincing would he make it that when he sat down he would have won, if not universal agreement, at least universal praise for courage, eloquence and power. Such the hope, the dream.

But then on a Sunday at Meeting Mr. Amling told him carelessly, even laughingly, how great would be the audience to hear him and how the Member for the Borough who was also the Minister of Defence (*Defence!*) was coming. 'Yes, and there's even talk of the Lord Mayor and Sheriffs of the City of London coming.'

Oh, my God! The nervousness was back in the centre of the room; nay, in almost all the room; and it was the speech that was now crowded into a dark corner. The Lord Mayor and Sheriffs! With their ladies! Oh, why ever had he got involved in this ghastly ordeal? These bloody Liberals!

He must go sick. Exquisite the relief, the healing, the peace that came with this thought of going sick and handing the speech over to someone else. Amling perhaps, since it was he who had started all the trouble.

But he didn't believe he would do this. Words and phrases came out of his past with the grand but deathly mud of the Salient behind them: malingering . . . dodging the column . . . skrimshanking . . . and he didn't like them. No, no; no escaping that way; no use of the cordite; he must go over the top with the others.

§

On the evening itself he began to dress far too soon. To begin dressing would be some distraction from the qualms which had possessed him throughout the day, spoiling his reading, blighting his eating, and breaking up his very breathing. It would be something to do; something to occupy his hands. The nervousness had been increased during the day by telephone calls from reporters —one from a national evening paper—inquiring what he would say. At once flattered by this and horrified by it, he suggested sending them a verbatim script, which, being the last thing they wanted, they politely declined, asking that he should just 'tell them in a few words'. He found that he hadn't the courage to tell these faceless voices that he was going to advocate national disarmament, so he said merely that he proposed to speak, partly as an individual and 'partly as a lifelong Liberal', on the 'problem of the hour', the danger of nuclear war.

'Oh, yes, sir. Thank you, sir.' The telephone clicked at the other end.

It was a distress that he had only a dinner-jacket suit and not the full regalia of white waistcoat, white tie, and tails, but he certainly hadn't the money to buy so expensive an array for a single occasion, however momentous. 'A pity,' he thought, as he dressed in the bathroom where the light over the mirror was good. 'A great pity because one can't wear one's war medals on a dinner jacket.' Not five times in forty years had he worn his war medals.

Since he would be an object for the public gaze he dressed with care, though less with a relish than in a kind of desolation. And there in her room was Gwen attiring herself with excitement, happiness and pride. Even joking sometimes when he was suffering. Once she called out gaily, while he was rearranging his tie for the seventh time, 'Now come along, Steve. I'm aching to hear you speak.'

('Oh, *shut* up!') 'I shouldn't expect anything very much. My speech is only one of several and a mere ten-minute do.'

'Still, such a tremendous occasion!'

('Oh, for God's sake, *do* keep quiet.')

'And have you got it all prepared? I hope so.'

'I've put a few notes together ... yes ... that's all. I like these things to be more or less impromptu.' Mr. Blaize the Liar. He had long ago written the whole speech out, committed it to memory, and rehearsed it before the clock, timing it. In one of the rehearsals, possibly the twelfth, he'd had a terrible moment when memory failed and he hadn't the ghost of a notion what came next. Supposing that happened on the night. Tonight.

'Aren't you nervous?' she called.

What a question! It stirred up his nervous condition as a chef's wooden spoon stirs up the risotto in its saucepan. It inflated the wretchedness as a bellows blows up embers that were temporarily smouldering.

'Oh. I don't know,' he said. 'It's only a short speech.' Mr. Blaize the Showman. Cool. Not easily excited. Composed. Sang-froid.

'Fancy speaking before the Lord Mayor and a Member of the Cabinet. I should be at death's door.'

'It's only a few minutes.'

'Well, I'm sure you'll do it beautifully.'

(Christ!)

At last he emerged from the bathroom fully dressed, hair oiled into place for the public eye, and collar tie straight. Taking the finished article into her room to show to her, he asked, 'Does this amount to a gent?' A small joke to mask his terrors from her. 'A gent of some distinction?' he pleaded.

'Oh you look adorable,' she said, and flung her arms around his neck. She touched his tie, brushed the silken lapels of his jacket and straightened his hair. 'You look a perfect dear. Nothing suits a man like black evening dress.' The first helpful thing she had said.

'It ought to be a white tie and tails.'

'Never mind. There'll be plenty of others in these days who've only got a dinner jacket.'

'Yes, but they haven't got to make a speech.'

Both ready at last, they walked out into the street, one talkative and merry, the other feeling like a captive walking with his escort to the public square and the guillotine.

Night after night in bed he had been practising his auto-hypnotism in the hope of achieving a freedom from nerves just as he had practised it in the hope of achieving a high morality. 'I'm afraid of nobody. I'm afraid of nobody. I'm not *going* to be nervous. Not *going* to be nervous. If only I can get shut of nerves it can be the speech of the evening. The speech of the evening.' He practised it again now in the Underground trains carrying them to Marble Arch, and as they entered the monstrous vestibule of the Marble Arch Hotel, all pink damask and gold chairs and lofty mirrors, where it was very necessary. 'I'm afraid of nobody. I'm not *going* to be nervous. Not *going* to be . . .'

But somehow it was now no help at all. Its power, if ever it had any, was lost. Left at home. Or dispersed in the night air of Oxford Street. All these golden chains on the breasts of mayors, all these lushly caparisoned ladies with little or nothing on their breasts, this loud medley of voices (from people who hadn't got to speak), the sudden glimpse of the Member for the Borough (and Minister of Defence), the medals, the starry decorations around necks and on coats, the waiters with their trays of golden drinks—yea, and the Lord Mayor over yonder in knee breeches and buckled shoes, with Sheriff standing by—oh, my God!—and the scarlet-coated toast-master bellowing out the names of guests, who *would* at this moment be 'Lord and Lady Sams and the Honourable Miss Daisy Sams'—all drove his 'I'm afraid of nobody' out of this vast hall—if it had ever consented to come into it from the street.

One had to pass the fringes of this assembly to come at the

Gentlemen's Cloak Room and get rid of hat and coat before being received by Lord and Lady Wetherloe. And in the cloak room, as he straightened his tie again, he played for the last time with the idea of staging a sudden illness. Say one of those things that attacked without warning. Appendicitis? Angina pectoris? A message to Gwen in her Ladies' Room that he'd been seized—at this of all moments—by acute abdominal pains—cardiac pains—what a cruel pity, my dear, just as I was going to enjoy a great occasion. Oh, it's most disappointing. *You* stay and enjoy yourself. I'll get myself home somehow. A taxi.

But his sense told him that many people would read this as 'cold feet' and 'wind up'. Gwen herself might wonder if this had been the truth; and the story, to his shame, would travel all over the Borough. Such a trick was but the other horn of a now inescapable dilemma. He went out to meet Gwen—and Destiny.

So in old days they went 'over the top'.

After being presented to host and hostess they mingled with other guests, and when a waiter came up with his tray of golden drinks, Mr. Blaize seized on a cocktail, hoping there was courage and strength for him somewhere in its glass. A little comfort did emerge from the depths of the glass, but no permanent cure, so he managed to arrest the progress of two more waiters as they threaded through the crush and to drink desperately from further founts of strength, before the toastmaster bellowed, 'Mr. Mayor, my Lord Mayor, Aldermen and Sheriffs, Your Worships, Ladies and gentlemen dinner is served.'

§

With such a chain of visiting mayors and their ladies it had not been possible to seat all the speakers at the top table. Mr. Blaize's place was at Table 1 which stretched at right-angles from the centre of the top table, with the other tables parallel to it on either side. Seated at the upper end of this table, he was thus at the very axis of the whole outspread assembly, surrounded, as it were, by the enemy. In the heart of his dislike for this midmost position there was room for aggrievement when he saw the Conservative speaker sitting down at the top table. Why the hell ...? Gwen was on the other side of this Table 1 but far down it, and he felt unhappily alone. It was comfort, however, to see that the wife of the Conservative was at Table 2.

The menu of that banquet will not be described because Mr. Blaize had no clear apprehension, at any time, what he was eating. The successive dishes interested him less than they offended him. He forced down a little from each plate, not because he wanted it but to appear at ease. Only the wines were welcome but they didn't do much for him—not as much as he hoped—and the waiters were sadly slow in coming round with refills. What the wines were he didn't know, or want to know. Similarly he had no adequate grasp of what the idiot woman on his left, with her enormous outworks of pink bosom and pearls, was saying to him. He had to repeat her sentences to himself before he knew what they had meant, and then to force out replies with shows of smiling. Sickening shows. She asked him what he was by profession (and he couldn't remember at first; what was he?) and how did he come to be present, and had he lived long in St. Mary Upbourne (Had he? It took time to remember) and was his wife here, and wasn't he terribly nervous if he was going to speak. When he denied—with one of the sickly smiles—that he was 'as nervous as all that'—the unspeakable idiot said the most demolishing thing of all; she said skittishly, 'Oh yes, I think you are. I can see you are.' (God *damn* the woman.) 'But don't worry. I'm sure we shall all enjoy it.'

'But wh-what makes you think I look nervous?'

'Oh, you seem so lost in thought most of the time——' (Damn the great sow)—'and you're a little pale, aren't you?'

'Am I?'

The woman on his other side was possibly no idiot but she could look idiotic because she was deaf and smiled deliberately whenever one said something—under the impression, it seemed, that whatever people said at a public dinner had to be funny.

Between the Pear Hélène and the Mushroom on Toast (repellent notion), as the time for speeches drew nearer, he was seized by a need, which quickly became a craving, to escape for a speeding minute to the accommodation in the 'Gentlemen'. But how? Placed as he was, at the focal centre of a seated congregation, and sideways-on to the Mayor himself, how could he rise up and walk out before them all? But ... it was becoming inevitable; and the more impossible it seemed, the more inevitable it became. His situation (and *situation* seemed the exact word) was now desperate. At last he leaned forward and said to the man opposite, 'Look. I've stupidly left my handkerchief in my overcoat pocket. How on earth can I escape and get it?'

'Oh, that shouldn't be difficult. When we're at the coffee and cognac, and just before the speeches'—horrid word—'you rise, make an elegant bow to the Mayor, and stroll happily out.'

'Oh, I see. Yes. ... Thank you.'

'Yes, that'll be quite in order. Nothing to worry about in that.'

'Thanks. I want to do things in order.'

Come quickly, Coffee and Cognac. They came, and after he had sipped from both once or twice, as a formality, he rose, turned towards the Mayor, bowed and walked out with a show of nonchalance—of neutrality, as it were. Nobody seemed to mind, so he took his time about this expedition. Three minutes later, relieved of one distress, he returned and, walking back to his place before the seated people, bowed gratefully to the Mayor and sat down again to the other pains.

'My lords, ladies and gentlemen, pray silence ...'

He did not know much of what the Mayor said in his speech, or what anyone else said. He did not consciously take in their words any more than he had consciously taken in his food. He could give no thought or interest to any speech but his own. But he heard enough from Lord Wetherloe and Tory and Socialist to become more and more certain—oh God!—that his appeal for national martyrdom, which a week ago had seemed so splendidly of the moment and profound—and which *was* of the moment and profound—would have an ugly reception. Certain of it. Certain. ...

And yet it was a good speech. Not a doubt about that; he'd studied for it in too many wise places, he'd borrowed too many good words for it from wiser men, he'd polished and polished it day after day. Not a doubt that it exceeded in significance anything the two other political speakers were offering. Not a doubt that it ought to be so deeply impressive as to be a sensation—but—but was it perhaps only a good speech for a man in the quiet of his study, not for an audience of festive and wine-excited minds?

But, whether it was or not, he'd have to stand up and give it. He had no other speech. No composing something else at this late moment. No rising from his place and departing 'sick'. No crashing to the floor in a simulated faint. Great his distress in these last moments, and yet he was restless to begin, partly because speaking would at least be a change of pain, and partly—very odd, this— because he was half looking forward to a scandalous sensation and to being the centre of it.

'My Lord Mayor, my Lords, your Worships, ladies and gentle-men, pray silence for Mr. Stephen Blaize, Chairman of the Liberal Association.'

He rose. And lo, he was the only perpendicular figure among all those lollers in their chairs: a kind of solitary lighthouse in a wide and listening sea. Suddenly, and most disturbingly, he felt ten inches taller than he was accustomed to be. He cleared his throat twice and hoped that no one had perceived so far that this was a perpendicular vessel of pulsing fears which now stood uphoisted in their midst.

He began with a little joke prepared days ago as a mask for his present shocking state, which he had known would be his.

'My lord'—here he turned with a bow towards Lord Wetherloe in the way he had rehearsed before his bathroom mirror—'you have most courteously invited me to speak as a Liberal. I certainly am an old Liberal, and this, I think, is perhaps a pity, because the Liberal Party of today is a party of youth and the future, and it would be better that a young Liberal should address you. We have our branch of the Young Liberals Association in St. Mary

Upbourne but as its uppermost age is thirty, I was in no position to join it——'

This was interrupted by such a roar of laughter that he was quite offended by it. It was not a very good joke, and he had expected only some titters; not this universal roar. Did he then look so terribly old that the jest was uproarious?

Still, the rich laughter was a small encouragement as well as an offence, and he proceeded a little more easily—but only a little.

'As it is, I shall try to speak of something that transcends all party programmes, and it may be that all I shall do is to demonstrate that among us Liberals there is perfect freedom of conscience. For I suspect that many of my Liberal colleagues would not agree with what I am about to say. Perhaps I am speaking more as a Quaker than a Liberal and you will be entitled to regard it as a merely personal statement.'

His voice might be shaking, and the hand that held his notes shaking too, but this was certainly an opening that had captured interest.

'I offer no apology for what I am going to say. The other gentlemen, at your request, my lord, have been as controversial as they wished in stating their politics; so I now propose to put before you what I conceive to be far and away the most important political question of all.'

So far, so good—except for the shaking voice and the hammering heart. So far without disaster. This might be a kind of living death but the Showman was producing a show of ease—always provided no one could see the sweat which had sprung from his hair roots and was moving slowly down his nape. And that they attributed the tremor in his voice to a nobler emotion than fear.

'You may find what I am going to say difficult to take. I do myself. For long my head has been at issue with my heart in this matter. The truth, as I see it, had to batter its way against the entrenched positions in my heart. But it has forced its way in.'

Yes, they were listening spellbound. Even gaping. As if wondering what dreadful thing he was about to say.

And this meant that there was a great silence among them. And that suddenly he heard his own voice as the only sound in the silence. And so strange and disturbing was this that, instead of remembering the next sentences of his speech, he was remembering the quotation, with some pity for that voice, 'Alone on a wide, wide sea' and trying for a second or two to recall what poem it came from. Then wondering how he had come to embark on this wide sea. And even wondering who he was. And where he was. And why he was where he was.

What came next? He had no idea. And this moment of amnesia launched the greatest attack of nerves yet. He discovered, in this ghastly emptiness, that if you learn a speech by heart, you may lose it, because your brain is not occupied by reasoning it out but only summoning memory. His heart was now a rioting rebellion in him but he hid this with a smile while he dived into his notes for a lifebuoy. Presumably this hiatus was much briefer than it seemed to him because the people waited comfortably while he swam for help.

Ah, yes.

'Ladies and gentlemen, was there ever quite such an hour in the long drama of humanity on the stage of our Earth? I can think of none. Within the lifetime of the youngest here the course of history has been violently diverted. History went over a watershed from one world to another on that day when a nuclear weapon was used in war.'

In the pause which he allowed here deliberately he saw that the deaf woman at his side was providing her smile as she looked up at him, in case what he was saying was funny.

'We are therefore all sitting here in a time of revolution—at a moment when there is a need for the greatest revolution in thought since—well, since man became a thinking creature—and I submit with respect that my Tory and Socialist friends tonight have seemed unaware of this. They have revealed only the outmoded attitudes of the past.' (One for the Tory lad and the Labour boy. He forgot which book it had come from.) 'The question before the world is nothing less than a choice between a splendid upward leap of the human spirit and a degradation of it, whose issue will be its death in shame and dishonour. I say "degradation" because there is today no longer any possibility of a "just" war, and because we are no longer able even to use this nuclear weapon as a threat without a degradation of the human spirit.'

It was now that he began to feel the impatience, the warm intolerance spreading over his audience like an incoming tide. But they were listening. Oh, they were listening all right. Just as Dr. Johnson said, 'Depend upon it, sir, when a man knows he is about to be hanged it concentrates his mind wonderfully,' so when men know they are about to be infuriated it concentrates their listening wonderfully. All eyes were on him. Unloving eyes, most. And now, for the first time he noticed Gwen: she alone was not looking at him, but down on her plate as if in a horror of embarrassment. This completed the work of turning his heart into a quivering jelly-fish. But he went on, he went on, voice trembling for all to hear, heart hammering for none to see, sweat dripping for those near by to see.

This was the hour, he said, for an uprising of the lonely human will against the very march of history. (Again a good sentence— where had he found it?) But while admiring it, he forgot the next sentences of his speech. Go on he must; the people were staring and waiting; so he went on, with a section of the speech omitted. Fortunately the point at which he resumed followed on in a possible sequence, so that none would know that he had dropped some of his luggage by the way. 'To anyone of simple sense the weapons of the great nations now are clearly useless. Why? Because their infinite destructiveness bears no relation to any objective that a war will seek to achieve. It will be like spending a million pounds for a pound's worth.' (His own, this.) 'And because of this lack of all relation between the infinite destruction and the limited purpose, never again, as I have said, can there be a just war.'

A halt in an awful silence. Then: 'And again, because of this, though I yield to none of you in love of my country, I submit, ladies and gentlemen, that the defence of Britain is no longer the most important thing in the world. The most important thing is the defence and saving of humanity.'

Muttering now, all over the room. Murmurs of 'Rubbish!' 'Balderdash!' Even a contemptuous voice, 'Oh, *sit* down!' All of which strengthened him a little by angering him. '*Sit* down' was especially offensive. His voice lifted; for a moment he had no nerves. 'Oh yes, gentlemen. And I go farther. I say, never again can there by such a thing as war, just or unjust, because a single day of nuclear annihilations cannot be called "war". It will be merely a day of genocide and suicide.'

Palpable, even audible, hostility now. Beating up against one who learned in this moment that he was not built for audible execration, he who wanted to be liked. And admired and praised. And here he was—he who had wanted to appear an orator and the speaker of the evening—giving a fair demonstration of a man all a-tremble with nerves. Hands and notes shaking, voice tremulous, breaths caught and tripped. The mental pain was heavy but it enabled him like a hurt child to stagger angrily to his conclusion. Where stood Christianity in this hour, he asked. 'I suggest it should realize that it once again stands alone in a pagan world. I suggest it would be the saving of Christianity if, instead of truckling to the powers of the world, as it has done more or less since the time of Constantine, it should now outlaw itself as in its first days and challenge the divinity of Caesar. Christianity should refuse this last impossible sacrifice to any Caesar.'

This was his well-prepared coda. It had seemed so good when he thought of it, and looked it up in dictionaries, but now— now it seemed all too like clap-trap, as he uttered it in a shaking voice and sat down, the sweat streaming between nape and collar.

'Yes, *sit* down,' advised a neighbouring voice, with scorn.

Otherwise total silence. No applause anywhere. People seemed afraid to start even a formal applause. If ever three seconds of silence proclaimed the hot rejection of a speech, these were they. To Mr.

Blaize, as he drew a handkerchief and touched his wet limp collar, this brief silence seemed like the silence over Arctic spaces.

But it was only three seconds of silence. Then the talk erupted, and everywhere, as he dabbed at neck and brow, hoping no one knew why, he heard the words of repugnance, aversion, hostility. His hearing, sharpened by disaster, seemed able to catch any words anywhere that were attacking him. 'Universal murmurings.' Even in this deathly situation his old love of nonsense was able to call this collective chatter 'murmurings in the wilderness' and, pat on its moment, a text appeared in his mind, 'I have heard the murmurings of the children of Israel. As truly as I live, saith the Lord, your carcases shall fall in the wilderness.' Why couldn't he get up and say this to them? It was as likely as not the truth, and it would be good for them to hear it. In this moment he rather hoped it *would* be the truth for them.

'Rubbish!'

'Shame!'

'Never heard such piffle. Ask the Hungarians what *they'd* say.'

'Are we to sit down and smile while the Reds come and liquidate us?'

'That's the idea. Not even to threaten them because it wouldn't be gentlemanlike.'

'Just to stand by and watch my daughter being raped by one Russian after another? No, *thank* you.'

'Highfalutin nonsense. Sickening sloppy sentimentality.'

'Yes, all pacifist cranks make me sick.'

'Yes, why can't he keep this muck for his Quakers? *We* don't want it.'

Rose a red-hot Liberal. 'My lord, I may be out of order in rising but the gentleman to whom we have just been listening spoke in the guise of a Liberal, and I, who have been a Liberal all my life, must insist that this fanatical defeatism which he has given us is no part of the Liberalism that most of us profess. Thank you.'

'Hear, *hear*! Hear, *hear*!' from many voices. And "ear, 'ear!' from a tipsy clown. 'Who the Blaizes does he think he is? 'Ear, 'ear.'

'Nor is it Conservatism,' from somewhere; and a louder chorus of hear-hears.

'Nor Socialism.' A smattering of hear-hears only; the Socialists were not many in the room.

'Nor Communism,' cried a loud and well-wined voice, almost certainly Tory (for there were no Communists among the Mayor's guests) and this drew again the loud hear-hears, even delighted hear-hears, from the Conservative faction. For once Tory and Communist, Blue and Red, were hand-in-hand.

Mr. Blaize's heart as he sat there, hearing these attacks, was like a blob of water bubbling within him. Never an hour like this in all his sixty-five years. Sitting here among three hundred, a lonely object of hate and derision. And covering the pain of it all with a sham smile. The memory of it would remain as a sore in his heart for ever.

Of course his reason told him there must be a few in this audience who agreed with him, but reason was powerless against the suffering in his heart. If there were those on his side, why did not one—not one—rise and say so? Was it that they were naturally quiet people, or were they overawed by the general hostility?

Oh, for it to be over! Oh, to be put of this place! To get to Gwen and explain to her that they were a lot of Philistines and why his speech had been good.

But he was no longer sure that it had been good. The murmurs among three hundred people had knocked it from its proud seat. Before this general condemnation he had known it to be good, whether acceptable or not, but now—now he sat with no such assurance. He was even, at times, attacking the Inward Light for having led him up the garden.

One grain of comfort. The idiot woman on his right made reparation for her earlier offences by touching his hand where it rested sadly on the table and saying, 'Very nice.'

'Oh, no,' he said. 'They didn't like it.'

'*I* liked it.'

'Oh, no, you didn't.'

'I did. I enjoyed it very much.'

He knew that this praise was only formal; that 'nice' was the least fitting word for what he had told them; and that only an idiot would have said she enjoyed it; but at least her offering was friendly, and he now loved the woman. His one friend.

'I began to feel their hostility, and that made me nervous.'

'You didn't look nervous.'

(Dear lady, if you couldn't see that I was dripping with nerves you are more of an uncomprehending idiot than I thought. But probably you're just lying.)

Even if he now loved her, he was impatient when she began to talk about other things, just as if he were not worried to death, and didn't want to stay apart with his worry. He wanted to be silent, thinking only of what had happened; going over it again and again; point by point, again and again. He forced himself to respond to her remarks even while he was telling himself, 'I shall never speak in public any more. Never, never, never. Can't go through this sort of thing again——'

'Oh, yes, she *is* a beautiful woman,' he agreed. 'I quite agree with you. Wonderful for her age.'

'Age! How ungallant of you.' She touched his hand in playful reproach. 'She isn't all that old.'

'Isn't she? No, perhaps not.' (But what the hell do I care how old she is. I shall retire from Liberalism. Sick of it and of all politics. I've finally learned my lesson that I'm not made for polemical speech-making because I can't endure open hostility. Others enjoy it, I suppose. It's part of the fun for them.)

'What do you think this wonderful party cost the Mayor? You are a clever man and probably have some idea.'

'Cost? I've absolutely no idea. All of four figures, I should think.'

'Would you really?'

'I certainly should.' (Done with Liberalism for ever. I hate the word. And anyhow I seem to have ruined the Liberal Party in St. Mary Upbourne for the next ten years. Not sure that I haven't done with the whole borough of St. Mary Upbourne. It will always be the place where I suffered a public shame. And not sure, come to that, that I haven't done with the whole of London. I never want to pass this bloody hotel again.)

'Yes, but I don't suppose a thousand or so troubles him very much. He has all the money in the world.'

'Yes. His ground rents must be a pretty penny.' (Marble Arch Hotel. I shall never want to look upon the Marble Arch again. I'd like to go far away into the country somewhere. When will this be over? Have I got to sit here for another hour, conscious that I'm an object of dislike to all these loathly people? Though surely one or two—one or two at least—must have agreed with me. How long, how long, must I sit here answering this idiot creature?)

Should he, when they were out in the corridors, talk with other guests and try to explain that he had meant well? No, that would meet with no success and only give him more pain. All he longed to do now was to get to Gwen and explain to her that he had sought, with no small courage, to speak an unpopular truth, but that perhaps this had been an absurd attempt, because they were an audience of hidebound, beef-witted Philistines.

§

The evening wore away at last and he was able to hurry forth to Gwen with his suffering and his explanation. But there was no chance of a proper exposition in the corridor with the departing people streaming by. Only when they were out in the dark street together, walking towards Marble Arch station—Marble Arch! Detestable name—did he feel ready to dilate at length upon the disaster. He waited at first for one word of her usual ready flattery to comfort him; he would know it for what it was, but he would try to forget this and believe in it and find in it a tiny measure of balm. She stayed silent. So he ventured, 'Well . . . if ever a speech was an out-and-out flop——'

'Oh, no,' she dissented. But it was plain this was said in wifely compassion rather than in real disagreement. And, after a pause, she began, 'But I must say, Stephen——'

'Say Stephen *what?*' he demanded warmly.

'I'm afraid I couldn't agree with what you said.'

'No, I didn't expect you would. No one did. No one would.'
He spoke as a man who drives yet one more knife into his heart.

She started to justify her disagreement but he stopped her. 'Oh, please don't say any more. I've had enough for tonight.'

'All right, all right,' she agreed, and talked cheerfully of enjoyable things in the party, which was yet more hurtful to him. She said how delightful had been the men on either side of her, and how they had made her laugh with their jokes. She actually told him their jokes. He tried to answer with 'Were they?' and 'Did they?' and 'Ha, ha . . .' but felt ever more exasperated with her for being merry and insensitive to his suffering. It was all very well for her to be in Abraham's bosom when he was in hell and its torments. Sometimes, walking silently through the darkness with his dark memory, he gasped at parts of it, and the pain was indeed like a small torment of hell.

Much of that night he lay awake with the memory, giving at times this involuntary gasp when its worst parts recurred. And out of this particular pain did Mr. Blaize, so prone to revelations as he neared his seventieth year, achieve a new one; not a large one like that Bo-Tree enlightenment in the Paris room but a sudden clear sight that was not merely accepted by the mind but felt and possessed in the deep of his soul.

He perceived—somewhere about three o'clock—that there would have been no pain at all in what had happened if only his single desire had been to speak an unpopular truth without one thought for the glory of Stephen Blaize. Then there would have been peace and pleasure even though they had cried him down. If only he had risen and spoken the hard unwanted things, and never mind the blame or the praise. *Athanasius contra mundum.* Stephen Blaize *contra mundum.* But it had not been at all like this. His dominant desire had been his own glory. All the time from the first composition of his speech to the moment when he rose to deliver it, he had been sitting, not in a fine Athanasian solitude with only his courage and fidelity for comfort, but in what he sometimes called his Wanting-to-be-Admired Department. 'The speech of the evening'! Oh my God! A small moan as he remembered these wholly self-centred words; and as he told himself, 'You can bear anything if you know that you've acted only for the truth's sake as you see it, and to hell with blame or praise. You then laugh and are happy. As *I* might be happy now—because I did believe it to be the real Christianity—if only I'd eliminated that wretched Stephen Blaize. I might be rejoicing in the fact that I've now experienced in my own small way the great truth that if you proclaim something too high for the normal instincts of men you will be reviled and howled down and possibly crucified. I might be feeling the joy of the martyr. Stephen, the last Christian martyr. Or at any rate the most recent.'

Exhaustion at length, and sleep.

In the morning he said to Gwen, 'Come. I'll do the shopping,' partly because 'when the devil is sick the devil a saint would be' and partly in the hope of getting a smile from some friends in the street and of feeling loved in spite of all. These two motives merged as he walked towards the High Street with his wheeled basket, his 'pull-me-round', behind him; he felt a drive to be gentle with all whom he would meet, both because this was to be saintly and because it would win him some love. 'Nothing like the chastisements of pain,' he told himself. 'They teach you to love everybody more, and to be less exacting with them, because you need them.' Perhaps he would meet someone who'd been present last night and would say that the speech had been good. Just one person. One would be enough—or almost enough. Perhaps tomorrow morning a letter might come from just one unknown sympathizer, and it would say 'Well done.'

But again and again as he pulled his basket between the shops, his head shook as he remembered that 'Oh, *sit* down!' and that foul, mildewed old Liberal who'd got up and publicly disowned him, to a chorus of delighted hear-hears. Some did smile as they passed him by, and he felt grateful to them and fond of them. But of course they hadn't heard yet that he was in disgrace. '*Who the Blaizes does he think he is?*'

Between the greengrocer's and the supermarket a new thought arrived: 'Oh, come, come. I must try to take this with humour and courage. I'm damned if I'll be defeated by it. I may yet speak in public again—but in a smaller way. Definitely in a smaller way. And I'll try to do it, caring only for the truth. I don't quit the field because of one deep wound. That's not me. I rebuild. They unhorsed me for a moment, but I mount again and ride on. What a gift for metaphor I've got.'

A funeral passed up the High Street, and he caught himself envying the dead man in the hearse because '*his* troubles are all over'. More than one baby went by, sitting upright in its pram among it's mother's shopping, and he caught himself pitying it, because 'it's got seventy years and more of life to get through before all pain is over'. His basket filling with cartons and jars of groceries, and his head (also pulled around) filling with alternate despairs and comforts, he went from shop to shop, often forgetting inside what it was he had come to buy. It was in the High Street, towards the end of his task, that a Bible verse, exactly appropriate, presented itself to his mind: 'It is good for me that I have been afflicted, that I might learn Thy statutes.'

Was not God notorious (if such was the word) for disciplining his saints by sending them trouble after trouble to strengthen their spiritual muscles and purge them gradually of self-regarding and self-pity? Perhaps that was what it had all been about. It had been God's discipline for one of His—for one who was trying to be better.

He would look at it like that.

Comforting. Comforting. Let us leave Mr. Blaize in the High Street, being purified by suffering, while he shops.

XV

Crime in Murry Walk

NEXT morning, when he went to the letters on the hall-door mat, he found one in a strange hand. Its postmark was local, its date yesterday. Abuse? Oh, he couldn't take any more. Bitter abuse almost certainly; and for some time he stood there by the mat alone, afraid to break the envelope. Then defiantly he tore it open.

Dear Sir [he read],
Permit a stranger who was present at the Mayor's banquet last night to offer his small tribute of applause for your courageous speech. If only there were more with your readiness to speak the truth fearlessly! The deplorable reception given to your words revealed the blind or blinkered indifference of the vast majority to the dark threat overhanging the whole world, and the need for a few brave men like yourself who will speak out loud and clear. You chose your place and your moment well, sir.

He felt like saying 'Thank God.' Only one such letter, and this one on paper headed 'Campaign for Nuclear Disarmament' but still . . . it was a touch of healing. If his pitch into misery after his exalted dreams about the speech had been a peripeteia downwards, this moment by the mat was a small peripeteia upwards. 'A dove to the ark,' he quoted, being ever ready with Biblical texts, and 'God has tempered the wind to the shorn lamb', which he supposed to be in the Bible, but which was not. He would not submit these texts to Gwen because, just as he had hidden his stage-fright from her, so had he hidden his grievous shames and pains; but he rushed down the kitchen stairs to lay the letter before her.

And as he went he wondered if in some circles the speech would become quite famous.

On Sunday, hoping to hear more good words, he went to Meeting and, after worship, left himself about in the vestibule so as to be ready for possible congratulations. Surely Quakers, of all people, would offer approving words. Such as 'I heard you made a very fine speech at the Mayor's Banquet'; or 'You delivered a great blow for Pacifism, I hear. . . .'

Not that he wanted any more to hear endorsements of his pacifism, for the aftermath of that disastrous speech in the heart of Mr. Blaize was a loss of all interest in—or a loss of all love for —the notion and very name of pacifism. Nor was his faith in the Inward Light what he had liked to believe it. Last night in bed he had told himself there was nothing left to him but a blind agnostic trust in some Purpose behind the world, and a certainty that he would continue his struggle to be better.

But it was difficult to be better. The Devil walketh about as a roaring lion, and could even be around in a Quaker meeting on a Sunday. Seeking whom to devour. No one was saying a word to him, and the self-seeking Mr. Blaize was disappointed. Had they not even heard about the speech? Had it been, not only a disaster, but also a matter of no importance? Was he, from now onwards, to have no more words of praise? But here at last—ah, good!— came Mr. Plaicey towards him, surely with a congratulation— perhaps 'Mr. Blaize, sir, I understand we have to thank you for speaking with great courage to the needs of the Hour. I gather that you really gave them that of God within you'; or perhaps, 'I under- stand, sir, that you wielded the sword of the Spirit to great effect at the Mayor's dinner'—but no, Evan Plaicey said none of these things. What he did say, however, was mysterious and exciting enough to drive aside any disappointment. He said, 'Could Miss

Diver and I come and talk to you about a serious matter one evening?'

'You and Sidonie? Why, certainly,' he answered, savouring a mystery. 'Do you mean privately or could my wife——'

'No, no, I think we'd rather speak with you alone at first.'

Better and better. This not only added to the mystery but elevated him above his wife; it put him in a class apart from her. 'What about tomorrow evening?'

'Tomorrow evening would be perfect. It will suit Miss Diver, I know.'

He could not ask, 'What's it all about?' because a tiresome woman came up, touched Evan on the arm, and said, 'Mr. Plaicey, please . . .'

'Hell!' he thought. 'Damned rude. *I* was talking to him'; and, pronouncing quite loudly, 'I thought Quakers had manners,' he went out into the street, angered, but happy with his mystification.

Next evening, having got rid of Gwen by suggesting that Mr. Plaicey and Sidonie were wanting to talk 'Quaker business', he walked about the drawing room, arranging it to look as expensive and dignified as possible—did the Devil, Father of Lies, come sometimes and walk around in the drawing room? Never were visitors awaited but Mr. Blaize the Showman gave pains and time to preparing and cleansing the room. Today he re-set the chairs and the ornaments, straightened the pictures, put out a few silver pieces, and gave prominence on side-tables or elsewhere to things that reflected distinction on the householder. All done in the drawing room, he came out and tidied up what he called The North-West Approaches, to wit, the front door, the hall mat and the passage.

These in good order, he came back into the drawing room and went once and again to the window to see if Evan and Sidonie were in view; and at last they were. Here they were, he tall, she small; and something in the way they came side by side put knowledge into his head. Good gracious! Could it really be?

They came in and sat down, Evan on an upright chair, pulling

his trousers over the bony knees of his too-long legs, and Sidonie
contenting herself with the mere brink of a deep easy-chair.

He gave them an inquiring smile. 'Well . . .?'

Mr. Plaicey, looking at Sidonie, said, 'You tell him, dear'; and
that 'dear' told him all.

'Well, Uncle . . . Evan has asked me to marry him. . . .'

'Oh, Sidonie, sweetheart—but that's wonderful!' and it was
certainly wonderful in so far as he was wondering if this was good
news or not. Such a grave, even such a grim, young man.

'And I—of course I'd like to, Uncle—awfully—but there's Uncle
Morley, you see. . . .'

'What's *he* got to do with it?' An unloving query.

'I don't like to leave him, old as he is, and Evan doesn't think
I ought to.'

'No,' Mr. Plaicey agreed, eyes very grave again. 'Her duty is to
him. I've given it great thought and sought guidance and I feel it's
my duty to wait for her.'

'Oh, hell,' thought Mr. Blaize, but didn't express his feeling
thus to a pious young man. He said, 'I don't think I agree. No, I'm
sure I don't. No young woman should be sacrificed to an old man.'

'It can't be for very long,' said Mr. Plaicey. 'Mr. Morley Blaize is
nearly ninety and, if it's not unkind to say so, he can't go on for ever.'

'I'm not so sure of that,' was Mr. Blaize's thought as Mr. Plaicey
continued, 'I shall be happy to wait for dear Sidonie.'

'But I still don't think she should be tied to him.' He looked at
Sidonie. She was thirty-five now, and he understood all. Mr.
Plaicey was not exactly an ideal beau but to a woman approaching
forty who'd been sought by no other man, he was, to state it
vulgarly, 'better than nothing'. And, to continue in the vulgar
tongue, she had probably 'jumped with joy at him'. He would be
a good husband and faithful and pious and kind. 'How do you
feel about it, Sidonie?' he asked.

'I feel I ought to do whatever Evan advises.'

(Oh dear! Already in train for the obedient wife. Sidonie, the
congenital disciple.)

'But we both thought,' she proceeded, 'that we'd like to ask you as his son.'

Mr. Blaize felt flattered. 'Does he know?' he asked.

'No, I've been afraid to tell him. It's the last thing he suspects and he's so unreasonable about Quakers. He gets so hot and rude about them. And for some reason he's got an especial grudge against Evan. He's properly got his knife into him. So I don't know what to do. You see, after that stroke, Dr. Blythe said he must never be over-excited or the result might be serious. He said to me more than once, "No over-excitement or mental strain".'

Yes, Mr. Plaicey would certainly be a mental strain for Sapper Blaize, thought the Sapper's son; an over-excitement, but he didn't tell this to the young man. Instead he said, 'But at that rate, Evan, he might hold Sidonie for years and years. You don't know my father. I always say he's immortal. There's no killing him.' This had come out as a joke, and he instantly felt it was unsuited to the ears of Mr. Plaicey. He regretted it. 'My dear father, Evan, might easily go on to be a hundred.'

At which Mr. Plaicey only shrugged. 'Yes, well . . . Miss Diver mustn't upset him in any way. I feel sure she wouldn't want to, and that I mustn't ask her to. She's an earnest young woman.'

In the whole record of the world's love stories had any young man hitherto called his beloved, in the first flush of their romance, an earnest young woman?

'But, Evan,' Mr. Blaize objected when in a condition to speak again, 'it's not only a question of upsetting *him*. What about upsetting her? He's a hell of a—I mean he's a very great strain on her. I can promise you I wouldn't live with him for a thousand pounds a week. What's your idea if he lives to be a hundred?'

After a silence Mr. Plaicey said, 'I can only leave that with God.'

Mr. Blaize tut-tutted to himself, sighed, ruminated, and then suggested, 'There must be plenty of good women in the British Isles, one of whom we could get to look after him.'

'Yes, but it's Sidonie he's used to and depends on.'

Now Mr. Blaize's foot moved impatiently as if to stamp.

'Heavens, man!' he thought. 'Don't you *want* the girl?' And, joking impatiently again, he asked, 'Well, what's wrong with his coming to live with you?'

'No, I don't think that would do,' Mr. Plaicey submitted in full seriousness; and Mr. Blaize, after looking at the young man, and remembering his father, thought, 'No, it wouldn't do.'

'I've meditated and meditated on it, seeking guidance,' said Mr. Plaicey, staring through his large lenses at a far wall, as if there might yet be found guidance there, 'and I can only say that I don't feel at ease about taking her away from him at this juncture.'

Juncture! What a word for a love story. The impatience swelled within Mr. Blaize, to the point of shaking his shoulders a little. If Mr. Plaicey's Inner Light was directing him thus, then Mr. Blaize, with respect, would defy it. 'Well, I don't know, Evan. Perhaps I'm far less noble than either of you—in fact, a rather bad old man——'

'Oh, no, you mustn't say that.'

(Good God, did he think I meant it?)

'Well, whatever I am, I can't think he has any right to keep two young people apart. I want Sidonie to be happy. She hasn't had much of a life with him. I'd like you to be able to marry soon.' Aloud he could not say, 'It's all right for you to be so noble, Evan; you're only just thirty. Sidonie's coming up towards forty. Can't you see it's different for a woman, you silly young man?' So he ended by asking, 'Will you trust me to go and talk to my father about it? I'll do it as gently as I can.'

'Oh, yes, *do*, Uncle,' Sidonie pleaded suddenly, and this showed where the earnest young woman's desires really lay, whatever might be her suitor's compunctions. 'But he's not going to like it,' she sighed. 'I can't imagine *what* he'll say.'

'Do you agree, Evan?'

'If you'll make it clear to him that I'm determined to do nothing which will render him unhappy.'

'I'll make that clear to him, Evan——' (but I'm damned if I'll stress it too far).

177

'Oh, it's good of you, Uncle,' said Sidonie, 'but whatever will happen when you tell him?'

As he followed behind them to the street door and saw them start along Denlow Road, she resting her small hand trustfully on his arm, he felt that, however serious the young man, he really loved them both and longed to help them.

Having their permission now to tell Gwen, he closed the door and dashed downstairs to tell her.

§

Mr. Blaize went to his father, not without pleasure in the thought of giving the old man a lesson—of punishing him, in fact, for plenty of bellowing at Sidonie and bullying her, and showing him that another man was prepared to be good and kind to her. Punishing him only mildly, of course, because he was very old now and it was late in the day to begin teaching him. A part of him even pitied the old man because he'd never, in all his eighty-eight years, had a vision of self-conquest and self-giving like his son's in a Paris room.

He went to Murry Walk in the morning while Sidonie was at the shops, because he didn't want her coming into the room and hampering his arguments by making him self-conscious.

There in Murry Walk he saw the old man leading Ah Sin up and down from tree to tree. Or, more accurately, Ah Sin at the end of his leash was drawing him from tree to tree along the grass verge, and from lamp-post to garden wall. Against tree or wall Ah Sin achieved the lesser more than once, but presumably, since his master did not pick him up to carry him home, the lazy little beast had not yet given his mind to the senior affair.

'Good morning, Father,' said Mr. Blaize, coming up behind the two of them.

His father stopped and swung round, while Ah Sin used this halt to prospect for heaven knew what interests among the grasses at his feet. 'Good God, Stephen. Need you jump my heart out of my body? Creeping up like that.'

'I didn't creep up. It's just that you don't hear.'

'*What?* What did you say?'

'I said it's just that you don't hear.'

'Justice is damned dear? Too true, but what's that got to do with anything?'

'Nothing,' said Mr. Blaize, and, having dissolved this difficulty, he asked, 'Can I come in and speak to you about something?'

'Come in and what?'

'Discuss something with you when Ah Sin is ready to return.'

'Ah Sin is ready to return when *I'm* ready to return. I don't allow my movements to be determined by Ah Sin.' He picked up the little long mass of fur and laid it, as usual, belly upwards, on his right arm. 'I'm glad you've come because I want to express my strong disagreement with what you apparently said at that Mayor's how-d'ye-do. I've been told all about it and I couldn't disagree with you more.'

This unexpected attack, on a subject happily out of memory, stung Mr. Blaize, as might a passing wasp. This was not what he had come for. He had come to teach the old man a lesson, not to be taught one himself. 'I never supposed for a moment that you would agree. But may we leave that subject? I don't think there'd be any profit in discussing it.'

'Maybe not, but at least allow me to say that I thought it traitorous talk.'

'Please . . . I——'

'It was no talk for anyone who's held the King's commission. You and I both fought for our country once. We were ready to risk our lives for it. We were lucky, both of us, to come out of it with our lives. It was not for want of offering them that we're both here. And now you advocate throwing all our weapons away and giving the bloody Reds a free run in. Not on your life! Not in a thousand years.'

Mr. Blaize still restrained himself and answered nothing as they went up the steps to the open door.

'Get in, Sin.' His father put down the dog and gave it a small

kick as if it were a pacifist (which it certainly wasn't). '*Get* inside.
Yes, it's all those damned Quakers, I suppose.'

An unpromising introduction to a discussion about Mr. Plaicey
as bridegroom. Best hold back any retort. Best contain oneself.

Ah Sin waddled ahead of them into the small living room. Mr.
Morley Blaize with a self-comforting sigh flung himself into his
large fireside chair and his legs at full length on to the pouffe in
front of him; and his son noticed the fine crease in the fawn trousers,
the clean beige cardigan buttoned neatly over his deep chest, the
matching cream shirt and brown bow-tie. Perfectly dressed as ever,
and perhaps one ought to admire him for it. Still well groomed for
this world, on the edge of ninety. With a further sigh of relief the
old man drew up his legs, removed his shoes, and then stretched
forth the legs again that the unshod feet might bow before the fire
like two acolytes at appropriate moments in the Mass. Meanwhile
Mr. Stephen Blaize had sat himself sideways on a chair with his
arm along the back. After a brief, horrified, but fascinated glance at
those two feet bowing their toes side by side, he averted his eyes
from a sight so oddly maddening. Even so, the eyes of his mind
still saw those upright twins on the pouffe, each at regular intervals
making its *inclinatio capitis* to the fire.

'It's about Sidonie that I want to talk.'

'*What?*'

'About Sidonie.'

'What the hell about Sidonie? I'm not at all pleased with Sidonie.
I don't know where she gets to nowadays. She's never here when
I want her.'

Oh, let him have it. 'She wants to get married.'

'And she still goes to those dismal, damned Quakers.'

'She . . . wants . . . to . . . get . . . married.' Mr. Blaize enunciated
it louder and more clearly.

'*What?* Married? You didn't say "married", did you?' His toes
stopped all bowing to the fire, as if they would hearken to incredible words. His eyes stared into Mr. Blaize's.

'Yes.'

'Married? What—soon? You don't mean soon?'

'Of course I do.'

'But, devil take it I know nothing about this. Am I just to be left? Am I not to be considered at all? What the hell!'

'That's what I want to talk about. About what arrangements we can make for you.'

'But who in the name of heaven is it she suddenly wants to marry? She never sees any man unless it's the milkman.'

'It's a young man you've met.'

'*Who?*' This 'who?' a pistol shot in the face.

'He came here once to talk with Sidonie.'

'I don't know who you mean. I tell you no man ever comes here to talk with Sidonie unless it's the milkman. Or the man from the laundry. Is it one of them she wants to marry?'

'His name is . . .' Mr. Blaize hesitated. 'His name is Plaicey.'

'What a damn-silly name.'

'Well, that's his name. Evan Plaicey.'

'Means nothing to me.'

'He came here once to——' but how insert the needle of this loaded syringe as gently as might be? He remembered Sidonie's statement that it might be fatal to over-excite him. 'He came here once to—well, he came from the Quakers to discuss with Sidonie——'

'What?' For once this syllable, fired straight into the eyes of a speaker, did not mean that he hadn't heard, but that he'd heard only too well. 'What? That upended tapeworm who came one day without my consent and walked past my nose downstairs to spend about an hour there gassing with Sidonie? *That* soppy-looking sawney? Are you telling me he's been getting at Sidonie behind my back? And probably down my stairs? Is he proposing, without a word to me, to walk her out of my house? She's more than my housekeeper, she's my niece. God damn it, to me she's practically a daughter.'

Mr. Blaize thought, 'Yes, and you've usually treated her like a terrified daughter,' but he only said, 'You hardly encouraged him to come and speak to you again.'

'I won't have it. I won't let her marry him. The whole thing's ridiculous. Some hare-brained idea that'll pass. Why, he's about ten years younger than she is.'

'Five.'

'Five. Well, the impertinent young devil. He must be daft. He looks about as fatuous as they make them. An elongated nincompoop——'

'He's a very intelligent young man, if a shade over-serious.'

'And Sidonie must be another fool if she's fallen for an elongated moon-calf like that. God rot these Quakers for coming and interfering in my house. We must stop this business for her sake. Her mother and I and you must stop it.'

'I certainly shan't do anything to stop it.' Mr. Blaize's anger was rising now and must soon be out of control. 'Sidonie is thirty-five, and if she wants him, well, he'll at least make her an honourable husband. If anything, he's too conscientious. He said he wasn't going to take her away if you really needed her.'

'Did he?' A sudden drop in the old man's fury was evident. And his next sentence revealed the only true root of his anger. 'Oh, well, what are we worrying about? I quite obviously need her and hope to go on doing so for a long time yet.'

This piece of concentrated selfishness so astonished and incensed Mr. Blaize that he no longer felt the power or the desire to restrain his words for fear of consequences. Let the selfish old devil have them good and plenty. 'But I don't think you ought to hold her back by saying you need her. It's not fair to her.'

'What about what's fair to me——'

'She isn't happy here. Anyone can see that. It's pathetic the way she moons about the kitchen and goes early to bed with her little transistor.'

'*What* are you saying? Goes to bed with a little Franciscan?'

'*Transistor.*' Mr. Blaize roared the word. '*Transistor.*'

'Man's sister? She can't go to bed with a little man's sister.'

'*Transistor. Radio. Wireless.*'

'Oh, I see. Yes.' And never able to resist a bawdy joke even when

182

in the worst of tempers, he added, 'I understood she wanted to go to bed with a long Quaker.'

'That she wants to go to bed with someone is probably the sheer truth of the matter. And it's not fair to hold her back.'

'But what about what's fair to me? I take it I have some claim upon her——'

'None, I should say.'

'And some right to protect her from a great long nincompoop?'

'No, you haven't. A woman of thirty-five must be allowed to know her own mind and manage her own life. *And* leave you just when it suits her like any cook or housemaid. You can't hold her back just because she's a relative.'

'Are you presuming to teach me at eighty-eight how I should behave?'

'Yes, I suppose that's exactly what I'm doing. Because you're being utterly unreasonable. Even wickedly unreasonable.' His words were running away with him. That warning of Sidonie's about over-excitement and mental strain was still in his memory but so far back now as to be little heeded. If he heeded it at all, it was to think, 'Oh, let the damned consequences look after themselves.' And with this came the thought—a shocking thought, spawn of the old evil thought—'A hell of a lot'll be solved for poor Sidonie, it'd be splendid for her, if the consequences are what the doctor said'—and he didn't fight it. He *couldn't* fight it because he was so angry and because he was wholly on Sidonie's side. And partly because he had suppressed a ferment of anger, some minutes ago, when the old man had been so rude about his speech. Let him have it all. 'I say it would be utterly wrong of you to take advantage of an over-conscientious young man's offer. I say you should tell Sidonie she can marry him as soon as she likes. I say it's the only decent thing to do. And, what's more, I don't propose to let you do anything else.'

'You talk to me like that? You dare talk to me like that?' There was now a change in the old man's face. It had whitened; the mouth was a straight gash in the whiteness; the lower teeth showed in the gash because the jaw was protruded; the lips were blanched.

A little frightened at what he had done, Mr. Blaize flung in mollifying words. 'Of course we'll find some good woman to take Sidonie's place. It shouldn't be difficult.'

But his father wasn't listening. He was repeating, 'You dare talk to me like that? You dare come into my house and call me wicked? I—I—— Will you get out of my house? Will you please get out?'

Mr. Blaize forbore to say, 'It happens to be my house, not yours,' but more because he was alarmed by the look on his father's face, and the quivering in that squared, pugnacious jaw, than because he was anxious to spare him an uncomfortable memory—though an element of this decency did beat somewhere in his angry heart. 'I will certainly go,' he said, 'since it's impossible to make you listen to reason or be other than grossly selfish where poor little Sidonie's happiness is concerned.' He walked to the door. 'And I promise you I shall advise her that she has every right to walk out of your house too, just as soon as she's ready to marry the man she loves.'

He left this with the old man and went down into Murry Walk, heart-shaken, face as white as his father's.

§

It was Sidonie who came round that evening to tell them that the old man was dead.

Sidonie had come into the room less than an hour after her Uncle Steve had left him. He had not greeted her or said a word to her when she came in, so she sat down in silence to admire some silk and lace trimming that she had bought for nightdresses, delighting in the knowledge that she could now prepare for a wedding on some distant day. He just continued to pace in front of her, a few steps this way and that. Happily interested in her purchases with their whisper of a strange new life, she did not notice any quivering in his face or any change in his gait. To careless eyes his posture seemed as upright and strong as ever. But the pacing stopped so abruptly that, like the stopping of a clock, it lifted her eyes to him. His right leg was stationary, the left moved slowly towards it as if it had found difficulty in keeping up with it; a hand flew to his brows; he swayed and fell sideways to the floor.

The rest was a repetition of the previous time. A dash to the telephone of the friendly Pearsons next door; a frustrated summoning of Dr. Blythe who was out on his visits; their gentle laying of the limp figure on its back and getting a cushion under its head till the doctor came; the doctor traced and arriving quickly—but this time he got no response from the recumbent figure, not even from a touch on his open eye. Uncle Morley did not, in fact, recover consciousness. Mrs. Pearson rushed round to Uncle Steve and Auntie Gwen but could get no answer from their maisonette or from the one above. For once in a way they had gone out to 'get a snack in a pub' before attending the afternoon round at the Palladian cinema.

So now in the evening Sidonie came with the news that Uncle Morley was dead. She sobbed as she told them, wiping eyes and nose, though never could an entry of Death have been more timely for her. Gwen wept too. But our whole business is with the thoughts of Mr. Blaize. Whatever he might be saying to the women, whatever becoming expressions of shock and grief he might be uttering, he was really asking himself, Had he, for Sidonie's sake, murdered his father? By furiously provoking a second seizure though aware that it could be fatal. Had the old evil desire caught up with him in a weak moment and helped him to a quiet but useful murder?

And there was Sidonie, red-eyed, red-nosed, and weeping, because her tyrant and bully had died. 'Weeping, when I've just done my best for her.' Marvellous things, women. He might have brought death to the poor old Sapper, but surely he had brought life to Sidonie.

As he talked with the sorrowing girl and with Gwen he was really hearing the case against himself (very strictly *in camera*). He was thinking he could acquit himself of murder but not, alas, not with any conviction, of manslaughter. No, as jury, judge, and criminal he was inclined to agree—in all these roles—that man-slaughter was the proper verdict. He'd had occasion in his Civil Service days to learn the difference between manslaughter and murder. 'It's manslaughter, isn't it, if you cause the death by gross or wanton negligence? The death may not have been fully con-templated, but the guilt or *mens rea*'—even in his rather worried state he was pleased at remembering this learned phrase—'the *mens rea* consists precisely in that failure to contemplate it. But, oh God, I did, for a second or two in that blazing row "contemplate the consequences"—is it not then manslaughter but . . . the other thing?'

Mr. Blaize the Murderer.

'I'll get a few things together, Sidonie darling, and come round and stay with you in the house. You can't stay there alone, and I shall be able to help you in making all arrangements for the funeral.' The word stopped his heart. 'You go home and . . . and . . . and be with him.'

'Yes, Stephen'll do everything for you, Sidonie. He's so good at this sort of thing. It's his Civil Service training. One needs a man for this sort of thing.'

'There's nothing very difficult to do, Gwen. And everybody's always so helpful on these occasions. So don't you worry, Sidonie dear. Nothing to worry about.' (It's only manslaughter, not murder, if death results from an injury inflicted under provocation and God knows the old devil was provoking enough . . . *but*—oh my God!—the provocation has to be by assault and battery and not by words alone if it's to reduce the offence to—but surely, surely, it was only manslaughter.)

'Yes, Sidonie dear. Gwen'll go with you, and I'll follow very soon. Poor old Dad. Still, he had a good innings. I must tell Evan, and he'll come along to comfort you.' (No one to stop him coming to that house now.) 'I'm so glad you've got him for a com-panion——' (Manslaughter! And the plain truth is I'm not feeling anything like as penitent as I ought to, surely. Less penitent than —let's have the truth of it—than—well, relieved and excited. But not *pleased*. Not exactly pleased. No; poor old boy. Remember his last joke, 'go early to bed with a little Franciscan'. And he not knowing it was a jest within minutes of his End. Poor old devil. No, not pleased. Not ... delighted. ... I mustn't let myself be delighted. I ... I'll fight against that.)

'Go on, you two, and relieve that poor Mrs. Pearson. Give her my thanks as his son ... and as Chief Mourner, I suppose.' Why had that phrase slipped out, a phrase that was as self-flattering as (at the moment, alas) it was rather insincere? Why should one be proud, even in a death, of being a Chief Something? 'Go along and help, you two. I'll be with you in half no time,' he said, dissatisfied with himself and resolving to be kind and help.

Not a thought yet—not for a long time yet—about a large increase to his income and a monstrous profit on that little house. Let him think only that a most unfortunate happening had at least set Sidonie free. But—Mr. Blaize the Murderer. Mr. Blaize the Manslaughterer. The Parricide. Still ... whether or not ... whether or not ... there was obviously no pleasanter way to die.

XVI

Two on the Menin Road

WELL, Sidonie did marry Evan Plaicey soon after this; and, what seemed very remarkable in Mr. Blaize's eyes, she produced a 'little Arthur Plaicey' just as promptly as possible. Within the distance, as the boxing fraternity say. Mr. Blaize was not only astonished by this achievement of the slender and over-earnest Mr. Plaicey but a little shocked by it. He had never quite lost his childhood's sense that all sex whatsoever was tinged with sin. 'In sin hath my mother conceived me.' Was such prompt work really quite right in a Quaker?

Still, a nice little Plaicey, to whom he now had dreams of being a very good uncle.

Mr. Blaize did make a massive profit out of the little house, so that now, what with the liberation of those hundreds he'd paid yearly to his father and with these few thousands of new capital, he and Gwen could spend more freely and live very pleasantly. He did have to live for a while with the recurring question, Had he really eased the old man out of the world so as to clear the path for Sidonie? Or, as the cruder parts of his mind persisted in mischievously phrasing it, had he 'polished him off for Sidonie's sake'? And had he polished him off the more readily because the old man had been rude about a pacifist speech? Not seldom, shaking his head regretfully, he thought the answer must be Yes. And I only wish I could add to this that his shame and remorse were as prolonged

188

as in that case they should have been. But, on the contrary, the truth is that he managed to live quite comfortably with them very soon. He was never sure of the answer, you see, so he decided that the only thing to do was to go on trying to be good. One mustn't be defeated by a tumble, even quite a big one; one must just pick oneself up and march on. Though, to be sure, if the answer really was Yes, it had been no behaviour for a Quaker. Recognizing this, he ceased, not without relief, to be a *practising* Quaker, though always calling himself one—much as his father had always been a proud but remarkably unpractising Catholic. There was not the same need to be the full Quaker now that the Catholic was no more.

He retained his chairmanship of the Liberal Executive in St. Mary Upbourne, and this had a most remarkable issue, which has no place in this story, but of which, perhaps, we will tell you all one day. Meanwhile . . .

§

A result of this new affluence and this undefeated desire to be good was a surge of generous ideas, one of which was that he would get Wally Bletcher and Liz to come far more often so as to relieve Gwen of almost all the work in the house. And he would insist on paying Wally the same as his wife. 'Can't have this double standard, Wally. Equal pay for men.' In the end it was arranged that Wally came three mornings a week, and Liz three and a half: Wally on Mondays, Wednesdays, and Fridays; the Smasher on the intervening days; and Gwen 'living like a lady' the while. He was very happy about this: paying Wally 'the rate for the job' and accepting pain with tight-closed eyes when he heard the Smasher at her demolition in the scullery.

One should perhaps add that these generous emotions were further helped by the thought that, if his present wealth was really the product of crime, then he ought to be altruistic with it and devote some of it to others.

Having Wally about the house three times a week and enjoying chats with him meant that Wally became, as a good servant does with a good master, one of his best friends. Often enough their causeries together, as Wally pursued a job in house or garden, strayed to that old topic which lay so deeply rooted in both their hearts, the Salient in '17. And when April came again and the warm sunlight, caressing the cheek, seemed to call one from pavements to open green places and wooded hills, Mr. Blaize would see, again and again, those placid fields and farmlands undulating gently upwards from the moated walls of Ypres—up towards the Ridge, now silent and tranquil beneath hamlet and wood, but bearing once the dark name of Passchendaele. The Salient, then but mud and glistening water from sky to sky, but now the far-spread Garden of Ypres.

And Mr. Blaize, remembering his visit to that haunted garden, was gripped by a new generous idea. It came one evening and he longed for the hours to pass that he might submit it to Wally in the morning.

The sun was bright in the morning, and Wally, looking up at it, said thoughtfully, 'Wurl ... if it's all right by you, guv, I'll be kind'a tidying up the garden. The beds could do with some hoeing, and them there turf edges want a trim. Not 'alf they don't. The grass fair shoots up with this sun and all.'

'Well, let's begin, Wally. I'm going to help. You take the hoe and I'll take the spade, and you give the orders what to do. I'm your navvy.'

'No, sir. You just watch, see? Watch that I do it proper. It'll be mucky work on them beds.'

'Rubbish. I love messing about with the earth and feeling it dry on my hands. It's a town-dweller's reversion, I suppose, to the ancestral peasant. Kind of atavism.'

This was too much for Wally, who said only, 'Oh, well, sir, just as you please.'

'You're quite a gardener, aren't you? The trouble with me is I've lived in London all my life and hardly know the first thing to do. You can show me.'

'Yurse, had to be a bit of everything in my time. And we got a tidy stretch of back-garden in Burman Street.'

'Well, lead on, Sarge. I'm the fatigue party.'

They went out with hoe and spade to the narrow bed beneath the garden's north wall and, side by side, began to turn over its London-black soil. In silence at first till Wally, resting on his hoe, said, 'If you arst me we could sow a larkspur or two, being as how it's April now, and put some lupins in front and then some nasturtiums, red and yeller, see? Look lovely.'

'Why, that'd be splendid.'

'And perhaps some chrysants and a sunflower or two, to come up later. But the soil'll want to be well worked for lupins and larkspurs.'

'Well, let's work it.' Mr. Blaize began to work it deep with his spade.

'Yes, and well manured for the sunflowers and chrysants. I must try and scrounge some stable manure. When I was a nipper I used to go out and collect it from the road with a shovel and a bucket. My dad give me a penny a bucket. But there ain't no horses now.'

More quiet work together, and then Mr. Blaize said, 'Wally, I'm going back to Ypres. I feel I simply must see Bellewaarde Wood again. Can't get it out of my head. What do you say to coming too? Coming and looking for your O. Pip.'

'Don't make me laugh, sir. I ain't got the money.'

'I'm not suggesting you pay. This is an invitation. I'm suggesting you come as my guest. I feel I'd like a companion who was there and knows all about it. I was lonely last time. And who knows it better than you? You at Ypres One, Two, and Three. I'd help you look for that O. Pip.'

'Never find it now, sir.'

'I don't know. There are still some standing in the fields.'

'It's very kind of you, sir, but I reckon it's abaht thirty years too late. Thirty bloomin' years.'

'Not at all. My hotel proprietor told me that they still come, the old boys. Getting a bit white-haired now and much fewer than they used to be, but they still come in the summer-time.'

'Damned few now, I should think. Well, I must say I wouldn't mind seeing the old place again. Perhaps I could find the money to pay for myself.'

'You'll do nothing of the sort. You're coming with me. To help me.'

'Well, your old guv'nor did leave you a tidy lot, I suppose?' said Wally, weakening.

Mr. Blaize smiled to himself. 'You could put it like that, yes.'

'Wurl . . . I don't know, sir. . . .'

'I do, Wally. I've got it all weighed up. You're getting on, you know, and you must go there before it gets too late.'

§

And it was on a May day some four weeks later that the two of them walked unnoticed on the old Menin Road along which Mr. Blaize had come some thirty months before. Unnoticed because it was morning and the traffic of lorries, buses, cars, vans and cyclists was roaring and racing in continental fashion along the straight pavé between the blown poplars, and many other pedestrians were hurrying to their day's business, unmindful of wars and histories, though it was unlikely they took three steps without treading where a man had dropped. Our two were also hurrying, but because they were very mindful of old things. They were excited about the memory-haunted places they hoped to find.

A mile along the Menin Road, and not only did the railway cross it at an angle but two side roads, crossing at right angles, made a carrefour. High road, side roads, railroad—they must make an asterisk on the maps, and no wonder that, once upon a time, the guns ranged perfectly on to it. Mr. Blaize, delighted at being guide and showman, slowed his pace as they approached the level crossing. Wally stopped abruptly.

'Gawd!' he said.

'Recognize it?'

'I'll say I do! How do anything else? Hell Fire Corner. Gawd! Bloody old Hell Fire Corner!'

He stared at the rusted rails and the sleepers lying among nettles, brambles, and dandelions (for the railway was almost dead now, only a freight train ambling along occasionally with a load of sugar beet).

'Wurl ... wurl ... will you only believe it? Hell Fire Corner! We called it Suicide Corner in Ypres One, but the High-ups soon put a stop to that. Nobody could never stop us calling it Hell Fire Corner.'

'It was Hell Fire Corner all right when I came by.'

'Yepp. And did I hurry past it like jimmy-o-goblin when I was coming back to the battery? I did, sir. I did. ... And I can tell you there were no dandelions there then.'

They stared together at cross-roads and crossing, and at the weedy rail-track running, straight as a measured mile, into the heart of the Salient. Loath to leave these things, they stayed there speechless, the heedless traffic streaming by.

'Well, come on to Bellewaarde Wood,' said the guide at last. 'It's a mile or more to go.'

'Yes ... well ... but I can't get over that being old Hell Fire Corner. ...' And 'Cor!' he breathed, as if still unable to believe what he had just looked upon.

They went on, Wally more than once turning his head to look back at the crossing with its tall hairdresser's poles reaching for the sky.

You will remember that Mr. Blaize walked about half a mile along the straight Menin Road before he reached the old Birr Cross Roads and, turning left, saw in the distance his Bellewaarde Wood. He did not fail now, before leaving the Menin Road, to point out to Wally that it began to mount, and mounted steadily here. This does not seem much to say of a road, but it was much to these two.

'Gaw!' said Wally, staring at that straight incline between its shadowing trees. 'The Ridge! The old Ridge! We never reckoned it more than a hundred and twenty feet high but it had us at its mercy all right.'

'You're telling *me!*' said Mr. Blaize.

Continuing to stare up the shadowed slope while the traffic rushed past him, Wally, nodding an appreciative head, offered at length, 'Gaw . . . lummy . . .' and 'Did you ever?'

They turned on to the country road and were soon alone in the quiet of the Salient. Fortunate in their day, they had an unclouded sun to irradiate the whole green sky-encircled landscape with what —to the private heart of Mr. Blaize—seemed almost a sacred light. After all, had not the poets called this a Holy Land of the British Nations—of Britain and Canada, Australia and New Zealand? In the days of Third Ypres it had been but mud, nothing but mud as far as eye could see; now what was it but the extreme opposite of sterile mud: young wheat spearing up, barley standing higher, flax and beet and tobacco plants emerging in a brilliant green as if the old mud nourished them well; the few acres of pasture all splashed with ladysmock and bluebell; cows cropping near the farmhouses and a young foal gambolling around; and in the far luminous haze two new spires: Langemarck and Passchendaele.

Passchendaele. . . .

Ahead of them now, crowning a low oval hill—a wood, tall, dense, and dark.

'See it?' asked Mr. Blaize. 'Bellewaarde Wood.'

'My Gawd! But are you sure?'

'Absolutely. It's the one place we can be sure of because of the little monument to the sappers of the Tunnelling Company who made the galleries under the wood.'

They came to the fringe of the wood, which the road skirted, and as they halted there staring into the trees, Mr. Blaize said, 'Somewhere down there were the galleries and the dug-outs opening off them and the orderly rooms and the electric light—somewhere under the tree roots.'

'Don't I know it?' said Wally. 'I was there once taking a message to Brigade and I fair lost myself in them passages. I come to a place where four of the passages met, and it was labelled "Clapham Junction". I come to another and it was called "Elephant and Castle". I didn't know where the hell Brigade Headquarters was, but I made it at last. . . .' He stared and stared at the thick, entangled wood, and the underbrush within its dark and crowded deeps. 'I wonder where Clapham Junction is now. . . . Gaw Christ . . . lummy . . . lummy!' This was all the poetry of which Wally was capable, but it was, in its kind, a lyric from the heart, and Mr. Blaize was satisfied with it.

'Now we must go and see if we can find your O. Pip. It was near Frezenhoek, you said. That'll be a mile or two along the Zonnebeke Road.'

'That's right. Our Line after Ypres One ran just in front of St. Julien and Frezenberg and Hooge, behind Langemarck and Zonnebeke.'

'Well, we'll look. We'll look.'

'Ah, but it won't be there,' said Wally sadly. 'We built it of concrete between the ruins of two cottages so that it could look like the walls of one of 'em. My officer had a peep-hole at the top and watched through it with his field-glasses, while I as his runner had to wait below, seeing bloody damn-all.'

Then began for them a day of epic wandering. They wandered about the fields and along the new clean roads and between the few concrete pill-boxes that still stood, spectral and grey, among the green crops, marking where once the German and the British Lines had wound about the Salient, and where was No Man's Land, St. Jean, St. Julien, and Zonnebeke saw them; and Hooge and Gheluvelt and Sanctuary Wood. The few at work in the fields with harrow, hoe, or plough, glancing at them as they wandered by, one tall and lean, the other shorter and plumper, guessed who they were, because, for some reason ever inexplicable, the English are recognized by continental brethren at sight. And they were old.

For Wally, it was a day of a hundred memories, memories of Ypres One, Two, or Three, but they never found his O. Pip. 'No, never find it now,' he sighed. 'You were lucky with your monument to the Sappers. They didn't put up no monument to me. My O. Pip might be anywhere, I suppose, and there's only wheat or barley now, or a cow, where it used to be.'

§

Fifteen minutes to nine, and early dusk in Ypres. The two of them left their little hotel in Station Street and went by the Butter Street to the Grand' Place, or market square, where the vast Cloth Hall, which had been but heaped stone rubble and gap-tooth fangs when as soldiers they came by, now stood before them, re-created, wide-shouldered, many-windowed, pinnacled, its bell-tower high in the sky again, and the whole edifice reproducing, in exact detail, the proud Gothic structure built by a proud city seven hundred years before. Of the Grand' Place as they had known it only the cobbles remained—the cobbles over which the British millions had marched to a duty in the Salient.

'It used to be a damn-sight darker when we come along with the guns,' said Wally.

'Yes, it was near midnight when I came by.'

They went the rest of the way through the Grand' Place in silence, Mr. Blaize almost a pace ahead of his longer-legged companion, so eager was he to guide him to his greatest moment of all. As they came out of the Place into the road that led to the Gate, he said, 'This next bit used to be called the most dangerous hundred yards in Europe.'

'Yes, and I reckon it was. Jerry knew we came this way every night.'

'I wonder,' said Mr. Blaize, looking at the nice clean houses and shops on either side of him, 'if the people here know that they live in what was Europe's worst hundred yards.'

The hundred yards brought them beneath the great coffered arch of the Menin Gate which, seventy feet high and more than a hundred long, spanned the pavements and roadway. The Gate with its fifty thousand names of the undiscovered British dead soared over them like the white vault of a Roman basilica, save that the traffic of a cobbled highway stormed through its nave, and pedestrians hurried along its footways into or out of Ypres. Few or none of them were interested in the white walls or the names cut on them as they hurried by. They were too familiar with them, or they were two generations later than the story which the endless writing in this great stone register told. Only Mr. Blaize, gazing around him and above him as he waited, built his own phrase to fit this great sorrowing arch, 'Britain's Sorrow and Sole Amends', but he kept it to himself, thinking it hardly in Wally Bletcher's vein. Mr. Blaize the Poet.

The people and the traffic went by, taking no notice of two elderly men, waiting there for something, like two spectators on a kerb.

Three minutes to nine, and Mr. Blaize was thinking of that heart-sickening speech at the Mayor's banquet. 'You know what your Liz's Quakers say, Wally: that we ought to have nothing to do with another war. Well, my head says they're right, but I don't know where my heart is. All I know is that if the next war was the same as '14 or '39, and I was young again, and they all went off, I'd have to go with them.'

'Me too. Sure enough. Every time.'

'So I think, but I don't know. . . . However, we needn't worry. The world has decided the question for us.'

'How d'yer mean?'

'No time, next time, to go or stay.'

'I suppose not, but listen, mate. If——'

'Stop.'

The two young buglers with their silver bugles had come under the arch. Different lads tonight from those of thirty months before, but their duty the same, the new nightly duty of the historic and resurgent City of Ypres. The two policemen appeared, one at the outer entrance, the other at the inner, and, standing in the highway, raised their hands and stopped all traffic. A sudden silence beneath the arch succeeded the storming of a continental traffic over the cobbles—those immortal cobbles. The buglers stepped on to the crown of the camber with their backs to the Salient, their faces towards the fifty thousand names, and their bugles at their sides. The chimes of Ypres struck and they lifted the bugles to their lips. The last chime died and the bugles blazed forth the opening notes of Britain's Last Post.

Snatching off his hat, Wally came smartly to attention; Mr. Blaize did the same at his side; and they stayed so, as the bugles sang on and on beneath the echoing vault.

It is said that the soldiers of the old armies, while finding words, often unseemly, for the singing music of other bugle calls, never touched with any ribaldry the Last Post, the call that ends the day. As 'Parade' sang out they might say or think, 'Fall in, A. Fall in, B. Every bloody companee.' To 'Defaulters', if happily it was not calling them, they might apply the serene words, 'You can be a defaulter As long as you like As long as you answer your name'; and to 'Retreat' which sings the sun down, 'You won't go to Heaven when you die, Mary Ann'; but to the Last Post no words at all because it is too beautiful; nothing; only silence and reverence. All the same, when at the end it sounds its two lengthened notes, and repeats them, some have heard the words, 'Lights out ... Lights out ...' or 'Come home ... Come home ... Are ye there?'

These last long notes died under the high vault, the young men lowered their bugles to their sides, the traffic came through the Arch again; and the two ageing men put back their hats and stood at ease. They were silent for a second or two, while the notes still echoed in heart and mind; and then Mr. Blaize said, 'Yes, I'm afraid I'd do it again, Wally; but History has taken it out of our hands.'